DOCTOR WHO

LONGEST DAY

MICHAEL COLLIER

BBC BOOKS

Published by BBC Books
an imprint of BBC Worldwide Publishing
BBC Worldwide Ltd, Woodlands, 80 Wood Lane
London W12 0TT

First published 1998
Copyright © Michael Collier 1998
The moral right of the author has been asserted

Original series broadcast on the BBC
Format © BBC 1963
Doctor Who and TARDIS are trademarks of the BBC

ISBN 0 563 40581 3
Imaging by Black Sheep, copyright © BBC 1998
Cover illustration by Colin Howard

Printed and bound in Great Britain by Mackays of Chatham
Cover printed by Belmont Press Ltd, Northampton

Dedicated to Rebecca Levene
for help, understanding and generosity
in a *Mêlée Confidential*

CONTENTS

PROLOGUE

Nineteen years ago

Then time crashes through, like a roaring wave of pale water over the far-off spindly trees, ageing them and pushing up new saplings in the blink of an eye.

'Run,' he says, but it's instinct, not a practical suggestion.

Taaln runs the wrong way, spins round as the crackling wave breaks on him.

Vost is caught, on a narrow strip that's safe, an eye in the storm –

Vost watched him die for hours.

The eyes staring back into his own were dry and wrinkled. Gradually they atrophied until there was only a steady stream of dust pouring from the empty sockets.

That alone must have taken a good half-hour.

Flakes of skin broke away from the face like tiny petals and fluttered gently to the parched earth below. He counted them as they fell in the silence.

Vost hadn't known Taaln long, but he'd seen how full of life the man had been, all that careless optimism. He'd had the best attitude, Vost decided. Take what you can when you can – there's little enough on offer after all. And you never knew when the payback would come.

'There're millions of futures down here, aren't there?' Vost said idly as he watched Taaln carefully connect his black box to the now secure device.

'True,' nodded Taaln, straightening up, 'but they're all borrowed, aren't they? That's no use. The only real future's the one you make for yourself, isn't it?'

Vost frowned as the younger man's face suddenly crumpled in fear.

'It's not a safe reading.'

'But the remote sensors –'

'They must have got it wrong!'

'Then what do we –'

'I don't know! The readings were safe before. Pick-up's not for seven hours!'

Vost tried to breathe slowly and deeply to fight back the panic. 'Well, it doesn't mean this chunk's going up, does it? It could just be rumblings. We could have *days* of safe time yet.'

He looked about him, nervously. It was almost perfect here, untouched. He could picture his own people starting again in this bright ghetto, safe from outside, the way they always wanted to be. Ignored. Isolated.

Little by little Taaln's features were losing their individuality. Eventually, they would lack any trace of humanity at all. Vost's mind felt numbed. It had to be some kind of side effect of this place. Ever since they'd landed here he'd felt... well, each memory was so vivid. It was as if his mind was a sponge soaking up every second that passed as he waited the long hours until the pick-up.

'I'd feel safer if we were further from the barrier,' muttered Vost.

'Can't wait to be desk-bound, can you?' laughed Taaln.

'I don't see why I'm needed down here anyway.'

'You've been recruited from the best of the best, Monitor-to-be, sir!' announced Taaln with a cheerful bow. 'They think it's a good idea you experience first hand what you'll be looking at on a screen for the rest of your life. Besides, not many people know about this place yet, and until our numbers swell –' he ballooned out his cheeks – 'all hands to the chronal assessor!'

'I suppose it's useful to have some first-hand knowledge of what I'll be looking over,' said Vost, grudgingly. 'Although God knows what I'm meant to do if anything goes wrong. Is it all like this?'

Taaln shook his head. 'There's a good third of the planet that's fit for nothing. The time instability's too great.'

Vost stared around at the sandy landscape stretching out flatly into the horizon. A few spindly trees swaying in the slight breeze. It was a little like home used to be, before the relentless homogenising of the Outer Planets began.

The red sky stretched angrily over them, a fat, burning orange disc framed in its centre.

'Is that really the sun, or just some historical record of it?'

Taaln's voice floated through the dry air as he bent to unpack some more sensor equipment. 'Hard to say. The distortion effect stretches some way beyond the planet surface, so the image of that sun is captured in time just like its reflection would be in water. There's probably a million days and nights going on as we speak.'

Vost laughed drily. 'The party never stops on Hirath.'

'Won't for us, either, once it's properly exploited.' Taaln was smiling. 'Think of the money...'

'That's a young man's dream.'

'I'm young enough to dream it.' Taaln pulled hard at the lead shell of the chronal assessor, exposing the connections within.

The veins seemed to push through the backs of Taaln's tanned hands now, but Vost realised that the skin was simply paring away layer by layer, fluttering off, tugged by a thin breeze. It ruffled his hair. Yes, things were returning to normal here. His device was still functioning, the data display reading massive chronal activity.

Just rumblings.

He stayed watching as Taaln's painted statue continued to peel under the bright light of the sun. In another few hours the pick-up would surely come, steering its calculated path through the time streams. Perhaps by then there would be nothing left of Taaln.

You had to take what you could while you could. You had to make your own future. Vost carried on watching as the sun beat down.

Now

He's still watching over Hirath, way up in space he can see it all. It's given him a good, if meaningless, living over the years but he's been so distracted of late. He remembers the day Taaln died and the years he seemed to spend watching him. He's tired, worn out now. He's sick of knowing too little and accepting too much. He may have made a mistake. He thinks of his future but he's uncertain.

Somewhere in a dark corner things untouched for hundreds of years are stirring, like responding to like. They're thinking about the future, too.

ONE WEEK LATER

CHAPTER ONE
A DARK SKY

The door slid open with a rasping hum. He wasn't here. Good. The last thing she felt like dealing with right now was more of Vasid's weird behaviour. Waking up in the middle of sleep break to find him trying out different entry codes on her bedroom door was bad enough. Finding things had been taken from her wardrobe rated pretty poorly, too. But enduring him in the rec room, the comments, the snide remarks, the stupid forced discussions on sexuality and frigidity - well, in the mood she was in now, she felt she would smash his teeth in and ask him to discuss that with a surgeon. Or a vet, more likely - slimy little rat.

She pictured him with an involuntary shudder. Sharp, pointed nose sniffing the air as she walked by. Wide eyes just crafty enough to avoid seeming gormless. A smile with no warmth, hovering hopefully like a premature apology for whatever stupid conversation would follow.

'Come on,' she muttered, looking at her own shadow lying thick and black in the rectangle of light in front of her, spilling through from the corridor. She slapped a palm to her forehead and watched the shadow do the same. The lights weren't working. Again.

She moved into the darkness of the room, silent save for a low hum from the drinks machine in the corner and the soft, comforting whine of the base generators. The emergency lighting usually cut in, but it looked like that was out too.

She stepped through the doorway. On the far side of the room was the observation window, a huge rectangle of glass set into the wall. Feeling around the area beside her, she located the window shield control and turned the ball in its socket. A low grating rattled the shutters back and spilled a little more light into the shadows. The outside world revealed itself through the glass at a ponderous pace, but she stood patiently by the door until, with a final, unhealthy clang, the shield was fully retracted.

She stared at the grey brightness of the planetoid's surface – craters, mud flats and mountains vying for a bored onlooker's attention under the stars and blackness. Why was the sky dark at night? She could remember asking the question when she was younger, but found it hard to imagine she'd ever actually cared about the answer.

Sighing, she padded softly over to the window, groping her way past chairs and tables, piles of news printouts, empty cups. A pink-hued planet sat in the dark, so far away, but still so big. She felt almost guilty, not actually having seen it with her own eyes for so long. Monitoring endless lines of checking reports in the control room had become quite enough to remind her Hirath was still out there, so why bother looking at it herself? Two seasons she'd been here now. One more to go and it was back to tuition, praise the deity. Back to a desiccated, academic environment with culture, study, chatter and gossip, enough tools to hold back the real world, and hopefully enough money to make the reprieve more enjoyable.

Two seasons… She thought of Vasid again. He hadn't been here half the time she had, yet his indolence suggested he'd never been anywhere else. Vost's company wasn't much better: he'd been so withdrawn of late. Perhaps her snipes about the way things seemed to keep breaking down round here had got him down so much he wasn't leaving his quarters. Well, he was Chief Monitor. He'd take the blame for what happened here, not she.

Anstaar sighed again. Full of complaints in an empty base,

with two losers and no one to take her seriously. And out there, shining a soft pink in the why-is-it-dark and the twinkling stars, the only reason any of this was there at all.

'Water,' she muttered, tiring of the silence. 'I said, "water"!'

There was a rattle and a loud clang as a tin cylinder was dispensed from the drinks machine. She winced as the noise reverberated round the room, then again as the lights abruptly switched on. A brilliant white bathed the metal walls, the rubbish-strewn counter top, the cleaning drone on its side in the corner and the abandoned chairs and tables. The room was suddenly as bright and bland as everywhere else on the base.

She opened the canister of water. It was frozen solid.

Sam looked in the mirror. 'I never wanted to be the fairest of them all, but... well, in the top million would do.' She sneered at her reflection and blew up at the tousle of fringe she had spent the last hour sculpting for herself. She still wasn't convinced longer hair was for her, but had become bored with the short crop that had seen her through her final years at school. It didn't feel like her now; she'd been back in London a while ago with this length hair, and it had made her realise that the Sam of Coal Hill School was long, long gone.

She dreamed of them all sometimes – schoolfriends, teachers, bullies, fumbling boyfriends... Sometimes she was recounting her adventures to them, other times asking about people she used to know. But they would get bored listening to her – they'd leave the room without a sound. She found herself shouting at them to come back, not to be so... so *rude*. Sometimes she woke to find she was shouting.

Like last night. She'd sat bolt upright in bed. 'Stop being so *bloody* rude!' she'd shouted – typically just as the Doctor had been passing by her closed door.

'I wasn't being rude!' he'd said, earnestly, as he'd flung the

5

door open, the very picture of fatherly bemusement. It drove her mad that, after all the adventures they had shared, he still felt she was a child. She could see it in those anxious blue-green eyes beneath the brow crumpled in concern, peering right into hers.

'Don't you ever go to sleep?' she'd grumbled, rubbing her eyes.

The Doctor had mused a little on this, as if considering it a genuine and pertinent question. 'Sometimes,' he'd said, smiling at her and nodding his head. 'Yes, certainly sometimes.' Before she'd had a chance to give a world-weary sigh at yet another of her friend's self-conscious forays into eccentricity, his face was hanging in a sympathetic grimace. 'Bad dreams again?'

'I'm fine, I told you.' Then she'd looked down, and realised the white T-shirt she'd worn to bed was practically see-through with perspiration. She'd looked up in almost comic alarm at the Doctor, but he'd already breezed off up the corridor towards the food machine. 'Hot chocolate's what you need! Just the thing for nightmares.'

So, a cup of hot chocolate from Daddy and a tousle of the hair was all she'd get to see her through the night. How could he be so like a man and yet... so alien? He'd shown her so many, many things, and she knew he'd shown hundreds of others a thousand other sights besides over the centuries he'd been around –

Centuries, right. The eyes gave it away sometimes – the bright burning of intelligence underneath, the sadness they could convey, and the strength. He looked so young, his skin felt so smooth, but there was a resilience there, a strength she could feel the ages had imbued him with. She wondered how he carried on, how he always carried on, when he'd seen and done so much.

Look at him on Earth. He'd been there so often that in any one year there were probably half a dozen of his selves wandering round the place righting wrongs or meeting people to name-drop about later. Probably in every year. Every year, right from the start. She felt almost afraid to be with him when she thought like that. Was a life that long a blessing or a curse? Her seventeen years must seem like a deep breath to someone like him. She was surprised – and so very, very proud – that she'd even warranted a place in his odd affections. She knew he'd give his life for hers without hesitation – the life of a misfit schoolgirl, with no idea what she ever wanted to be, was worth more to him than his own.

She told herself it was just the way he was. He'd probably sacrifice himself for a ladybird: all life was sacred to him. She was nothing special. Even so…

One day the Doctor might just take the time to look *into* her less and *at* her a little more. Hopefully when she had this hopeless sodding fringe right.

'So the lights aren't working properly?' Vasid looked at Anstaar as if she'd announced the end of the world.

'Again. Just tell me it's not you doing it, all right?'

'Why would I bother?' Vasid spun round in the swivel chair, turning his back to her.

'Why would you bother sticking my underwear in the eating-room sink? It's the sort of pathetic thing you do.'

'I'll remember you want them back unwashed next time.'

I'm not going to rise to it, she thought, breathing deeply. I'm not.

'Anyway,' he added, 'go and tell Vost if you're that worried.'

'I would if I could find him,' rejoined Anstaar, frostily. 'He might give me some sense.'

'He certainly wants to give you something.'

'That machine in the rec room gave me ice instead of water.'

'It knows your nature.'

'It isn't working.'

Vasid gave a gesture that unpleasantly suggested Anstaar was lying. 'I know you're trying to freak me out with this "everything's going wrong" stuff. I know you put the rust in my water.'

'You think I've got nothing better to do –'

'And the scalding-hot shower, that was a good one, wasn't it?'

'Why would I want to risk the sight of you, naked, running out of a –' She stopped, and closed her eyes, smiling coldly. 'This is so pathetic, Vasid. You're like a child.'

'And Vost's like a man? Is that why he won't answer his call-out signal, you've worn him out?'

'What are you talking about?'

'Don't try to deny it,' muttered Vasid. 'You think I'm stupid?'

'Yes. I meant, what about the call-out signal?'

'The monitor's been flickering again so I tried to summon him.' She realised there was fear in his pale eyes. 'He didn't answer.' Suddenly he raised his voice. 'But then he wouldn't, would he? Because you two are just trying to freak me out.'

Anstaar turned and walked away in exasperation, thinking hard. The base wasn't that big, so if Vost wasn't answering his call-out tone he wasn't in his room or his office. As Monitor, he shouldn't really be anywhere else for any significant period of time, and he'd not said a word to either of them.

She heard a glugging noise, and turned to see Vasid pouring narcomilk down his thick throat.

'That's not allowed and you know it. You're meant to be on duty, Vasid. If Vost finds you –'

'If Vost finds me he's not likely to do much, is he? 'Cause if he tries anything, well, I'll just tell his family how he's been monitoring the aptitude of certain members of his staff. You know. The *special* services.'

Anstaar turned and walked out without another word. She

heard his voice. 'And don't think I don't know it's you who's been mucking up the maintenance programs on the computer!' he yelled after her. 'I *know* it's you!'

In the rec room, the lights flickered on, and then off.

Liquid flowed from the drinks machine, forming a huge dark puddle on the floor.

The bulk of Hirath sat resolutely in the dark of the observation bay.

'I'm losing control.'

Tanhith's voice was steady, betraying nothing of the panic that had gripped most of the crew. He looked away from his instruments and into Felbaac's dark eyes.

'And I'm losing patience.' The sound of the ship's engines was a grinding scream, and Felbaac found himself shouting to be heard. 'Can't you compensate for the slippage?'

'Compensate?' Tanhith stared in disbelief. 'How?' A jolt flung some of the ten-strong crew to the floor, and Tanhith turned back to the mad rush of flight data filling his screen. 'It's like finding a needle in the dark.'

'We haven't come so far just to be stopped by this planet's freaked-up atmosphere.'

Tanhith smiled faintly. 'That's very inspiring talk, but unless you can do a better job of flying this –'

Another huge lurch sent Felbaac and his men sprawling forward. Yast, Felbaac's right-hand man, was thrown against the back of Tanhith's flight chair. Tanhith heard the little man's voice in his ear, a low whisper over the screeching of the ship's helpless flight.

'Please... please get us down.'

A section of bulkhead above them flickered into flame. 'You try shutting up, and I'll try my best,' muttered Tanhith, flicking switches seemingly at random.

Felbaac was studying a screen at the opposite end of the flight deck. The noise as they ripped their way through the time currents of Hirath was so loud now that he had to stagger back to talk to his men.

'The time framings are definitely out. The safe path's shifted.'

'Bad information,' twittered Yast. 'I knew it.'

'It can't be.' Felbaac shook his head, then shook it more violently as a cluster of sparks flew from a thick power cable above him and threatened to set him alight. 'Get that under control!' He ducked out the way as two of the crew rushed over to deal with the overload.

Tanhith wiped a hand across his face and tried to stifle a coughing fit as a cloud of fumes began to fill the flight deck. 'Are the framings stabilised, or are they still shifting?'

'I don't know.'

Tanhith smiled. 'I might just get us out of this if we turn back now and take the same way out. I can't guarantee we'll get out the other side if we go on.'

A steady vibration had started to shake the ship. Felbaac leaned heavily against a bulkhead for support.

'Well?' asked Yast, his voice cracking.

After taking another hefty swig of narcomilk, Vasid spat on the floor. 'Drinking on duty's an offence,' he said, mimicking Anstaar's low and sensual voice very badly, then swigging down half the bottle in one go. He cursed. Where in the deity's pit was Vost? It was possible, of course, that he'd gone to the landing-pad reception area for something. Maybe something had come up there. No supply ships were due. The next ship on its way here would be the one carrying him back home to sweet civilisation. And people would take him seriously this time.

His hand flicked over the click pad. 'You're so smug,

10

Anstaar,' he snarled, looking through his narcomilk haze at her on the main screen – an image grab he had procured of her with his trusty old portacam. She was so prissy that she never even went out of her room for water in the night without getting properly dressed. He'd been waiting for ever to capture the moment she slipped up.

He laughed, then coughed. She couldn't look at him like he was dirt when he could look at her like this. Unguarded. Unaware. The picture was unflattering. She was just opening her eyes from blinking, long face turned slightly as she headed for her door, pinched little nose barely visible, long black hair blurred with the movement.

He swallowed another gulp. He should take it easy: he didn't have much of the stuff left, and it would take days to brew more up. He didn't have much of anything, he thought with a drunk's self-pity. He looked at blinking pixelated Anstaar. Her picture would do until he'd worked out a way to have her.

He tried approximating her voice again. 'Never gone anywhere, never done anything.' That's what they'd said at home – bad enough his parents, but his friends too? They'd drifted away, good Homeworld boys, off to explore, to enlist, to work, to start being adults. In such a rush to start living. To grow old.

Well, it wasn't for him. Just look at Vost. He'd been places, he'd become the Monitor, here. His family and friends were probably very proud of him, thanked the deity for his success and for his safe return at the end of his duty period. And what did that count for? He was growing old in this place. Right now, he was probably huddled up down in the docking lounge, drunk. Blind drunk. Yeah, this place would drive you to that – if you weren't so inclined in the first place. He grinned at the thought, and took another swig.

Vost just didn't want anyone to know, that was it. It would

undermine his authority. Imagine what Anstaar would say. Probably wet herself at the thought of two drunks for company. Maybe Vost could even turn out to be something of an ally.

The main screen juddered and the image spun and wobbled before the vision application abruptly cut out. Vasid cursed again, inputting a variety of basic query codes. 'Stupid –'

Vasid punched the digitpad again in frustration as the screen filled with meaningless symbols that refused to clear. Then he punched the console surrounding it, and finally threw his cup at the screen. Thick yellow syrup dribbled down it on to the metal worktop beneath.

He jumped to his feet and kicked his chair. It rattled and shifted forward a little way. A cleaning drone hummed over to clear up Vasid's mess, but he lashed out another booted foot and sent the thing spinning into a bank of machinery. Undeterred, it simply righted itself and tried again.

Vasid sighed wearily. Leaning on the chair, he looked up at the wide screen. A false-colour image of Hirath squatted in its centre. In front of the central control dais – where the drone was quietly mopping up his mess – Vasid took in the never-ending flickerings of the suggested probabilities and nano-possibilities the computer core was assimilating based on the readings from Hirath. He knew that each tiny one of those algebraic notions – which no one understood in the slightest – could foul up half the galaxy if not allowed for and moderated.

If the tiniest turbulence was detected on the planet surface the computer core would explore it, allow for it, accommodate it or counter it while at the same time keeping in check forces that, if not properly balanced, could shred him – and everything else – into a million pieces over a thousand parsecs.

And now the computer was trying to freak him out.

He turned round and hit the intercom to Vost's quarters, and to the reception bay. So what if it *was* the middle of the night? Vost was paid to deal with this sort of rubbish. Responsibility. Vost and that prim little bitch could haul it between them.

There was no reply.

All he had to do was get hold of Vost, let the old man worry about it. Then he could go and get *really* drunk.

No reply.

The screen flickered, then filled with incomprehensible symbols. He spat at the cleaning bot, then hit the general emergency buzzer.

A ship that could go anywhere in time and space, visit any planet in any time, anywhere. And he made it look like a cross between an old cathedral and a music hall and filled it with junk.

Sam smiled, even while one hand fiddled with the still-petulant fringe. How could she ever tire of this? She wondered what the original owners of the TARDIS would say if they could see it now. Candles and clocks jostled for attention in the murky-blue light that fringed the central console, along with ornate antique chairs and piles of discarded books. On a small occasional table sat a pair of binoculars, a telescope, and some opera glasses, and tied round a bronze effigy of a humanoid figure against one stonelike wall was an optician's eye chart. The Doctor (presumably) had used a big black marker to corrupt two lines so they now read FREE MONOCLES. She had no idea why.

Above the bronze figure hung a huge decorative seal, shining out brass and black. This was an important symbol on the Doctor's home planet. Once he had told her it reminded him of what he had to rebel against – but on another occasion he had spoken quietly about sometimes needing to remember where he'd come from.

A huge row of filing cabinets covered one side of the room, holding everything from first-edition Dickenses to unfinished drafts of Alpha Centaurian poetry. Some were held on diskettes, some were huge bunches of paper wrapped in elastic bands, some looked as if they were stored on bits of Lego. Closer inspection had revealed that they *were* bits of Lego. When pressed, the Doctor had announced, rather defensively, that it was his Lego file.

So it was quite a sight, and quite a state, this 'borrowed' ship of his. The rightful owners would be appalled.

Except that they were dead, of course.

They had to be. The Doctor had stolen the TARDIS when he was young. Hundreds and hundreds of years ago. She felt a shiver run down her as she watched him wandering round the ornate bronze-and-wood, five-sided console that guided them through the vortex, saw the angular lines of his face bathed in the electric-blue light of the time rotor as it moved up and down to signify their flight.

Over a thousand years old, and still like a child. She could see the pleasure in his eyes and the simple happy smile as he polished at the brass housings of an instrument bank. He prided himself on his rapport with his ship. It was as though he was driving an old steam train through time and space: he knew when to push her, when to ease her back, how much pressure to apply and when.

Not for the first time she realised she was beginning to think what he'd be like if –

'Sam, come here,' called the Doctor without looking over to see if she was even there.

I know, she thought, as she jogged over to him, you don't want me to think about it either.

'Trouble, skipper?' asked Sam, saluting. Then she straightened, warily. 'Don't even think about asking me for a

14

cup of tea.'

The Doctor looked up, offended. Then he sniffed. 'I don't like the way you make it, anyway.'

'What?'

'It takes hundreds of years to learn how to make a really good cup of tea.'

Sam seethed inwardly. Sometimes she felt he was doing this on purpose, reminding her of how utterly, pathetically different they were, as if –

– as if he knows what I'm thinking –

She froze, but the Doctor seemed to notice nothing amiss. 'We're out in space, quite a way out, as it happens. And something very odd seems to be going on.'

He looked at her as if sizing her up, waiting for her to say something. The same old game. How cool would she be?

'Makes a change,' she said, airily, feigning uninterest. It was a fairly weak parry but she hadn't been sleeping well lately.

'Ah, but this is really odd,' said the Doctor, deadpan.

Sam thought. Then she looked at the indication display. Thankfully, this version of the control console – there were others dotted around the ship – was quite obligingly user-friendly, with most of the controls named. She was staring at one with the legend FORWARD TEMPORAL PROBE engraved beneath it. A red digital display like that of a cheap service-station watch was showing a rapid succession of numbers, skittering about feverishly. A display screen hanging from a heavy metal chain anchored to somewhere in the blue-and-gold infinity that made up the impossibly high TARDIS ceiling read:

EX-THANNOS SYSTEM
RELATIVE YEAR 3177
ERA UNKNOWN

She looked at the Doctor, who was still looking at her with his arms folded, his face by turns sinister and politely attentive as the blue reflections danced across it. No clue that she was on the right track, but she looked back at the forward temporal probe display.

There seemed to be no correlation.

She looked back at him, and folded her arms in imitation of his stance. 'A time eddy?'

'Sam!' The Doctor smiled, arms flung suddenly wide open in delight. He squeezed the tops of her arms and looked proudly at her. 'No.'

Sam's bubble of pride popped, and she narrowed her eyes at the Doctor as he rubbed his hands together and moved round to the other side of the console. 'Some kind of time disturbance, though, surely,' she continued, determined not to come right out and ask, or to admit she was entirely wrong.

'My first thought,' said the Doctor. 'But I've scanned the area. It's a bit of a backwater, really, the Thannos system. Quiet, inoffensive, nothing much of note to the seasoned traveller.'

'But on closer inspection?' Sam had picked up the opera glasses and was studying the Doctor through them.

'On closer inspection, the forward temporal probe –'

'Which you use when we're in the vortex to get an idea of what year we'll materialise in –' Sam was determined to salvage something from this latest bout.

The Doctor picked up her sentence as if he had been banking on the interruption: '– but which can also be used in real time to probe for temporal disturbance if aimed at a spatial target –'

'Uh huh.' News to her and he knew it, but never admit defeat.

'– reveals that this,' and he flicked a switch on the heavy, hanging monitor of the external scanner, 'is the cause of our temporal fluxing.'

Sam waited, feeling impatient and a little excited as the cathode-ray tube inside the metal box warmed up and first interference patterns, then a hazy black-and-white image started to form on the screen. As colour seeped into the picture, she realised she was looking at a pinkish sphere, a thin crescent of its surface lost in shadow.

'A planet,' she said, blankly. Then she decided the game was up. 'Is it?'

'Yes. It's the planet Hirath, apparently. Never heard of it, and I wish I hadn't had to.' The Doctor walked round in front of the monitor, his mane of light-brown hair seeming to leave dark trails of motion against the brightness of the screen as he shook his head from side to side. 'I don't understand how, but Hirath appears to be a mass of conflicting time fields. The whole planet's cut up into little pieces of the past and future.'

'Like paddy fields.' Sam drew herself up to her full five foot three and said, in a low voice, 'The paddy fields of infinity.' She laughed, then stopped under the weight of the Doctor's stare, feeling more four and a half than almost eighteen.

'Sam,' began the Doctor, solemnly and quietly, 'this is more than just a quirk in space and time. A planet's biosphere seems to be in a manipulated state of temporal flux. There's no way this can be stable, and the forces being brought into play on Hirath to make it like this, well... I wouldn't want to hazard how hazardous they must be.'

A heavy silence filled the console room, punctuated only by the occasional clicks and whirrs of the TARDIS flight systems. Sam broke it.

'So I guess we're going to have to find out for sure, right?'

In Vost's bright white office with en suite sleeping quarters, Vasid's alarm cut through the silence, screaming for attention. No one came.

The drone of the signal would surely have driven Anstaar

quite mad had she not disconnected it after the last time Vasid had used it to lure her outside in the night. Instead, she was asleep.

And nobody heard the whispering, rushing and then painfully grating sound of the blue box's alien engines as it began to take material form.

CHAPTER TWO
ABANDON

No answer.

So what would that mean? You're not so stupid. You're not.

Vasid wiped his pointed nose. No Vost, and now Anstaar wasn't answering. There was no way off this base. Nowhere to hide.

Which meant Vost and Anstaar must be up to something.

What?

He swigged more of the sickly narcomilk, and turned off the emergency buzzer. No Vost, no Anstaar. They probably *were* lovers. No wonder she was so uptight, so dismissive of him. If she was with Vost, well…

So that really was it. Vost wasn't answering the call because he was in Anstaar's bed, and they were still keeping it secret from him. That was why she treated him like –

Depression seemed to flood into his mind. He felt it like a fluid, pouring into every crease and fold of his brain until his head was bursting. His nose dribbled and his eyes streamed salty tears, which he wiped and licked at. He felt like a small child, left out and ignored. It was the drink doing this – no, it was Anstaar. It was drink and Anstaar. It was –

A calmness descended on him. The shuddering breaths stopped. Something approaching rationality called him from the shadows.

If you're right, then you're right and you can get them. But make sure you are right. You don't want them laughing at you any more.

Making sure he was wrong entailed a long walk to the reception bay to find Vost drunk. He knew Vost wouldn't be there, and it seemed like such a pointless waste of energy.

But the vindication gained would make the long blurry walk back worthwhile. You've got to make your own future, take what you can when you can – that was what Vost had always said.

Tanhith rubbed frantically at his eyes as the ship careered and spun through Hirath's lower atmosphere. He knew below him were parts of the planet distanced by hundreds, thousands of years, cut off by dangerous forces of incalculable power. Would anything notice their passing, a bright scratch against the sky? Below him were forgotten things: waste, prisoners, exiles, people written off for scrap and stored out of sight and out of mind.

Felbaac had to be out of his mind himself to make them do this. The ship struggled against him as he tried to keep it on course, until a deafening bang numbed his senses and the ship was pitched into a moment of total blackness.

When the emergency lighting came on in caustic grey brilliance it was as if his sight had become a worn-out holovid, jump cuts and scratches all over it. The co-ordinate corrections were coming too fast; the jumping of his vision was disorientating him. Blink and he'd miss the all-important signal to alter course or speed, and he couldn't keep – this – up –

It was always at that point he woke from the delirium that passed for sleep on Hirath.

Felbaac's mocking words floated back to him: 'You always were a dreamer, Tanhith.'

'It's no dream,' Tanhith whispered to himself, realising how infantile he sounded. 'It's just this place.' Some kind of time slip, he was sure of it. The poison of this planet was in the air, the water, in every ruined molecule. It was ruining him, too. Every moment since the flight down, he could remember it in such detail that it exhausted him. Stealing his sleep.

'If only you could wake and find it'd all been a dream,' Yast had once said, looking out of the window of the support hut at the blackened hull of their ship in the distance, silhouetted against the bright pink sky like a desecrated statue. It was a ridiculous cliché, but then clichés were only clichés because they were so often accurate. The dead ship outside the window was like some monstrous memorial to their attempt at revolution. Over now, forgotten like everything else on this ludicrous patchwork planet.

Yet the curse was that this place wouldn't *let* you forget anything. His senses had never been so acute. Everything lingered, particularly soon after sleep. Then every blink seemed to be taking hours. He could remember each fleeting thought, then remember remembering. His thoughts chased their own tails and they had too much time in which to do so. It could never be over.

A fact Felbaac, apparently immune to such feelings, seemed determined to capitalise on.

'Travel the universe,' came a girl's voice from inside the police-box-shaped exterior shell. 'See –' Sam flung open the blue double doors and stood poised on the threshold, as the Doctor's voice floated over her shoulder – 'an empty metal room.' She turned around and looked archly at him. '*This* is Hirath?'

'Did I say this was Hirath?' The Doctor came and joined her in the doorway, breathing deeply. 'Not much air. I wonder where we are.'

'You don't know!' Sam's words were more an exclamation than an accusation, but the Doctor still reacted to the triumph in her voice.

'Oh, Sam, Sam, Sam, Sam, Sam. I know where we are globally, just not exactly where locally, that's all.' He closed the TARDIS door.

Sam seemed amused by his cheek. 'That's like being a kid on Earth lost in a supermarket but knowing he's in England.'

'We're on the moon.'

'The moon?' queried Sam in surprise.

'Sorry, I was forgetting. *A* moon. Of Hirath.'

'Nearest in or furthest out?'

'There's just the one. Mind you, the TARDIS instrumentation indicates that it used to be far, far closer but was nudged out of line some time ago.'

'By the same trauma that made the paddy fields?'

'I doubt it. Your moon is doing the same thing, you know. Its orbit takes it another few inches away every year.'

'Poor moon,' said Sam, without a great deal of sincerity.

The Doctor continued his little lecture. 'This place is a long, long way out now. Hovering round the planet in geostationary orbit.'

'Only visible from a small area of the planet, then,' Sam added, casually, pleased with herself once again.

'If at all,' said the Doctor, running his finger down one of the walls and then tasting the end of it. 'Do you know, I don't know what you'd see in the sky on a planet with fractured time frame. I suppose it might vary. I've never been on one before.'

Sam gave in and asked the obvious. 'So why haven't we landed there, then? What are we doing in a metal coffin?' She was feeling a little dizzy, and put her hand to her head.

The Doctor's high forehead crumpled into concerned furrows. 'Oh, Sam, I'm sorry. First things first. There's not all that much air in here.'

'Stale, too.' Sam sniffed. 'There's not all that much of anything,' she added, looking around the empty room. It was like a cell. 'Can't we hop back in the TARDIS and get some gas masks?'

'Peering through them, we might lose little clues such as these,' murmured the Doctor. 'Look.'

She joined him, squatting on the floor. 'So? Scratches. Mice, probably. They get everywhere.'

'Deep scratches. In metal. I'd say somebody's moved a lot of equipment out of here at some point.'

'Or been a bit too enthusiastic with a Brillo pad.'

'Possibly, possibly.' The Doctor nodded absently.

Sam tutted. Her dizziness was getting worse. 'Look, Doctor, if there's no fresh air, does this mean we're in a sealed-off area?' She considered. 'Area of what, though? Where are we?'

The Doctor fished out his sonic screwdriver from his bottle-green, crushed-velvet frock coat and started to remove a panel. Sam hadn't even noticed it, it being flush to the wall and almost invisible. As he pulled out a tangle of wires and some expensive-looking crystals he talked. 'We're in an outpost on this moon. I don't know who built it but I certainly want to know why.'

'Why?'

'Precisely, yes, "why."'

Sam rolled her eyes and wiped her clammy forehead. 'No. I mean why do you want to know why so badly? Shouldn't we be where the action is?'

The panel beeped noisily at him. 'I believe Hirath's interesting condition is being manipulated from here.'

Sam tried to concentrate. 'You used the temporal probe thing to tell you that?'

'The disturbance faded to just above omega from this very spot. No doubt about it, this is a controlling system of some kind. Ah!'

With a sudden loud whine, an opening appeared in the wall. Sam staggered forward and hung her head out of it, breathing the air noisily and gratefully. 'Good job whoever was here didn't come back and catch you knackering their lock. If they're strong enough to mark metal like that.'

The Doctor thought on this, then beamed at her. 'I was born lucky!'

Sam could find no trace of irony in his words.

There was a banging on the door.

Anstaar turned over in her bunk and slid further under the covers.

The banging continued, and suddenly she sat bolt upright. 'Vost?' She'd been uneasy about his absence. Where had he been?

'No. Vasid.'

Oh, praise the deity. The pervert on a squalid little night errand. 'Vasid, last time you tried to get in here I got you a penalty report. Try anything now and I'll fist your face open. It's nothing personal – I just find you utterly repulsive. Leave me alone.'

'I think you ought to see what's happening in the control room.'

Anstaar frowned. Vasid's natural cockiness seemed to have drained away from his voice. A trick, she thought, but said nothing.

'Just come and see.' Then she heard his footsteps fading away down the corridor, at a leaden pace.

Anstaar felt suddenly afraid. Things just weren't right. She thought back to the pink globe in the depths of the observation screen. Thought of the people who lived on it.

Thousands of people.

And three of us looking after all of them.

And one of them missing, and the other drunk.

'Corren Anstaar, champion of the universe,' she muttered, wryly, and hauled herself out of bed.

Vasid swayed slightly as he walked. He felt sick. Something

was wrong – badly wrong. There was nothing he could do – and nothing he even wanted to do any more. Everything was becoming clear.

Vost was gone. Vost wasn't in with her. He could tell. And it was nothing to do with him, therefore it – had – to – be – Anstaar.

She'd called out Vost's name but that was just a trick. She'd known it was him, because he was the only one left. All the time he thought he'd been watching her, she'd been watching him. And Vost. Monitoring the Monitor. He giggled to himself at his weak joke, then anger took hold of his features and squeezed. He punched the wall – holding back, hitting it only lightly as he walked. Then, after a second of hesitation, again, harder. The pain shocked through the haze in his head.

He shook his hand as if something was on it, then wiped it across his sweaty forehead and through his hair. He had to think clearly, had to know exactly what he would do next. Vost was nowhere on the base. Nowhere alive, at any rate.

Anstaar. She'd got him propped up in her cupboard. Or under the bed. For when she needed a stiff who wouldn't offend her by opening his mouth. She hated men, he knew it. He'd seen the way she'd looked at him. She was like most women. Uptight. Too smart. He'd thought she was frigid – wrong. She was a psycho. She'd killed Vost and she wanted more, and now there was only him left.

He pictured her looking at him. Thought of the image on his screen. Saw the disgust on her face as she watched him, marking him for death. It all made perfect, horrible sense.

His fist lashed out at the wall again, savagely. The noise of the impact echoed dully round the corridor. He sucked his knuckles, feeling them throb, and his numbed taste buds recognised the salt and iron of his own blood. He shambled off back towards the control room, wiping a tear from his eye. Sniffed loudly, walked faster. It didn't matter any more.

When Anstaar showed her face, he would show *her* he was too clever for her.

The ship seemed to hug itself almost foetally as it moved silently through space, its warp motors shining yellow, searing the void around them with their vivid glow. Its surface was dark and pockmarked, as if whatever materials made up its hull had melted and failed to reset before it had ventured on its voyage. An arms turret, twisted and brown, pulled itself away from the protective coil of the body of the ship, a wicked-looking point piercing the space before it like a scorpion's tail ready to sting.

Inside the ship, fetid air dank with moisture and fumes hung around the gnarled consoles and monitors. When the creatures inside spoke, their voices sounded as if they were forcing a way through the must and the fumes.

'Target ahead,' said one, its voice deep and strained. 'We have found it.'

Another glared with crusty orange eyes at controls seemingly welded into the organic-looking walls. 'Agreed. Close on nearest habitable area.'

The first creature to speak emitted a low crackling, like filthy deranged laughter. 'That *is* target, Leader.'

The other creature swung its massive head as if confused, then slowly curled its lower lip, narrow teeth bared, white and pointed. 'Close on target.'

'What a state!' said Sam.

'He needs help,' agreed the Doctor as they peered after the staggering figure. 'Or a black coffee at the very least.'

'Maybe we're on a wine-tasting ship!' Sam piped up, quite surprised at how buoyant she was sounding. That bloke had given her the creeps. 'Yeah, the different time zones are there so they can pick up different vintages on the cheap! Bit like a

Dover-to-Calais run –'

'Sam,' interrupted the Doctor, waving a hand for silence. 'There's something very bad happening here, I'm sure of it.'

'There's something bad happening everywhere we go, isn't there? I don't think some lush wandering round a place as boring as this –'

'He came from that way,' said the Doctor, pacing up and down past the little streaks of blood on the wall and holding his fingers to his forehead. 'Saw something, perhaps, something that made him angry.'

'Come on then,' said Sam, setting off confidently along the corridor. 'I could do with something to ruin my good mood. Could do with a drink, come to think of it! Maybe we'll see whatever he saw too and become booze brothers.'

The Doctor followed Sam off into the gloom.

It took Anstaar only a few minutes to get ready. She started brushing her thick black hair, then looked at her reflection in the mirror and stopped. Why bother making the effort this time of night? She'd see whatever stupid thing Vasid wanted her to see just in case it was something to do with Vost. She'd never felt so uneasy. There was only Vasid around, and he'd sounded so strange. What was going on at Temporal Commercial Concerns the day they'd taken on Vasid anyway? His psychoscreening must've shown how socially inept he was. Or was that why they'd tucked him away here? Or if he was a dangerous psychotic he could probably fake the screening anyway –

No. Vasid was *not* a dangerous psychotic. The notion that he was had lodged itself under her thoughts, constantly there of late as if her mind was always working on two levels. It reminded her of the only time she'd ever fallen in love. Whatever she was doing would seem to have her full and undivided attention but another part of her was able to consider, imagine and generally concentrate a variety of emotions on her lover at the same time.

The thought of Vasid's sociopathy being the same as an image of love made her feel sick and extremely annoyed at herself.

She thought of the call button in the control room. How long would it take TCC agents to arrive for an investigation. A few days? What was she meant to do in the meantime? Lock herself in her room? If only she had an IX link, a way of transmitting her reports directly into the TCC net... Why was recognisable technology so scarce in this place? The computer had been so erratic of late – bolted on like an afterthought to that science-fiction mainframe, but not taking. It was like a graft that was being rejected, it was –

'I talk some rubbish,' she said out loud, hoping for the comfort of her own voice, disappointed to hear it come out sounding so scared and unconvincing.

The door hummed open as she pressed the exit button. Outside in the corridor, a few feet from her door, a cleaning bot was humming away, spraying a sandlike material over a puddle of grey liquid. Anstaar smelled narcomilk and vomit.

She sighed. 'Stand by for great conversation,' she muttered. Irony sounding a lot more convincing than nervous supposition, she strode purposefully off towards the control room, leaving the bot to its labours.

The corridor seemed to go on for ever. Sam was still striding off ahead but feeling less and less sure of herself. She subtly shortened her stride, but, glancing over her shoulder, she could see that the Doctor was always the same distance behind her, never catching up, never standing still. There were stretches of the corridor that were dimly lit at best – usually the parts with sharp turns in them, so it was impossible to see what was coming round the corner.

The Doctor's voice suddenly rang out in the sterile silence of their surroundings. 'You know, when you've wandered up and down as many corridors as I have, it's quite soothing to find some as dull as these.' He yawned, loudly. 'This soft lighting is making me sleepy.'

'All we need is some soft music and a sofa. We could have some fun!' Sam grinned over her shoulder. I don't believe I said that, she thought, embarrassment suddenly making her toes curl in her battered trainers as she walked.

'Quite,' said the Doctor, vaguely. Sam quickened her pace, turned a new corner, and stood stock still.

'What is it?' Suddenly the Doctor was there at her side, body tensed, moving her behind him protectively. Then he relaxed. 'Airlock,' he said. 'Pressurised area ahead. Shall we see what's inside it?'

'Yeah,' said Sam with exaggerated enthusiasm. 'Tell you what, though.'

'What?'

She gestured proudly forward. 'You go first.'

The row of flickering screens flashed harsh squares of blue-white light into the darkness. A sound like static filled the air. A few red lights winked and flickered on the far side of the room as if dancing a frenzied code, begging for attention.

Anstaar peered into the blackness. She sniffed. That could only be Vasid. Her ears strained for some sound of him, her forked tongues flickering over her dry lips nervously.

'Is this your problem, Vasid?' she began, challengingly, thankful there was no tremor in her voice. 'The light's not working? I think you'll find a service bot can deal with this for you if it was my advice you wanted at this idiot hour of night.'

Silence. The flashing of static on the screens.

'This is so funny, Vasid.' Where was he? Hiding? Crouching in the dark? 'I just wet myself laughing. Good night.' She turned around to leave. Then a thought struck her. What if Vost was behind this? What if –

'You're paranoid,' she told herself. Then the hands grabbed her by the throat and propelled her into the control room.

CHAPTER THREE
SPLIT

Too shocked even to try to cry out, Anstaar tried struggling, but the pressure didn't ease off. There was a sharp crack and she realised her head had smashed against one of the monitors. Vasid's face drew close, dark blue and shadowy in the erratic light from the flickering screen. His breath was foul and his forehead glistened with sweat.

'I'm not paranoid,' said Vasid, relaxing his crushing grip slightly and smiling as she whimpered for breath. 'I know exactly what you are.'

He twisted her neck round and pressed close against her as her body attempted to turn with it. Her face was pressed up to the glass of the screen. She could see her features reflected in it, saw the fear in her own eyes and the manic gleam in Vasid's behind her. 'Got bored with Vost, did you?' he gurgled in her ear. A dribble of his saliva landed on the bare skin of her neck and she shuddered. 'Didn't he come up to your standards?' He grabbed her hair, pulled back her head and bumped it against the screen. She stayed silent. 'I know where you must've put him,' he grated, twisting her arm behind her back. 'I've worked it all out. I *know*. And I'm going to make you join him!' He pulled savagely on her twisted arm.

The pain brought with it anger and disbelief. This was Vasid, for the deity's sake! She brought her heel down hard on his foot, and with a cry of rage untwisted the arm he was holding, grabbed his wrist, and pushed. Vasid stayed silent as he crashed into what was probably the command chair, overtoppling it and landing, by the sound of it, underneath it.

There was nothing then but blackness.

31

Run.

No, nowhere to go. Vasid knows this base as well as I do. I can't stay in my room for ever.

Send help signal.

That's in this room, somewhere in here, but in the dark. And Vasid's here.

She felt her way round the hard edges of the console, grazing the skin of her wrist as she found the corner and moved stealthily round until the bank of machinery was between her and her attacker.

And the door.

She looked behind her. The red lights were still bouncing around in the blackness as if in distress. What were they, anyway? She hadn't noticed red lights before. Vost was in charge of operationals – he was the only one who needed to know the real ins and outs of –

Ins and outs.

He thinks I've sent Vost down to Hirath. In pieces. Those red lights. The matter transmitter.

He's going to send me there. To Hirath.

Nothing moved in the black silence.

The steel grey of the corridors had given way to a dirty pink luminescence beyond the airlock. A beige sofa with a tiny back to it sat on squat legs on a white rug. A cream plastic chair and a similarly coloured plastic desk with an array of dials, LCDs, and switches built in took centre stage in the modestly sized room.

'Tacky,' declared Sam. 'Tacky and very nasty.'

'There's your sofa,' said the Doctor, blandly.

'But still no music,' said Sam, equally blandly, but turning away as she felt herself blushing. The Doctor started humming something operatic to himself, and Sam walked over to the rug. Artificial fibres. Nice one.

Someone seemed to have plonked a computer screen in the middle of the desk. Sam walked over and scrutinised the digitpad. 'Two steps up from your average PC keyboard by the look of it,' she said sniffily. But it seemed barely used, with no trace of grime on the ivory-coloured touchpads. 'Maybe that geezer just had a bad day at the office. Hard to imagine a good one, here.'

'TCC,' the Doctor read aloud. He gestured to Sam at the enormous legend inscribed on the wall facing the desk in huge, clean, modern letters. A strange-looking bird that could have been a dove loomed over the letters, wings stretching to either side of the room.

'Tasteful logo,' said Sam, and nodded as if deeply impressed.

'Do you think so?' asked the Doctor with surprise.

Sam just glared at him, refusing to be taken in by his apparent misapprehension. 'What does TCC stand for?'

The Doctor abruptly turned and walked over to the desk. He started up the computer. 'Tee-Cee-Cee' blared out in a synthesised voice to a brief snatch of orchestral choir. 'Oh, very nice.' The Doctor nodded as if in appreciation.

'Do you think so?' asked Sam, drily.

The Doctor hummed the TCC theme to himself in the same operatic fashion, as a grandiose corporate home page faded up on to the digital screen.

'Aha!' cried the Doctor, leaning back in the chair and swinging his battered leather shoes on to the desk. 'TCC. "Temporal Commercial Concerns. We've got time for you."'

'Catchy. Like it,' said Sam with a challenging smile, but this time there was no rejoinder. The Doctor's face had grown hard.

'I don't like the sound of this,' he muttered to himself.

A file seemed to be downloading on to the monitor, and he read aloud. 'Hirath is the choice for races everywhere with problems too large for their living space. Rent the safest

33

house of all for depositing all your darkest secrets. Space is plenty and time has no meaning in a land barricaded by the most natural and effective barrier of all.'

'Go on,' said Sam, nodding encouragingly.

'Time!' snapped the Doctor, slamming down a hand on the array of switches and meters to his right.

Sam jumped as a loud hum permeated the room. An invisible join in the middle of the dove-bird revealed itself as almost the whole wall split in half, each half retreating away from the other, revealing a huge glass observation screen.

'"Where does it stop? Look for the sign of the lollipop",' muttered Sam under her breath as the Doctor moved round to join her in front of the starlit night filling up the window. Several geometric strips of silver metal stretched over the immediate foreground of the surface outside, then they gave way to bare rock and distant crags and mountains. The huge shadowy pink globe of Hirath sat balefully in space. 'Surprise. It's the scary alien planet stop.'

'So,' said the Doctor, doing his best to disguise what was clearly great unease. 'This is some kind of reception lounge. I imagine this computer is used to order up occasional supplies and that strip outside gives any cargo ferry something to land on, probably bringing new personnel every now and then. Skeleton crew I'd imagine, given we've only seen one person.'

'Doctor,' began Sam, realising what had been puzzling her on their journey here, 'why would a skeleton crew need such a lot of space?'

'Hmm?' said the Doctor, still staring out at Hirath.

'Well, all those long corridors. You'd think they'd want something pokier to get about faster.'

'Well, maybe they like a bit of space to get away from one another at times,' reasoned the Doctor. 'Running an operation like this, they're probably highly trained and intelligent.

Bound to want their own space at times. Bound not to get on on occasions.'

'Stay away, Vasid,' Anstaar called out, her voice rising with panic, 'or I'll break every last bone in your body and cut off –'

'Shut up.' Vasid's thick slur of a voice came out of the darkness. He was much closer than she had thought. She had heard him padding softly about straining her ears and eyes for some clue as to what he was up to, trying to remember where the matter transmit was. It was used only occasionally for beaming down the test probes and instruments to check for temporal stability, atmospheric abnormalities, and other little matters affecting all life on the planet. It was large enough to hold a child. Or maybe a person. Just.

She could think of better ways to travel than being dissolved into thin air and transmitted through space and several hundred thousand units of temporally ravaged atmosphere on to a schizophrenic planet.

There had to be a way out of this. Talking to him had achieved nothing. He had clearly hit the narcomilk hard – how many bottles she didn't want to think. As well as heightening strength and aggression, the stuff made you hideously paranoid. Several times now, in the darkness, she had theorised that Vasid had just fallen into a drunken sleep or lost consciousness. But then a tiny sound had given him away, or a tiny movement of shadow cast by the faint flickering blue of the faulty monitors.

By the sound of his voice, Vasid was still at the other side of the central console, just about. If he kept moving round, and provided she didn't bump into anything or trip, she stood a chance of making it to the far door before he could stop her. Then she could reason with him in the light – or see her way while she was running, if he still wouldn't listen. Wait for him to collapse into a stupor. Talk to him sober and make him tell her what in the deity's name was going on.

But a panicking voice at the back of her head gibbered and gabbled at her that she wasn't going to get the chance to do any of these things. She was going to die. Or be sent out of here, out of the safety – safety? – of the base, out of the warm, electronic, artificial world she had lived in for so long to go down there. Down to Hirath.

Tears welled up. No, she told herself, don't show you're scared. You'll inflame him – excite him, even. You know what he's like. Think about it, work it out, stop him – you can do this –

Her choked sob burst out into the blackness, and she heard Vasid snigger.

With a few acrid wisps of smoke, a glutinous screen dissembled from the side wall of the murky vessel. A circular icon, bleary and pulsing, appeared in the middle of a shimmering grid. Small dots of light appeared around the flashing circle, and a short list of alien symbols began spelling themselves out next to each of them.

A towering figure stamped across the command area to the navigation wall. 'Which is our target?' came the gravelly whisper.

'AB456, Leader,' reported the technician. Its speech was slow and laboured, as if its vocal cords were straining against each other.

The Leader snorted. 'And in the local tongue?'

A pause. 'A moon of the planet AB455.'

The Leader hissed in the fetid atmosphere. 'Where is the soul of a scientist?'

The technician raised its ovular head. 'In facts.' It returned to its work, before uttering 'Leader' almost as an afterthought.

The Leader revealed the pointed teeth sheltering behind his leathery lower lips. 'Have the Lost Ones sent us the required access codes?' he inquired.

'Some time ago,' rattled the technician.

'I was not informed.'

'You were at rest, Leader. We did not seek to disturb you before helming so important a mission.'

The technician bared its teeth in a smile and gestured at the crew, continuing their monitoring of the toffee-like controls that sponged out from the sticky walls. One of the tiny points of light glowed more brightly on the display screen. Then two pincer-like graphics closed round it until it was eclipsed, and black as jet.

'Something's coming.'

Sam looked over at the Doctor, then at the door, in quick succession. 'That bloke again?'

'No.' The Doctor's face was rapt as he stared at the computer screen. 'No no no no no no. A ship – a craft of some kind. It's heading our way.'

'The supply ship, surely? We should get out of here before they mistake us for porters or something.'

'No, Sam. None of the correct codes are being transmitted. That's why this computer's getting the jitters.'

Sam jogged over, absent-mindedly chewing her nails. 'What's it up to?'

'I think it's about to put up a force shield of some kind.'

With a sudden grinding of gears, the shutters over the observation window began to close.

'Show-off,' muttered Sam. 'God, that machine's a bit jumpy, isn't it? Could be anyone popping in for a visit.'

'I suspect that this place is kept rather quiet, off the beaten track – probably for some very good reasons.'

'In which case, I guess whoever's coming doesn't just want a guided tour.'

The Doctor remained silent, drumming his fingers on the

desk, waiting for any further information to flicker on to the screen. Sam began to feel vaguely irritated. With a noisy hum, the shutters finished sliding back into place.

'Doctor, what is this place?'

In a blur of movement, the Doctor had moved to the door. He politely waved a hand to suggest that Sam should go through first. 'I think it's time we asked someone exactly that. And to see if anyone knows who's coming to dinner.'

'Wait,' said Sam. 'How are we going to find anyone on a base this size?'

'Well,' began the Doctor. He made a show of thinking hard. 'We go yodelling through the corridors until someone tells us to be quiet?'

'Too risky,' said Sam, as if taking the idea extremely seriously. 'They might be too drunk to care. Or wearing headphones. Or they might be deaf.' She looked at him pointedly. 'Or tone deaf.' Then her face brightened. 'Tell you what – we'll take this huge map of the base with us.' She gestured triumphantly to a laminated sheet of paper stuck up in a recess next to the door leading to the landing bay itself. 'Better plan?'

The Doctor's mouth opened in mock astonishment, then snapped shut. He smiled. 'Keep your eyes open and your mouth shut. Admirable advice. If only I could remember who said it.'

Sam couldn't help feeling deeply smug at her discovery. Travelling with the Doctor, you had to learn timing. Reveal your amazing find at the right dramatic moment for best effect. It was the game they played. And she had to give him credit: he was never a bad loser.

'Sam, we have a problem with your map.'

'What's wrong with it? The fact that I found it first?'

'Take a look.' The Doctor shoved his hands deep in his pockets as he watched her scrutinise the map.

'What am I meant to be looking at? It's what it says it is:

"Base layout". There's the control room, sleeping quarters, a monitor station – whatever the hell that is – and this is the corridor we came down.' She stood on tiptoes to point to an intersection. 'And that's where we were standing when Legless the Lush waltzed past us. And…' She trailed off. Then she turned and looked at him, urgency shining in her blue eyes. So where's the room we landed in?'

'Well, if this map is to be believed, we landed outside – or in the lining of the hull.'

'But we didn't!'

'True.'

'And those scratch marks – they led away from the way we got out –'

'Which would suggest there's quite some area unshown on the plan, yes. Maybe they ran out of paper.'

'Maybe that's just *part* of the base,' reasoned Sam, doubtfully, although she suspected the grey shading filling the rest of the paper represented the dull landscape outside. 'Maybe there's another map somewhere else showing the rest of it.'

'Hope so! I'd hate to think we'd landed in a figment of our imaginations.' He frowned. 'But you'd think they'd put up that map near to where we came out ourselves. And why make the door invisible?'

'Maybe there're places here visitors aren't meant to know about,' said Sam, remembering the approaching ship. She shivered, then smiled. 'I'm spooking myself here.'

'We really do need to speak to someone, don't we?' The Doctor strode back over to the other doorway. 'I refer my friend to the exit I was due to make earlier!'

Sam pulled down the map. 'We'd better split up. We'll cover the ground quicker that way.'

'We'll just head for the control room,' said the Doctor, breezily.

'What if it's automated?' protested Sam. 'I'll take the control room. You take the sleeping quarters. Looking at this map, our mate the drunk could've been heading for either. And there's bound to be someone in one of them.'

'All right,' agreed the Doctor. 'But take care. Explain you're here to sack their cartographers.'

'Or,' smiled Sam, 'that I'm peddling Alka-Seltzer.'

'Right, that's it. I've had enough.'

Anstaar tensed herself. What was the lunatic talking about now?

The lights suddenly flared into life. Anstaar gave a cry of alarm and fell back, holding her eyes. The back of her head connected with something hard and pointed, and, had she been able to see anything in the sudden onslaught of the fluorescent lights, she reckoned it would be stars.

'Got you now!' came a snarl from across the control room.

The black speckles finally left her vision. Vasid was clomping towards her, the stealth he had tried in the darkness abandoned now, the pent-up frustration finally manifesting itself in an exclamation of triumph. He grabbed hold of her and pulled her to her feet. She tried to push his face away from her, but one of her fingers found its way into his mouth. She suddenly realised he was sucking on it, slobbering like a baby.

The revulsion gave her strength. She kicked him hard in the crotch, and backed away. She realised she'd been biting one of her tongues, and that she was swallowing blood. Anger.

No, she wasn't going to back away any more. She'd done that enough, and now she was going to fight back. She looked behind her for some kind of weapon.

That was when Vasid brought the distress-call handset down hard on the back of her neck and everything went black once again.

And that was when Vasid bundled her up into a fleshy ball of legs and arms and squeezed her into the matter transmitter.

The Doctor walked briskly back along the corridor to the intersection. He wasn't happy about letting Sam go alone, but she was right. They needed answers in a hurry. And if she did run into trouble, well, it wouldn't be the first time. She could handle it.

His footsteps echoed all around the dull metal of the walls and floor. Suddenly he came to a halt, skidding slightly on the smooth flooring. He turned to the wall and ran a hand over it, firmly but gently. Then the other, almost as if trying to polish the wall with his palms. He peered at the surface as if appraising a painting, looking first one way then the other.

'Striations?' he whispered to himself. 'Scratches?'

Like the ones on the floor where they had landed. In that room.

Sealed off but surely recently used.

Forgetting about the staff quarters, the Doctor hurried back in the direction of the TARDIS.

Leaving the muggy hut, Tanhith had to shield his eyes against the glare of the sunlight. Everything withered before a cruel, brilliant sun. There was an oppressive stillness in the air.

His 'quarters' were on the periphery of the settlement; it was an outhouse for supplies that had long since been used up.

He shared it with two other members of the crew, Maadip and Elb, but at least it was better than sharing with the prisoners. Felbaac was so determined to prove to these poor worn-out men he was one of them that he was bedding down in the communal dorm. Yast, of course, was by his leader's side, while the two other crew members were based in the

41

rocket, working to put things right. An order from Felbaac – one he knew couldn't be carried out but gave anyway, just to keep them occupied. It fooled no one, of course, but at least the scourge of the Thannos Multiplanetary Government was leaving Tanhith alone.

He considered heading towards the settlement centre, then changed his mind and decided to head away from the shabby shacks and the beaten men. Elb and Maadip must be training up some of the inmates now. Tanhith had watched the first couple of sessions and found them too painful to keep attending. Felbaac was giving them dreams that he was in no position to deliver. He thought of the government's own campaign of disinformation. The Outer Worlds were backward. Their beliefs were primitive, their right to self-determination proven unnecessary. Yast insisted that you had to turn that disinformation back on the enemy – and if that involved lying to your allies, then so be it. Tanhith himself had doubts as to what was true and what false.

Still, it remained a fact that one by one the Outer Worlds were being reconstructed, homogenised to the Inner World ideal. The old architecture, the old ways, all gone. The minerals and resources left as waste in the wake of the terraforming were being dumped on Hirath for reclaiming sometime in the far future when they were viable once more. And the people dissenting, those who would not claim temporary habitation on a pinprick government rock while waiting for repatriation, were dumped here, too. Perhaps they could be reclaimed at some point in the future.

Otherwise, a chunk of Hirath came cheaper than fashioning a prison planet. And it was *so* much more humane than allowing dissidents to share the government stockades – the message was clear: they would be victimised and killed. Life in the holding camps on Ipmuss had been hard enough, but even the presence of callous K'Arme guards reminded you

you existed, you mattered even if only as a hindrance, an object of hatred. You could feed on that, gain strength from it. When they shipped you to Hirath, you were forgotten. Nobody.

He paused and looked at his reflection in the grimy glass of another storehouse. His long blond hair was matted over his tiny ears. His face was weathered, the skin pockmarked. He allowed his long eyelashes to knit together, blotting out the sight. He felt he'd been nobody for years now and couldn't be bothered to fight against it the way Felbaac did.

At least here he was in good company.

Sam was running. She'd got bored with walking, just like back on Earth. Fair enough, you had to get from A to B, but she always felt the time in between was such a drag. She always wanted to *be* somewhere rather than just be going somewhere.

So she ran. There were times in Coal Hill when she'd just wanted to run and run and never come back. Leave behind the narrow little streets, the narrow little viewpoints, the hanging around on street corners. Well, she thought wryly, at least I managed *that* in the end.

She remembered the head teacher asking her to run for the school. Remembered how cool her friends – and her enemies – had thought her for saying no, for telling him she just wasn't interested.

She ran for herself, that's what she'd said. Not for Coal Hill School. Her mum and dad hadn't minded. They'd said it was good not to feel loyalties. It was good to be your own person. That's why they'd lived in Shoreditch, she'd always thought – a reaction against *their* own parents.

So, lesson one: rebellion was a healthy part of growing up, and continuing to rebel reminded you of who you were and what you were about. So instead of the life her mother had so *tragically* endured – fit in in some rural backwater, go off to university, feel morally obliged to get the best job you could to make your family proud – Sam had been stuck there, in Coal Hill. And was that better or worse?

She took no pride in it. She hated it. She could do the lessons, no problem. She could take the flak from friends and foes alike for not smoking, not even touching pot with the rest of them. But it made it so hard to be typical and teenage, and to rebel. Drugs frightened her. She'd dabbled once, and it had scared her to death. She hadn't known how they would work on her, how she'd react. She'd been OK – that time. That was all the risk she was prepared to take.

Then it had been no caffeine. Abstinence. She'd already said no to gelatine, no to meat. No drugs, and if that had meant no friends, she was sticking with it. Her parents had understood in that uninterested way of theirs.

She felt just the tiniest pang of guilt at the thought of them sitting alone in the living room, wondering if she would be coming back *this* night. Then again, wouldn't they be secretly a little pleased at this new, unexpected rebellion?

You couldn't stay away for ever, could you? She could come back. Carry on as normal. Take it all on again.

But with hair like this? She brushed her fledgeling fringe off her perspiring forehead, panting lightly, staring round her at the dull metal walls but picturing the huge planet hanging in the black sky beyond, billions and trillions of light years, or light decades, centuries –

She knew then that she wasn't going back.

She'd run away from it. Was running. She was still between A and B. Probably somewhere between C and X, knowing the Doctor. But just *knowing* the Doctor…

That was a bit more like belonging.

A shrill shriek suddenly tore through her thoughts. She stopped sharp. A woman's voice, screaming with fear, not pain.

Taking a deep breath, she pelted off again down the corridor, following the sound.

Anstaar was crammed in, her head forced down against her legs. She tried moving, but she was shut in so tight she couldn't even squirm. She screamed again, although she knew it was pointless. Who was there to hear? 'Vasid! Please!'

'Shut up. Just shut up!' Vasid's voice was slurred, unnecessarily loud. 'I can't concentrate.' She heard him curse, then the sound of him slapping his temples – and a low chuckle. *That's* right.'

She saw his head appear over the top of the console, a dribbling smile plastered on his face. 'Happy landings, you whore!'

Sam skidded to a halt in the doorway of what had to be the control room. No sign of the Doctor, but there was the woman who must've screamed. She was packed in a box so tight it was a miracle she could speak at all. The woman seemed quite attractive, her skin smooth and coffee-coloured, hair long and dark. But her eyes gripped Sam's. They had no eyelashes, just a tiny covering of some wispy material. The fear seemed to shine out of them.

Some bloke had his back to her. Had he put the women there? Then the clincher: 'Happy landings, you whore!'

Cue dramatic entrance. 'Well that's absolutely bloody charming, isn't it? And who are you, then, the cock of the north?'

Anstaar was somehow even more terrified to see the new arrival staring at her so intently. Then the voice: rough, demanding – and angry by the sound of it.

Maybe *this* was Vost's killer, thought Anstaar as the milky-coloured light began to disseminate through her cell structure. Oh deity, let her kill Vasid too. Don't let him get away with it.

Anstaar found herself giggling. She'd never have imagined the process would tickle. Then it was as if her eyes were retreating down into her head, her neck, into her torso. She saw her insides, organs, soft translucent fibres. Skin, flesh, and sinew paring away, huge wounds opening up with no blood, no pain, just fading sight. Just her life, her body oozing away on this ticklish, this – no, not any more –

No feeling any more.

Sam couldn't believe it. The woman had just faded away bit by bit, her skin, her insides, then even the bones. There was a smell of something burning, like something left in an oven too long. She felt suddenly sick.

The man, too, was sniffing. He wiped the thick string of drool from his mouth and focused on her. 'Organic. It's not meant for living things. That must be why she stank us out like that.' He sniffed again, loudly, and giggled softly.

'Vasid, I take it.'

'Yeah, that's me.' He stared at her, his thick eyelids hanging down heavily in a suspicious squint. 'How did you know?'

Sam clenched her fists. 'She screamed it at you with what I'd guess was her last breath.'

Sam suddenly wondered what the hell she could do next. What had she barged in on? Was she jumping to conclusions?

Then Vasid growled and threw himself at her. Eyes wide in surprise at how quickly he could move, she went down under his sweaty bulk, winded.

Even gasping for enough breath to fight back, Sam found time to reflect ruefully that eight or nine times out of ten in this game, your first and worst suspicions were often proved right. If you didn't jump to conclusions, they'd save you the bother and jump first.

* * *

46

The Doctor scrutinised the area of wall behind which the TARDIS presumably still stood. The tiniest of cracks in the metal alerted him to where the door was, and a few small dents to its left at eye level were all that remained of what was presumably once an entry coder. 'One way only,' mused the Time Lord. The TARDIS must've landed them in some part of the base sealed off long before, and now presumably forgotten about. There was no map here suggesting what lay beyond. Presumably the sonic screwdriver could help him gain entrance back to it, though. Interesting. Just what had been cleared from that room further into the bowels of the forgotten area?

The Doctor twirled round on one heel. He was torn between going to the staff quarters, going to see if Sam was having any luck in the control room, and going to explore a likely room which might hold some records of the partitioned-off area. The staff may well prove to be as ignorant of this extra *lebensraum* as the map suggested. In which case, while Sam kept them busy with questions and probably violent alarm at her presence, he could nip along and surreptitiously look for a real record of what was going on.

Which would mean a trip to the Chief Monitor's office. Which if memory served…

The Doctor tossed a coin, stared at the result anxiously, and moved back down the way he had come. Then he froze, tossed the coin on to the floor and stalked off in the opposite direction.

In the Chief Monitor's office, a persistent beeping noise rang out from a small black plastic box buried in the bottom drawer of a nondescript plastic desk under a pile of diskettes. Had anyone been there to respond to the beeping and picked up the box, they would have seen scrolling red letters of liquid crystal swirling about the data screen on its flush black surface.

Something was trying to make contact.

'Get off me, you sick piece of –'

Vasid's thick fingers clamped over her mouth. 'It was you!' he snarled. 'All the time you made me think it was – it was her. Anstaar. You *made* me send her down there –'

'Down where?' gasped Sam, breathing in as much air as she could, squirming against Vasid's sweaty bulk, nearly gagging at the stench of his body odour. 'Hirath? You sent her to Hirath?'

'You made me send her,' squealed Vasid. 'It was you. You!'

Sam struggled harder, then let herself go limp. Vasid looked down at her, and Sam swallowed hard. 'Yes. You're right, I was. I wanted to get you... alone. All to myself.'

Vasid stared at her, his rodent-like teeth peeping from behind his rubbery lips as he scowled in disbelief. 'What?'

Sam took a deep breath. 'You heard me.' She looked into his eyes, kept her look strong and sure. She felt his grip on her body lessen a fraction, but did her best not to show any emotion.

Vasid stared at her.

Sam continued holding his gaze and pouted the pout she'd rehearsed in the TARDIS mirror so many times to such little effect. 'I've been watching you, you know. I came in on the last shuttle.'

Vasid shook his head. 'All that time?'

'All that long, lonely time.' Sam softened her expression, attempting puppy-dog eyes. It wasn't an expression she was used to and she had no idea how convincing it looked, but Vasid sat up, confused. 'I had – I can't –'

Sam nodded sympathetically, rising up a little by pushing back on her hands, attempting to look provocative but steeling herself to grab his arms if he tried to push her

48

down again.

But when he slapped her hard across the face, she didn't even have time to react. The force of the blow was such that she barely seemed to feel it for several seconds, until the metal taste of blood in her mouth seemed to usher a ringing in her ears and a hot stinging in her cheek. He was shouting at her again.

'So you *did* kill Vost. It's got to be you. You were just saving me till last!'

'I didn't, I didn't!' shouted Sam, cutting across Vasid's hysteria. 'That was – that was the Doctor.'

'What?'

'The man who came here with me.' Sam's breaths were coming in deep gasps. 'He's – he's a spy. He's been spying on *you*. I was helping you. Really, it's true. I started off doing as I was told, but the more I watched you –'

'You can't fool me!' Vasid spat. 'What do you take me for?' He scrambled inelegantly to his feet and grabbed hold of Sam's hair, ignoring her squeak of protest. Why didn't I keep it short? she thought, as he pulled her up by it. Then she realised Vasid's face had twisted as if in revulsion.

'You've only got one tongue! But you're a girl!'

Sam just stared at him speechlessly, still trying to pull away and wincing from the man's grip on her hair.

'Well, you can't fool me,' yelled Vasid, as if desperate to convince himself. '*You* need a doctor, you freak. There's no one else on this base!'

The Doctor pushed open the metal door and peered warily into Vost's cabin. He'd heard the insistent beeping for some time, and had begun following it like a bizarre Morse code trail of audible breadcrumbs. 'Something of a disappointment, after all that,' he muttered, sadly, taking in his surroundings.

A functional office. On one wall was a fake window with

patterns of light dreamily playing in the glass, half obscured by steel-coloured shutters. A desk stood at the far side of the room, and a chair was neatly tucked under it. To the right of the desk was a door leading into sleeping quarters. There were no pictures on the wall, no adornments to enhance the functional grey of the place.

Moving over to the desk, the Doctor isolated the sound and pulled at the drawer. Locked. He shook his hand theatrically like a conjuror, then put it in his pocket and pulled out a hairpin. Realising there was no tumbler locking mechanism on the drawer, he self-consciously pushed the hairpin into his long light-brown hair. 'You're good for those locks at least.' He sighed and pulled out the sonic screwdriver. With a brisk twist of the shaft and a high-pitched whine, the drawer sprang open.

The beeping noise stopped. The Doctor's jaw dropped. 'That always happens!'

He fished around until he picked up the unit. It appeared to be part of the same range of equipment as the computer in the docking bay. A small, vivid blue square at the back of the machine sparkled in the weak light, and reminded the Doctor there was no need to skulk about in the dark. It was quiet as the grave, and at least the sudden luminescence triggered by his command of 'Lights!' dispelled some of the gloom accompanying that metaphor.

'It's a digital transmitting device,' he announced out loud, bored with the silence. 'And a receiver. But for what?' There was no answer save for the gentle, omnipresent hum, but the Doctor continued speaking regardless. 'What were you picking up, hmm?'

He studied the object closely, his fingers moving over the keypad underneath the crystal display as he walked from the room.

* * *

Sam fought down panic. It hadn't worked. She hadn't helped the woman and she couldn't help herself. She was history, and would probably end up being present and future too.

'Stay there!'

She was squeezed into the tiny compartment, legs bunched up to her chin, neck cramped, arms behind her back. It didn't seem real to her. This was something she often found: at a moment of extreme danger – and this was clearly one of them – things became less real. She and the Doctor would bluff their way out, things would just *happen*, as if someone else was calling the shots for them. Luck has no place in a rational universe, she remembered reading. But then to her mind neither did half the hideous monstrosities she'd run up against. Maybe your luck was determined by how far your mind could accommodate the thought of the hideous creatures and situations that must dominate the universe. Or maybe she was just rambling to take her mind off her impending –

Suddenly, the lights flared. She tried to turn her head but it was blocked into the tiny chamber by her shoulder. The brightness carried a heat that burnt her skin. She heard Vasid howl. What the hell was happening?

The Doctor came to an abrupt halt and covered his eyes as the corridor flooded with light. He reached out a hand to the wall for support as he instinctively ducked, then snatched it back with a gasp as the metal burnt his skin.

The onslaught lasted about thirty seconds. Then the lights faded back down to their former level.

And began to dim further.

The Doctor quickened his pace, feeling for the outline of the receive/transmit device in his coat pocket.

'Was that your doing?' Vasid swayed about, groping the air.

'Can't say it was, gorgeous,' Sam retorted. 'I can't quite reach the lights from here. Or hadn't you noticed?' She struggled furiously to get out of the cramped container, to slide the flimsy glass partition along with her fingers. While he was distracted…

'Why can't things just be normal? Why did you have to get rid of Vost? I'm sick of trying to think, sick of it!'

'Vost probably buggered off 'cause he was bored listening to your whining,' called Sam. She was starting to get a purchase on the glass. A little more time and she might just do it. *I believe in slug-headed giant porcupines that want to conquer the universe. I believe in giant pig-bee hybrid creatures that cruise round the galaxy in huge metal sties, and I'm going to get out of here.*

'I'm going to get rid of you and I'm going to get some sleep,' slurred Vasid. 'I'm sick of all this. You're probably not even real. I don't think any of this is real.'

'Oh, it's real enough, I assure you.'

Sam's heart leapt at the familiar voice. 'Doctor! I'm here!'

Vasid whirled round, and almost fell over. 'She was telling the truth!' Then he started giggling. 'A doctor? You're too late to help the others. You here to see me?'

'Well, you're clearly in a bit of a state,' said the Doctor, gently but firmly. 'Sam, are you all right?'

She almost smiled to hear such concern in his voice. 'Half left,' came her weak quip. She cringed as the words came out. She had to work harder on her tight-corner dialogue.

The Doctor tried to look at her predicament more closely over the bank of instruments, but Vasid lurched towards him. The Doctor held his ground, and stared challengingly at the flabby figure before him.

'And who might *you* be?' he inquired, politely.

'Vasid,' called Sam. 'He's mental.'

'Doesn't matter how many of you I send down, there're

always more of you, aren't there?' Vasid shook his head as if feeling sorry for himself, then his eyes started watering as paroxysms of laughter shook his body.

'Send down?' The Doctor's voice was suddenly hard. 'You've been sending people down to Hirath?'

'Wait your turn, I'm next!' piped up Sam, but the Doctor ignored her and Vasid just carried on laughing.

The Doctor took a step towards him and his voice cut through the smaller man's inane cackling. '*Tell me*.'

Vasid stopped, and shrugged. 'Couldn't – couldn't have her on the base. She got rid of Vost.'

'I never!' called Sam.

'You did, you liar!' Vasid shouted back, angrily. 'You made me get rid of Anstaar.' He turned to the Doctor, imploring him to believe. 'She made me get rid of Anstaar.'

'All right, now just calm down. Listen to me. I'm just going to get Sam out of there, and then we can all talk about the extreme danger I believe we're in.' As he spoke, Vasid could see the newcomer's eyes flickering between the central computer terminal, the flickering monitor screens, the matter-transmission booth and the instrumentation on the far wall.

Vasid sat down heavily in the control chair as the Doctor turned away with a tight smile.

Sam could just discern the Doctor striding towards her, his face full of concern. She smiled, broadly, but he couldn't see with her shoulder in the way. 'Knew I should've taken the sleeping quarters,' she muttered.

She saw the Doctor smile reassuringly as he moved his hand to the glass partition. But as he began to pull, his figure seemed diffuse with yellow light. A soft, gentle light that made her smile, giggle – no, it was like a tugging, as though she was being pulled on from within, and surely the Doctor could see her smiling so widely now, even though he seemed to be fading away, for her shoulder had gone and there was just bone there now, and now even that was gone –

Then her sight went with her reason and it was like drowning in a cold black stream.

'What have you done?' The Doctor grabbed hold of Vasid's shuddering bulk, incredulous, and shook him. 'You idiot!'

'You know what I've done,' said Vasid, dreamily, turning up his nose at the smell of burnt meat wafting through the control area. 'I sent her *down there*, like a probe. Everything will be under control.'

'Snap out of it.'

Vasid giggled again, and the Doctor slapped him lightly across the face. 'There's no time for this. Snap out of it, man! Where did you send Sam?'

Vasid stared at him, then slumped back in his chair. '*Down there*. I just need to sleep.'

The Doctor straightened up and began pacing round at almost comic speed. 'I've got to get her back. Sam, Sam, Sam, Sam, Sam…' He spun on his heel and pointed at Vasid. 'Is there anyone else on this base?'

'Not any more,' giggled Vasid.

The Doctor thumped his fist down on the desk with such force that the empty narcomilk bottles rolled off and smashed on the floor. 'Things are very wrong here, and unless *I'm* very wrong we're running out of time fast. You're going to help me. *Now*.'

Vasid saw real anger in the newcomer's wide grey-blue eyes, and cowered back in his chair.

He had the feeling he was not going to be allowed to just sleep off this trip.

In the chocolaty dark of the alien ship, the Leader sat in his control chair staring at the display of data flickering over the mesh screen before him.

'Signal flare,' came the technician's thick sibilant voice. 'We now have exact co-ordinates.'

'Close in,' rasped the Leader.

'Recognise this?' asked the Doctor, holding up the box he'd taken from Vost's office.

'No. Never seen one before.'

'Not standard issue, then, interesting. All right, question two: you saw the light surge, I take it?'

'Yes.' Vasid held his head in his hands, his thick fingers rubbing at his reddened eyes. The Doctor had ordered some water from a drone and forced it down his throat, splashing it over his face, gently cuffing him and coaxing him into a state approaching semi-consciousness. Vasid couldn't understand why this newcomer was actually being civil to him. He was feeling numb and ashamed, but despite that, deep down, a tiny piece of him was feeling a little proud. He'd never been so forceful in his life. It hadn't been too difficult, either – until this Doctor had turned up. And the Doctor was bigger than he was.

'It's this whole place,' he said. 'It's all going wrong. Has been for ages.'

'The machine stops, eh?' The Doctor looked up from his work dismantling a section of the control desk and ignored Vasid's blank look. 'I rather think it's dying, actually.'

'What?' Vasid shook his head to try to clear the thick fog he seemed to be thinking through.

'Dying.' He theatrically slumped forward on to the desk, then straightened back up. 'Fading fast. On its last legs. *Dying.*'

'What do you mean, dying? What are you talking about?'

'I think that surge of power was a last cry for help. A kind of warning. And I have the unpleasant thought that something out there was listening.'

'What?'

'There's an uninvited guest on the way. A ship, heading to this area. It's a long way off, but this base is designed to act early to seek proper authorisation. The ship refused to transmit access codes.' He looked down at the mass of circuitry and wiring lying on the desk. 'Of course, the ship may not even have known it had to *send* access codes for authorisation. But either way, the terminal out there has recognised the ship as unfriendly and has transmitted an incredibly complex hyperspatially bounced set of co-ordinate corridors to mislead the ship as to our precise location.' He smiled grimly. 'It could've sent that ship on a fool's errand halfway to the next system – a foolproof defence against any craft with a technology level comparable to your own.' A thought seemed to occur to him. 'Now, were you aware of that safety feature?'

'I'm not even aware of what you're talking about.'

'Precisely. So it wasn't you. And it wasn't me. And it certainly wasn't Sam or that poor girl you sent away.' He looked sadly over at the matter-transmission booth.

'Anstaar,' said Vasid, vaguely. He shook his head and carried on quickly. 'What wasn't us?'

'It wasn't any of us that caused that gigantic power surge. I'd imagine this place stood out like a sore thumb while all that went on.' He paused. 'To anyone who was looking, anyway.'

'Could've just been a glitch in the life-support. A natural surge.'

'Of that magnitude?' The Doctor shook his head. 'No. So unless the base did it all by itself...'

'How?'

'I don't know. But as I was saying earlier, it's had a critical effect on our surroundings. Your sending Anstaar and Sam down to Hirath –' Vasid shivered under the Doctor's icy glare

– 'has pushed this place over the edge. You've drained more or less the last vestiges of power in these circuits. Which means I can't follow her down there. Which also means the systems that are currently keeping Hirath stable will be running down. And *that* means that this entire sector of the galaxy may soon be torn apart, and I'm afraid there's no way of knowing if the life-support systems will hold out long enough for me to try to fix it.' The Doctor suddenly grinned. 'Whoops, eh? Looks like you might have killed us all.'

Vasid looked at him with scared eyes. 'What do you know about it?' he sneered at last. 'Nothing!'

'I know, *Mr* Vasid,' said the Doctor, his eyes flashing, 'that you prefer to live in your head rather than the real world, but that's just not possible now. Unless you start helping me to understand what's going on round here, you may find a bruised and battered cranium rather less comfortable accommodation for your little dream world than before.'

Vasid squirmed in his chair. 'Is that some kind of threat?'

'No.' The Doctor's voice was hollow. 'I'm just speculating as to the nature of our incoming visitors.' He frowned. 'And what they'll want when they get here.'

CHAPTER FOUR
CONFUSING RIGHT WITH WRONG

Tanhith's lungs prickled as he breathed deeply and slowly, staring out over the plain.

It was the same view as always from this preferred point of solitude. Mudflats giving way to small rises of soil and sand. Huge boulders strewn about like bizarre effigies left in the infinite past for a long-dead god to look upon. Here and there, a few scrubby bushes littering the baked red landscape, their tiny yellow flowers clogged up with dust and dirt.

There wasn't much else to see. A muddy trickle of water snaked its way from his wet feet beneath him through a furrow in the plain and into the base of a sheer cliff side towering in the distance. A few mountain birds wheeled around in the warm dirty air. Tanhith imagined them flying too near that fat sun one day and igniting, bursting into huge orange flames, falling like blazing arrows to the ground.

Dying in flames.

He was more sure every day that he would die here himself. Ever since the forced landing, the memories had been re-creating the event so vividly and so often it was like living through the last few minutes of a scared and desperate life. Enough was enough, and perhaps the burning birds would be the key. He wanted to be in their path – to die that way – when it happened. When it was time.

Just then, a movement caught his eye.

Something arose from behind one of the giant boulders nearby, hauling itself up into view. Tanhith rubbed his eyes, and took a few steps back, the splashes of his footsteps in the water drowning out what the creature seemed to be saying.

'Oiwadeaminnit.'

Tanhith cocked his head to one side, his eyelashes fluttering against his cheeks as he blinked in consternation, a look of astonishment on his face. The thing – the figure – was holding out its arms. Its voice was high-pitched and cracked, but clearer this time. It sounded desperate.

'Can you direct me back to the moon please?'

The figure crumpled to the hard sandy floor. Tanhith frowned.

He looked up once more at the circling birds, then moved cautiously towards the fallen figure.

'Hopeless. There's not enough power.' The Doctor slumped back on to the console and looked at Vasid. While his voice was calm, his eyes betrayed his anger and frustration. 'Tell me about Hirath.'

'What about it?'

He gestured around them. 'What is all this for? What do you keep down there, and why? What's Sam up against?'

'Depends where she is,' said Vasid, shrugging. 'Some use it as a storehouse. Some to tuck away their undesirables. TCC has got clients all around the local systems. Beyond that for all I know.'

'It's a shame you don't know more,' sighed the Doctor.

'You could do with talking to Vost. They recruited him quite early on. They took a lot of the initial workers from the Thannos sector. Strong central government. Order. Vost did a lot of the survey assessments, checking which bits were stable enough to support life and which could only be used as a dumping ground.'

'Plenty of takers for that, I suppose. Why drop on your own doorstep what you can drop on someone else's without protest?' reasoned the Doctor. 'And are many of the areas amicable to life?'

'No. But the transmission terminals the other end were only constructed in those areas in case we needed to check up on them on the owner's behalf.'

The Doctor baulked visibly at the term 'owner', but seemed relieved nevertheless. 'So this Vost, your boss, did you know him well?'

'No. He just ran things. He was all right, I suppose, for a repatriot.'

'I'm sorry?'

'Word is he started life on Venel.' The Doctor looked blank, and Vasid began to feel a little more like his old self at the revelation that the Doctor wasn't as clued up on local knowledge. 'You know, one of those arsey little Outer Worlds the government took back a few decades ago.'

'Was it theirs to reclaim?' wondered the Doctor, innocently.

'Of course it was ours. Everything in Thannos is rightfully ours. Anyway,' Vasid continued, 'Vost wasn't so bad for one of them.'

'Ironic, isn't it,' said the Doctor, smiling sadly, 'how much you miss the normality you've spent your life railing against when it's torn away from you? Things aren't so easy, are they?'

'Like I say,' muttered Vasid, 'he was all right.'

'Someone was communicating with him using this.' The Doctor held up the receive/transmit device. 'Possibly our visitors. Go to his office and have a good rummage about. See what you can find, see if he kept any records.'

'I just want to go to sleep.' Vasid yawned. 'You're crazy.'

'Do it.' The sudden authority in the Doctor's voice had Vasid on his feet before he even realised it. He glowered at the weird man in the green coat.

'And what are you going to do?'

The Doctor slapped a palm down on the console. 'Wait a minute! We were going to ask you, weren't we, Sa–' His head spun round to the empty matter-transmission device, and he sighed. 'Oh, Sam…' He looked hard at Vasid. 'We were going to ask you if you knew about the concealed area in the corridor.'

Vasid's voice rose in irritated disbelief. 'What? What are you talking about?'

'On the outer rim of what's marked on your plan as Sector C1. There's a concealed doorway leading to a whole new area, possibly pressurised.'

'No, there isn't.'

'There is. My transport's there right now.'

'There isn't. You *are* crazy.'

The Doctor carried on, eyes closed, shaking his head and speaking quickly, ignoring the fresh fear in Vasid's voice. 'No, no. A fool perhaps, but not crazy. Maybe Vost *did* discover it. Maybe he's discovered something *in* it and is there now.'

'I don't believe you. How *could* there be a concealed area?'

'Very easily. Embedded in the surface of this planetoid, perhaps. But who concealed it? And then those scratches on the walls and the floors…' He beamed at Vasid. 'How very interesting. Do you know, I'm beginning to think that you and your bosses are cuckoos in the nest.'

'Cuckoos?' Vasid stared at him. 'What are cuckoos?'

The Doctor attempted an impression, but Vasid just stared blankly. 'Vasid, you don't want to listen to my wild theories, so please just run along to Vost's office and try to find out what he was up to.'

'And you?'

'This equipment needs a boost if I'm to get Sam back. And I need something from my ship. So I'm off to the part of this base that doesn't exist. Won't be long.' He flashed a sudden smile. 'Oh, and Vasid?'

'Yes?'

'Be quick. I don't think we've got too much time on our hands.'

* * *

The room was almost stifling. The brightness of the day outside shone in through chinks in the stone walls. Felbaac found himself squinting as he faced the small assembly, and curled up his eyelashes to filter out some of the light, a frown on his high forehead.

'Not used to these conditions, eh, Felbaac?'

'Not such relentless sunlight, no,' came the immediate response. 'Where I was incarcerated on Ipmuss, the sun was so distant you could barely distinguish it from any other star in the sky. We dug and we mined rock and earth that was frozen for fifty metres down, for two years. So yes, this *is* quite a change for me.' With a small, tight smile Felbaac finished his carefully measured tirade, his voice even, rich and sonorous.

'Oh, I didn't for one moment imply you were a stranger to the toils and hardships of your fellow rebels, Felbaac. Not for one moment.'

Felbaac swallowed back his annoyance and smiled once more at his persistent heckler, deliberately ignoring any intended sarcasm. 'Dwynaar, we have all toiled. We have all suffered. But let us never lose sight of who we are struggling against.' His voice rose at last, confident and booming about the rough-hewn walls. 'They can dump us on forsaken rocks in space, they can try to sweep us out of the way – out of time and space altogether – but they can *never* crush us! They can never crush the spirit of *anyone* who knows their destiny is not bound up with the machinations of a corrupt, depraved –'

'I only asked if the heat was bothering you,' said Dwynaar with a shrug, a crooked smile on his whiskery face at the round of low laughter that followed.

A little awkwardly, a smaller figure, his hair jet-black, rose to his feet. 'Perhaps now is not the best of times for speeches,' he announced, to no one in particular.

'Fair words, Yast,' replied Felbaac, the tight smile returning to his gaunt face.

'Yes indeed, Yast,' rejoined Dwynaar. 'We don't need reminding how we came to be here.' He looked pointedly at Felbaac. 'Not from anyone.'

Felbaac moved from his position at the front of the shack, fed up with shielding his eyes from the glare. A few faces in the crowd turned to follow his movements, but the rest, like Dwynaar, stared sullenly at the ground. He'd seen it before. He'd been in enough prisons and known enough men who'd lost their hope, their conviction, even their faith in the ideals that had landed them there. The correction treatment was very effective. But, while a few would be repatriated and forced to publicly denounce their allegiances for propaganda value, the only reward most got was to die as restored citizens of Thannos with a decent state burial, instead of having their carcasses chucked out to rot on some pinprick planet far from anywhere.

So you had to *restore* faith. You had to lead, firmly but with compassion. Your decisions could never be wrong. You had to play deity to them, be unassailable, unbeatable. Wherever possible, give them a miracle.

He knew the score. He'd been one of Somaath's band for years. Somaath had pulled Felbaac off Ipmuss when there seemed no hope. He remembered the gruff man's burning zeal, his insane courage. The countless feats of heroism that made him an icon to millions, fighting the K'Arme across the system, bursting into speeches the way a show chorus would break into song. A righteous man, and then a hero.

But Somaath was dead now. And, as his only trusted confederate and partner in rebellion still fighting with any degree of success, Felbaac was finally becoming known system-wide.

So this rabble could damn well show him some respect.

'All I'm saying,' he began again, his tone urgent, 'is that you must be ready. You'll be needed to fight the fight again. We all will.'

'You've been here... how long?' Dwynaar made an elaborate show of counting his fingers. 'Two months? Well, we're all up for fighting the good fight once again, Felbaac, but where are we going to fight it? Out there in that red desert? Not many souls to save out there.'

Felbaac cut across the rising murmurs of agreement with Dwynaar. 'It's our *own* souls we have to nurture for now. You've been left here now almost twenty years. I know what that does to men. Believe me, I know. But you've survived, took what little they threw at you and made yourselves strong on it –'

'We've kept ourselves alive,' snarled Dwynaar, rising to his feet.

'And what for, eh?' Felbaac stared at him with burning eyes. 'Have you kept yourself alive for so long just to give in and die here?'

Yast walked nervously across to Dwynaar, shooting embarrassed looks at Felbaac. 'We're already retraining you. We're going to equip you, too.'

'We're going to let you fight back!' Felbaac shouted.

There was a long silence. Dwynaar broke it.

'*Let* us fight back? Or *make* us?'

The sheet-iron door was kicked open with a loud bang and the squeal of rusty hinges. Framed in the searing brightness outside was a tall figure, panting with exertion.

'Tanhith!' Felbaac exaggerated his concern, grateful for the interruption. Then as his squinting eyes adjusted to the light, he realised the man was carrying something. Something slight and blonde.

Tanhith lowered his burden to the dusty floor. Coughing saliva noisily from his throat, he looked up at his leader. 'I found her out there in the desert' He coughed noisily, again.

'She's not dead. Not yet.'

The men in the room stared in silent disbelief. Then a babble of astonishment swept the room, and chairs scraped noisily across the floor as the men crowded round the new arrivals.

'Back! Get back!' growled Tanhith, crouching protectively at his find as hands reached out to poke, prod and feel. 'Get back!'

Dwynaar swung round from the periphery of the crowd and marched over again to Felbaac. 'This another facet of your brilliant master plan?'

Your decisions could never be wrong.

Felbaac looked directly into the older man's eyes. 'Perhaps.'

The Doctor reached the part of the corridor with the hidden section, and aimed the sonic screwdriver at it, trying it on different frequencies until at last the door opened. He kept it in position by implanting a small loop of sonic oscillation in its opening mechanism.

All was as he and Sam had left it. The battered police-box shell of the ship stood in the corner. He wondered, not for the first time, if it had an aesthetically aware circuit that made it materialise in a tucked-away location each time, and smiled.

Cautiously he moved behind the police box. A few traces of a brown mucus-like material stained the wall in vertical streaks. Peering closely, he thought he could detect another hidden door in the wall, partially obscured by the hardened slime.

'A pressurised area between the forward and aft sections?' mused the Doctor. 'Fascinating theory, Doctor. Oh, do you think so, Doctor? Absolutely, Doctor.' He sighed noisily. 'This sort of thing is lonely without a companion.'

Turning back to the door, which was still open, the Doctor made some rough measurements, just like an artist trying to gauge perspective with his thumb. Then he walked outside and stretched out his arms either side of him in the wide corridor, before walking back, apparently satisfied, opening the TARDIS doors and going inside.

A short time passed, then there was the roar of an engine igniting, subsiding to a steady purr.

The Doctor drove his purple Volkswagen Beetle from the TARDIS. Popping out to close the ship's doors, he happily patted the car's roof and then clambered back in. He drove round the corner and along the corridor towards the control room.

Vasid asked himself almost constantly what he was doing and why he was doing it. And he kept coming to the same basic answer – he had no idea what else he *should* do.

So he rummaged through Vost's belongings. Nothing particularly dodgy, no filth. He picked up a glass frame that held a vidprint of Vost and what was presumably his family, enjoying a few moments of celebration and happiness in an endless loop. Sneering at the scene, Vasid threw it to the ground, where it shattered.

So much for authority, he thought. So much for Vost.

There was a grey plastic diskette holder on Vost's desk. Vasid dropped it to the ground and stamped on it. Then he began to throw out anything that wasn't fixed down against the floor. He pulled off the sheets from the bed, threw clothes around the room in a tantrum and smashed a huge mirror, panting harder and harder and feeling tears well up inside him.

There was no one to stop him doing whatever the hell he liked. He could do anything. No one cared. No one was there to stop him.

He felt sick.

Rubbing his eyes, he glanced up at the broken mirror.

Behind some of the fragments still fixed to the wall there was something taped – a small package. He pulled it from the wall, a shard of the glass cutting into his thumb. He cried out and sucked it.

This whole place must've stood out like… that was what the Doctor had said.

Shivering, he opened the parcel. Data disks.

Vasid started up the machine on the desk, too worked up even to register the cheery TCC start-up tune with the usual cringe, and inserted the first of the small pile. The disk's tinny datavox announced that the first file had been created just four months ago.

Within a second graphics filled the screen. Vasid just stared. Then a chill ran through him.

PRIORITY K'ARME
THIS MESSAGE PROPERTY SPECIAL K'ARMEAN
HUNTDOWN DIVISION.

The message was from the Most High Commissioner of the House of Beckal. It held confirmation of some kind of transaction.

For a time Vasid did nothing but stare. Then, involuntarily, he looked around at the mess he had made of the room. Without thinking, he began clearing things up, hands shaking but making small piles of half-broken objects.

He didn't want to think how powerful Vost's allies must be.

The Doctor could hear the beeping of a communications unit as he approached the control room, even over the throaty growl of the Beetle's engine. The car wouldn't fit through the doorway, so the Doctor pulled up on the handbrake, turned off the engine, flung open the door and skidded over the bonnet to answer the noise. He looked around, trying to ascertain exactly what was beeping. Then he strolled over to the slim grey grille mounted in the wall near the control console.

'Vasid, is that you?'

'Who else would it be?'

The Doctor almost flinched from the fear in Vasid's voice. 'Vasid, what is it? What have you found?'

'Vost. I can't believe it.'

'What?'

'He's an agent.'

The Doctor stared blankly at the grille. 'A cleaning agent? An estate agent? What do you –'

'Vost is an agent for the K'Arme. He must be.'

'The who?'

'The K'Arme, you idiot. The Justice Control Force from the Homeworld.'

The Doctor frowned, then nodded furiously. 'They're your police?'

'They *own* the police throughout this system. And who knows what else?'

'Let me guess: they helpfully make all your government's decisions for them, control the populace by covert means and lurk menacingly in the background at every state parade.'

'You can joke, Outer. No one knows exactly how powerful they really are.'

'But your people like to err on the side of caution. Look, why don't we talk face to face? You can show me your evidence then. I'm feeling silly talking to this grille.' There was a pause. 'Vasid?'

'Wait.' Vasid's voice was hoarse. Tension and dehydration, the Doctor decided as he wandered over to the car and slid across its bonnet to get to the boot. The grille remained silent, so the Doctor called across, helpfully, 'I'm still here!'

The silence continued as he pulled the long tangle of jump

leads from the boot and then reached inside to release the bonnet clamp. As he was finishing connecting one end of each lead to the Beetle's battery, a bizarre sound echoed out from the speaker grille: wild laughter.

'Vasid?'

'This is crazy. Oh, Vost. No wonder you left us to it.'

'What is it? What have you found?' Silence. 'Vasid!'

'Vost got mixed up in something big. So much for the proud repatriated citizen. He did his deal for the K'Arme after they found out he'd been helping the rebels.'

The Doctor stared bemusedly at the grille as the unsettling sound of Vasid's laughter filled the control room.

The curled-up slug of a spaceship powered through the void, compensating almost instinctively to stay on course despite the distant pull of Hirath's sun.

The Leader lay back on a wire-mesh bunk, trying to rest. They were close now. So close. He had to be prepared.

With a mechanical belch, a small point of light began flashing on his monitor screen.

'Another ship?' he ventured.

'Yes, Leader,' came the rumble of the technician in the darkness, as if praising a small child. 'At the periphery of our forward scanners.'

The Leader ignored any intended patronising. 'What is its intended course?'

'Early indications suggest Hirath. It is too far out to attack unless we change course.'

'No,' sighed the Leader. 'We must not attract undue attention here. It is unimportant to our mission.'

With a familiarly crushing sense of disappointment, he contemplated the tiny speck of light and their inability to wipe it out.

* * *

Tanhith looked down at the figure on the bunk, wiping a hand through his thick blond hair, feeling how damp it was with sweat. A rush of frustration surged through him at the relentless heat. He saw the perspiration standing out on the young creature's forehead like little beads, and wiped his finger in a circular pattern over them to crush them.

She was alien; but rather than being repulsed, he found himself fascinated. He parted her lips, and saw one tongue lying slack inside, not two. Yet he was sure she was female. Her bones were small, she had a thin waist, her chest was clearly designed for suckling the young. But the yellow hair, the blue eyes with their tiny lashes, the single tongue... Even the nose was larger than the narrow pinch of skin bestowed upon the women of his race.

He turned away and went to the shuttered window. Outside the men of the camp were working as the sun shone balefully down. Most tended the neat rectangles of crops that littered the settlement, the brukweed that kept them alive. While some squeezed the fleshy stems for drops of sweet water, others carefully removed the leaves with a well-practised clipping movement. A group of younger men were digging deep under the sandy topsoil for the more fertile ground beneath. And there was Dwynaar, the grizzled old bird, hefting up the foul-smelling mud in an improvised basket and carrying it to different patches of bruk, piling it up around the base of each plant, then moving back to collect some more.

He coughed, noisily and turned from the depressing sight. These men were living from day to day just for the sake of it. But in that case, it wasn't really living, was it? It was survival.

He knew how they felt. Some men, surviving battle after endless battle and living through a whole parade of pointless skirmishes, became veterans. He still felt like nobody, nothing. A set of responses, not a man. Just like those men out there.

Except that Tanhith was no longer scared of dying. He felt it in the warm, fetid air, in the dusty soil on his boots. This place welcomed death, it knew all about it. He thought of the burning birds, and of the old wishes for blazes of glory, for his name to be remembered in hushed tones. And now dreams of accidental death, or a quiet funeral pyre, burning in silence. A private death in nobody's name.

He turned back to the girl on the bed, and brushed a bruk leaf against her sun-reddened face. She troubled him, this alien girl from nowhere.

'How much glory is there in you?'

The door was kicked open with a rasp of metal on stone. In the doorway stood Felbaac and the ever-hovering Yast.

'Tanhith, you were meant to be with Maadip and Elb training group E.'

Felbaac wasn't bothering to hide his irritation, but equally Tanhith couldn't be bothered to disguise his lethargy. 'Those men aren't interested, Felbaac. They don't care.'

'Then you *make* them care. We *have* to have a fighting force.'

'Then we should've got here a few years earlier. What have they got to care about?'

Felbaac strode over and almost spat out the words. 'They've got the lawless swine who put them here to pay back. They've got the freedom of their people to fight for.'

'In other words, they've just *got* to care. Because you can't use them if they don't.'

Felbaac turned away. Yast hovered indecisively between the two men.

'This is a lost cause, Felbaac.' Tanhith gestured outside at the workers, then suddenly stopped, and drew himself up to his full height. 'Ours is a lost cause.'

Felbaac spun round, surprise and anger flickering across his face in rapid succession. Yast stepped in.

'We all feel like that sometimes, Tanhith, we all do, with all that we've done.' His voice was low and soothing, but his eyes flickered about nervously. 'But we must never voice those thoughts. We must never give in to self-pity. There's too much at stake.'

Tanhith smiled, ignoring the smaller man. 'These men won't fight for you, Felbaac. Look at the state of them.'

'By the deity, I'll *make* them fight!'

'Face it, your information was bad. A grade-one penal settlement for top political offenders?'

'And so it was.' Felbaac was on the defensive.

'Twenty years ago perhaps. When Somaath was barely starting out.'

'So why place them so quickly on Hirath? Cut off from the rest of the galaxy and policed long-range by approximate number only?'

'I imagine there was less of a waiting list back then,' said Tanhith drily. 'Or perhaps they're here as a decoy precisely for men like you. Maybe that's why Somaath was never stupid enough to –'

Felbaac raised his fist and Tanhith instinctively backed away. Yast flapped his arms up and down between the two of them, and just then another voice rang out.

'Look, when you've finished beating each other up, how about getting me a glass of water and telling me where the bloody hell I am?' The three men gaped at the alien girl, who raised an eyebrow. 'You mean this isn't room service?'

CHAPTER FIVE
IN A JAM

Luckily for Vasid, the Doctor had warned him about the purple thing blocking the doorway to the control room. He peered over its metal shell and saw the Doctor reaching down into the bowels of the control desk by the computer. Seeming to sense Vasid's arrival, the Doctor pulled himself out and stared at him.

'I take it the rebels have little chance of changing things in this system?'

Vasid glanced furtively about as if expecting to see hidden portacams recording his every word. 'All of the Thannos system belongs to the Homeworld. Outer scum, that's what they are, dangerous influences.'

'You don't feel something of an affinity with them then?'

'No!' Vasid bellowed. He tried to calm down. 'Why do you care, anyway?'

'Oh, I'm a bit of a buff on rebellion, oppressive regimes, that sort of thing,' said the Doctor, breezily. 'So, this place – and Temporal Commercial Concerns – is of entirely alien origin?'

'Yes.'

'But which aliens?'

Vasid shook his head. 'I don't know. The Thannos sector of TCC runs this place for them, but doesn't own it.'

'Ah, the caring human face of alien technology.'

'Human?'

'You know what I mean. Well, that at least explains what I've found here.' The Doctor gestured at the pit in the control desk. 'Someone, presumably TCC, has attempted to augment this computer. They're very advanced circuits, but still crude in comparison with the original. And I'll tell you something else. A few things, in fact. First, this machine has developed some kind of personality.'

'What? Do you speak nothing *but* dross?' Vasid stared insolently at the Doctor, who continued speaking with a pleasant smile on his face.

'No, it's quite true, I assure you. I don't mean personality in the way that you and I – well, in the usual sense. But the components in this machine easily lend themselves to a simulation of something similar – a complicity, if you like, an understanding. But perhaps "developed" was too polite a word. These circuits have been overcome by something – something else.'

'It's probably just broken,' said Vasid, uneasily. 'It's been acting up for ages.'

'What, giving out strange messages, that sort of thing?'

'Just not making any sense. Piece of rubbish.'

'Hmm.' The Doctor began to pace up and down again, and Vasid rolled his eyes. 'It's probably just finally given up and gone mad. Torn between regulating that mass of time fields down there and trying to hear itself think, it's given up on either. Which leads me to point two.'

'Is point two as boring as point one?'

'Very probably,' beamed the Doctor. 'There's enormous temporal leakage in one part of Hirath, by the look of these readings. It's dangerously unstable. Chances are it's even responsible for the state the whole planet's in.'

'I can't be bothered to listen to all this.' Vasid turned to go but the Doctor grabbed him and sat him down in the control chair.

'Then don't listen. But talking aloud helps me think, and I always do it best to a sentient audience.' Peering intently at Vasid, he sighed. 'Anyway, suppose that that temporal leakage is like an embolism, or a clot in time, poisoning what's around it. What if that machine was meant to be curing what caused it but instead has been *communicating* with it?'

'How?'

The Doctor scratched his head. 'I honestly don't know. But it's an intriguing theory, isn't it?'

Vasid banged a fat fist on the table. 'Shut up with your theories! What are we going to do?'

The Doctor looked at him gravely. 'We're going to get back poor Sam and Anstaar, and do everything we can to save the lives of everyone else on Hirath. We're going to think of a way to stop that planet tearing itself apart throughout history and wiping out a large portion of this galaxy with it.'

Vasid turned away but the Doctor was relentless. 'We're going to persuade whoever's on their way here that they really *don't* want to come in after all, and perhaps then we can think about staying alive ourselves, because I really don't think that life-support is going to function much longer.' He smiled, and his face softened. 'So if you'd like to turn the key inside my vehicle over there to start the engine, I can see what I can do about jump-starting the regulators.'

Vasid shuffled off, pasty-faced, to the Doctor's machine.

'Hey! Have you seen it?'

Dwynaar looked up from his pile of mud, spitting a gobbet of thick saliva at the bruk in front of him. 'What d'you want, Sost?'

'The sun. It's not shifting.'

Dwynaar automatically stared up at the sun, his eyelashes bending upward to shield his grey eyes. 'You're crazy.'

'Maybe.' The short younger man smiled uneasily at him. 'But I've been working in my shadow for what feels like hours now. And I know how much work I get done in a day.'

'Yeah. Not enough.'

Sost ignored the joke, pushing a long length of wet brown

hair out of his eyes. 'I tell you, that sun's not shifting.'

'Well, what in the deity's name does that mean?'

'Beats me,' muttered Sost, digging at the dusty ground once again. 'Just thought I'd mention it.' He smiled grimly at Dwynaar's worried expression. 'Could be a long day.'

Sam put down the metal cup of water, licking her lips much to the fascination of her audience. She became suddenly aware of the scrutiny she was under, and cleared her throat. Her skin felt tight and sore, and prickled in the wet heat of the stone room. 'So…' She couldn't think of much to say. 'Thank you for getting me out of the sun. I feel half cooked.'

Felbaac smiled tightly. 'Thank Tanhith here. He found you.'

Sam looked at the tall, willowy man with his long droopy lashes and pretty green eyes. He smiled a little awkwardly. 'Thank you, Tanhith,' she said, and smiled herself. 'So this is Hirath then?'

'Yes. Although you'll find that anyone left here long enough comes to think of it as hell,' announced the other man with well-rehearsed melodrama.

'Well, I've heard that hell is other people. At least it's less crowded in here now the little bloke's gone outside,' Sam said.

'That's Yast,' said Tanhith, helpfully.

Sam swung herself off the bunk and paused, eyes scrunched up, as a wave of dizziness passed over her. She swallowed thickly. 'And who are you, then?'

'My name is Felbaac.' He folded his arms as if waiting for a reaction. When none came, he continued. 'Perhaps you've heard of me.'

'Sorry, no. Should I have?'

'Well, you are an alien, of course.'

That tight-lipped smile again. Sam raised an eyebrow. 'Of course.'

'So now perhaps you'd like to tell us who you are and how you come to be here.'

Tanhith called over from his spot in front of the shuttered window. 'She needs rest, not an interrogation.'

'I'm fine,' said Sam, a little more grumpily than she'd intended. 'My name is Samantha Jones and as for how I come to be here… well, do *you* know what this planet is?'

'It's one of the places our so-called government puts away its undesirables, anyone who dares to speak out against its imperialist policies.'

Tanhith closed his eyes as he felt another speech gaining momentum and interrupted. 'It's a planet cut into segments which are rented out to the highest bidders, no questions asked. Each strip of land is caught in its own separate time zone.'

'So – explain to us how *you* got here.' Felbaac repeated his question with heavy emphasis on each syllable.

Sam eyed him, casually. A high forehead, dark eyes. The same droopy eyelashes as Tanhith, but blacker, less attractive. He could've been handsome in a way, but overall he reminded her of a dodgy salesman. 'From the control centre,' she began, hesitantly deciding that honesty was the best policy. But how much did they know? 'Up on the moon. I was sent down from the place that keeps this planet ticking over.' A shock of realisation hit her. 'Hey, there wasn't anyone else out there with me was there? A woman?'

'No,' said Tanhith with a small smile. 'Good job too. I couldn't have carried both of you.'

Felbaac carried on. 'It's ridiculous. You couldn't have come from the control centre. No one can steer through the time fields without the authorised co-ordinate codes.'

Sam's head hurt. She was fed up with this bloke's attitude. 'Well, you got here, didn't you? Maybe I got them from the same place you did.'

'Vost? You mean you –'

'Shut up, Tanhith!' snapped Felbaac. 'You idiot! We could've found out if she was telling the truth if she'd told us herself!'

'Well, actually I didn't.' Both men stared at her. 'He was long gone by the time I arrived. Missing, believed dead. I think.'

Felbaac and Tanhith looked at each other.

Sam continued. 'I was sent down here through some kind of matter-transmission device, I think. Judging by its size, it's not meant for people. Didn't stop some psycho having a pop, though.'

'She's gibbering,' said Felbaac. 'It's the heat.'

'It's the truth,' snapped Sam.

Felbaac continued to stare at Tanhith. 'Come outside,' he ordered, moving to the door. Tanhith shrugged at Sam, and followed him out into the oppressive heat of the day.

Sam looked at the door as it closed. She rubbed her burning eyes, wincing as the dizziness returned with a wave of nausea. Then the clanking of a chain being wrapped around the handle filled the air. 'Surprise, surprise,' she muttered.

'She's not going anywhere. Where *can* she go?' protested Tanhith as Felbaac finished coiling the heavy chain round the door handle. 'Everyone's a prisoner here, remember?'

'So Vost's gone. He'd have wanted to get away, I imagine.'

'What are you talking about?' asked Tanhith.

Felbaac looked at him. 'Do you really think she came down via a matter transmitter? What was she doing there on Vost's base anyway?'

'Well, perhaps we should try asking her. If you don't believe her story, why do you believe Vost isn't there any more?' Tanhith followed his leader's example and ploughed on without waiting for an answer. 'We know aliens made Hirath the way it is. Maybe she's one of them.'

Felbaac said nothing. 'I wonder if she knows how to get

back from here? The safe path?'

'That wasn't much of a safe path,' retorted Tanhith. 'Those co-ordinates were constantly fluctuating.'

'Vost warned us it was a hazardous route without the very latest updates. He did his best for us.' Felbaac smiled, grimly. 'Maybe your piloting just wasn't up to following them.'

The memories sat heavily in Tanhith's mind once again, distracting him. He tried to concentrate. 'I… I got us down alive, didn't I? When half the thrusters aged to dust, I still gave us a landing.'

'And I'm grateful, Tanhith,' smiled Felbaac, smoothly, looking over the other man's shoulder. 'Now here comes Yast. Perhaps he'll have news for us on the repairs' progress.'

The diminutive man bustled over, wringing his hands. 'The latest batch of circuits don't patch in either,' he whined, apologetically. 'Even the brightest here are employing methodology we outgrew twenty years ago.' He looked down at the red dust swirling round his boots. 'That ship's not taking off again.'

Tanhith smiled grimly to himself and glanced at Felbaac, whose face was impassive. Then Yast began twittering again.

'And the men here, Felbaac. They seem to be working themselves up about the sun. They think it's all down to the alien in there.' He gestured with distaste at the chained-up outhouse.

'What do they think is down to her?' demanded Tanhith.

'I told you, the sun.' Yast blinked at them. 'They say it's stopped moving.'

'It's no use,' said the Doctor, wiping his hands on his trousers. 'This machine has lost the will to live.' He looked over at Vasid, who had connected the black box from Vost's quarters to a small monitor screen and a data disk loader borrowed from Anstaar's quarters. 'How are you getting on?'

Vasid shrugged. 'Hard to say. Vost kept his dealings brief. But I think he was selling the co-ordinates of how to get through the time barriers to somewhere on Hirath.'

'Where on Hirath?' demanded the Doctor.

'A penal colony –'

'No no no no. I mean where geographically?' The Doctor threw over a small chart of Hirath that had been mounted on the wall. Vasid gestured to an area near the planet's equator. 'Round there, I think.'

'Hmm, not far from the temporal leakage then.'

Vasid shook his head. 'First he sold a safe path to the rebels, then gave the information to the K'Arme. Different co-ordinates second time. The same rough area, but –'

'I'd imagine that any safe path through that desolation would change and shift with some regularity. Especially with this thing –' he tapped the computer – 'playing up. If you don't get in and out pretty sharpish, you're in trouble.'

'The last lot of data was transmitted only a few hours ago,' mused Vasid, rubbing his red-rimmed eyes.

'Preprogrammed to answer your K'Arme's signal, I'd guess. I suppose Vost wouldn't have wanted to risk making the transmission himself if he was on duty.' The Doctor scratched his head. 'Even if he was worried that his double dealings would be found out, where could he run?'

'Found out by whom? The K'Arme?'

'I think he probably told the K'Arme exactly where the rebels were. If any of the rebels had ships about to observe the K'Arme craft, it wouldn't take them long to get a little suspicious.'

Vasid looked up, almost hopefully. 'Could that be the K'Arme's ship approaching?'

'No. They'll be heading for Hirath, remember, not here.'

'The rebels then, coming for Vost?'

'Both they and the rebels would have been thrown off the

scent by the automated defence.' He looked at the dismay on Vasid's face and smiled ruefully.'That rules them out. Sadly.'

Vasid jumped to his feet, aggressively. 'Think you know all the answers, don't you?' he began.

The Doctor sighed.'Vasid, I really haven't the time for more helpless paranoia. And neither do you. Just sit down and be quiet.'

Vasid swung a fist at him. The Doctor ducked under Vasid's arm in a blur of movement and grabbed hold of the back of his flabby neck, squeezing it gently.

'I can't move,' squealed Vasid.'Let me go.'

The Doctor shook his head, sadly. 'As I say, there's no time for this. Why not make a little more of your own life instead of trying to take from the lives of those around you?' He let go, and smoothed down Vasid's stained tunic. Then he turned back to the gutted console. It was as if the incident had never happened.

'It's no good. I'm going to have to divert power from the hidden part of this ship to keep this thing on line.'

'What do you mean, "ship"? I never know what you mean,' moaned Vasid.

'This isn't a base: it's an alien spacecraft. This must've been the flight computer. The vessel either crashed or was buried, but whoever took possession only needed certain systems. So they stripped out this part of the craft and made it nice and cosy for you and your fellow crew members.' The Doctor's voice lowered to a conspiratorial whisper:'But I'd estimate a good two-thirds of this ship is still as the makers intended.' Then he looked up brightly. 'Terrible waste of power if you ask me. I think we'll divert it to where we need it. Do you agree? Good.'

'You *are* mad.'Vasid backed away. He looked as if he were about to cry. 'Well, you can just leave me alone, all right?' No answer.'All right?'

Vasid stormed over to the doorway and clambered over the vehicle. But, fishing around with connections in the bowels of the control desk, the Doctor barely even noticed him go.

A sudden shudder vibrated through the console, and a hum of energy rose from the control desk. The monitors flickered back on. Images of Hirath annotated with swirls of red graphics clarified from a snowstorm of pixels. The central computer powered up, and the Doctor gave a satisfied nod.

'That's that.' He frowned. 'Now I wonder what may come crawling out the woodwork as a result.'

He walked over to the clear perspex booth of the matter transmitter. Taking out his sonic screwdriver, he set to work.

Vasid staggered off up the corridor. Huge sobs racked his body, and tears flooded his eyes, drowning them, making him blind. Nothing made sense any more. With everything turned upside down, all he could do was hide until his world had finished falling in.

Self-pity gnawed at him. He wished Vost would suddenly appear, explain that it was all a big joke, that the Doctor was an old friend of his and that everything was fine. Tell him to get some sleep, then to get back to work. Life as usual.

He wandered aimlessly, not knowing where he was going, at times breaking into a stumbling run, at others slowing down and gasping for breath. Then, wiping hot tears away with the back of his hand, he came to a standstill as a dark, massive shape blurred into view close ahead of him.

His heart missed a beat and he stopped breathing.

He got the impression of something huge, some kind of creature, almost reaching up to the ceiling. Its skin was dark, brown and shiny, with the texture and smell of charred flesh.

Vasid didn't know whether to scream or start crying again. While he made up his mind, he turned and ran desperately along the corridor.

* * *

The sun was still sitting like a huge welt in the pink flesh of the sky. Sam reflected on the men milling about outside, talking, arguing, all the time shooting suspicious glances up at the sky as if expecting the sun to have leapt half a mile across it and for everything to be normal again.

But then, she couldn't blame them. It was frightening. As simple as that. Somehow, fighting Krotons, Daleks, whatever – however scary or deadly they were – you could understand them. They wanted to kill you, or to subjugate you, or to do something undoubtedly very unpleasant to you, and you either resisted or gave in.

The sun didn't give a bugger what you did. If it wanted to stop, well, what the hell did that mean?

Shivering despite the heat, she sat down on the bunk again, wincing at its unexpected hardness against the small of her back.

The chain suddenly rattled against the iron door, and she tried to assume a pose of studied boredom for her imminent visitor.

It was Tanhith, and she relaxed. 'Hello. Nice day, isn't it?'

'I think we've all had enough of it,' said Tanhith, smiling grimly. He sat down, eyelashes swaying as he positioned himself on the stone floor. Sam couldn't help smiling, and he noticed. 'What?'

'Those lashes. Unbelievable!'

Tanhith stared at her. 'What do you mean?'

'Have you any idea how many of my old schoolfriends would kill for lashes like those?' She started laughing as Tanhith distracted her by suddenly flexing them so they performed a small Mexican wave under, then over, his eyelids.

It was strange, to suddenly laugh like that, and it fleetingly occurred to her just how happy it could make her to be a traveller in time and space. 'That's a neat little trick.'

'Elementary grooming. We're taught it at a young age. It's a custom in the Outer Worlds.'

'Well, Tanhith, I am well accustomed to customs, and I still say it's a neat little trick.' Her smile dropped a little. 'Why am I locked up here?'

Tanhith shrugged. 'Felbaac's reminding us all he's in charge, I suppose. Deity knows, he does it often enough.'

'In charge of what?'

'Of everything we are. He is the custodian of our cause, and of our selves. Of the entire rebellion, it seems.'

'Rebellion, eh?' Sam nodded. 'Is that why you're banged up here?' Tanhith looked blankly at her. 'Stuck in this dump, I mean.'

'Obliquely, I suppose,' said Tanhith, wryly, stifling another hacking cough. 'We aren't prisoners any more – not officially anyway. Our ship was damaged as we descended into this inferno. It seems we can't get back out again, nor get our...' He tailed off, and smiled a little sadly. 'Felbaac brought us here because we need a small army to help us in our attack.'

'Attack?' Sam's voice was unapologetically harsher.

'Well, in our struggle to assert and maintain the liberty of the Outer Worlds, then.' He was well aware of the disappointment in her eyes. 'You are quick to judge me, Samantha Jones.'

'Sam,' she said, a little hollowly. 'No. I'm sure you fight for what you believe in. Just as whoever you're fighting against is oppressing you in the name of whatever they believe in.' She looked down at her feet. 'Even a bloody Dalek fights for whatever it believes in.'

'A Dalek?' Tanhith made a show of being affronted. 'Now you are *surely* doing me a disservice.' He held out both arms in front of him, pointing at her, and moved the eyelashes of both eyes into one black circular tangle above his long, thin nose. 'EX-TER-MIN-ATE!'

Sam smiled again and shook her head at how bizarre things

could get. Wherever you were in the galaxy you could bet your life you'd find someone willing to share scary Dalek anecdotes. The evil little sods had probably broken the ice at more parties across the universe than anything else. 'I'm sorry. That *was* probably a bit a much,' Sam said at length, 'but spare me the details. I don't want to get into the rights and wrongs right now. I'm tired. Is that OK?'

'That's – OK.' Tanhith pronounced the letters falteringly, but seemed to understand their meaning. He smiled at her again.

'What are you doing here, anyway?' Sam was suddenly suspicious. 'Is it time for part two of the interrogation?'

'I just wanted to warn you. I think those men out there think you're responsible for this odd little mystery with the sun, and I've a feeling they might want to ask you some questions about it.'

'What?' Sam looked scared as well as exasperated. 'How could *I* be affecting it?'

Tanhith shrugged. 'They've been here twenty years. It's inevitable that reason must give way to superstition.'

'Well,' said Sam a little bitterly, 'thanks for something new to worry about as I lie here by myself. I'm beginning to wish you'd left me out in the desert.'

Tanhith looked pointedly at her one last time before closing the door. She tried to puzzle out the expression on his face for some minutes after the chains had been put back in place.

Felbaac kicked at the ground, sending a cloud of hot red dust into the air. 'This distraction is just what we didn't need. It'll be harder than ever to get them interested in the battle training now.'

Yast looked at him nervously across the table, his voice timid and joining Felbaac's in echoes around the low stone walls of the council chamber. 'What do you think it means? Could it be that blonde thing?'

'Oh, don't be ridiculous. It's just some localised time distortion. Some freak effect.' He banged his metal cup down hard on the table. 'Deity knows, this whole planet is a freak effect! What are they getting worked up about?'

'It's never happened before in twenty years.'

'Well, maybe that's because it only *happens* once every twenty years.'

Yast's voice was barely more than a whimper. 'Or maybe they've run out of their allotted time here. Maybe that's all the government paid for. Twenty years. Maybe now the sun's going to just sit there for ever and ever and ever and –'

'Shut up, Yast!' yelled Felbaac, throwing his mug at the weaselly little man. He calmed himself down. 'That can't be. The government wouldn't just let them die like that – there's far more capital in stringing out these people's lives, rehabilitating them and parading them around the Inner Worlds as tame little pets.'

'You don't really believe that, Felbaac,' muttered Yast.

'I do. And this bunch will let them do it, too.' He paused. 'If we let them.'

'They know you're stalling them.' Panic tinged Yast's words. 'They know you'd take them off-world and train them somewhere with proper facilities if you could.'

'While they stay here, the government's long-range surveillance won't register anything's wrong. There's nowhere safer for them than here, they know that.'

'No, Felbaac, no. They've guessed you're stuck here now, just like them. They've seen us to-ing and fro-ing to the rocket. They've guessed and they're right. We're all of us stuck, even the damned sun, so what are we going to do?'

'You just don't understand, do you, Yast?' Felbaac sneered at the little man. 'You really think I'd be so unprepared? You really think I'd risk telling anyone my plans?' Suddenly the kindly public face of the revolution was back, borrowing

Felbaac's swarthy features. 'Trust me, Yast. All we need do is wait a little longer. I'm sure of it.' He rose and walked over to the window. The yard outside was bright and still, the air shimmering in the heat. 'We're not beaten yet.'

'Doctor!'

Even distorted through the grille at high volume, the voice sounded desperate as it blared out into the control room.

The Doctor left the lash-up of equipment around the matter transmitter and was at the wall communicator in seconds. 'Vasid! Where are you!'

'There are – *things* here!'

The Doctor swallowed hard. 'What kind of things?' Silence. 'Vasid, this is important! What things?'

'Creatures.' The word was barely more than a throaty whisper.

The Doctor frowned. 'Hostile?'

'I don't know, I don't know.'

'How many?'

'I don't know. I've seen two of them so far. Oh, please save me, Doctor.' The Doctor shut his eyes as Vasid tried to choke back his tears. 'Please save me.'

'Where are you?'

'I – Oh, no –'

The communicator went dead. 'Vasid? Vasid!'

The Doctor leapt over the bonnet of the Beetle and ran full pelt down the corridor.

CHAPTER SIX
THE HUSKS

Vasid had seen another one, a third creature, and had run away. He could tell the creature was different. It was a little shorter, but thicker, and the huge eyes were dark and oily. He'd watched the huge head swinging from side to side with such frightening force that he could imagine it flying right off the spindly neck.

It had looked as if it was hunting something.

Now, eyes closed, Vasid edged along the metal wall very, very slowly. He barely managed to suppress a cry when his hands left bare metal and slid into something soft and sticky. He looked down. A brown morass clung to his fat fingers, almost sticking his whole hand to the wall. He pulled it away – it still ached from his striking of the wall earlier – and wiped it against his already soiled top. Thick strings of goo stretched between hand and fabric, and his stomach turned.

He had to get to his room, lock himself inside. Hide under the bed, in the shower, in his cupboard, anywhere. Stay alive.

He didn't recognise where he was. Then he worked it out – and realised with dread that a doorway must've appeared from nowhere, next to him.

'This shouldn't be here,' he whispered to himself in confusion. 'This was just corridor. Anstaar used to exercise here. I – I set up the portacam there and –'

He peeped inside. A large blue box stood in front of another doorway beyond. The air felt heavy and smelled rancid. Vasid was suddenly gripped by a fresh twist of fear and turned to run yet again.

But the creature with the dark eyes and the hunting head

had followed him. It was moving slowly along the corridor, its thick white tongue flicking out to taste the air as it walked. Vasid swung himself round the new doorway, wincing as his body slushed into more of the brown deposit on the walls. He tried to breathe deeply. There was no way he could go back out into the exercise corridor without the creature seeing him.

He would have to go through the doorway and give it the slip, then double back. That wasn't impossible. He'd got rid of Anstaar and that other one – he could do it, he could do it.

Vasid moved past the blue box into the dark, slimy space beyond. It was like another world. Not the clean, metal, comforting base. It was fibrous, glutinous, sticky. It stank. He realised that the walls were crusted with what was probably the same stuff he'd found in *his* base, only layer upon hardened layer. Sticky strands hung down from the faintly glowing ceiling above him, and even the quiet, comforting hum of the place he knew so well sounded muffled, suffocated in here. Frightening.

He waited in the dark, eyes fixed on the patch of bright white light cast through from the base lights outside. Then the shadow of the creature appeared stark and black in its centre.

Vasid shuffled off into the dark with a low moan of panic.

The Doctor skidded to a halt. There were sticky brown marks on the floor and walls outside the personnel cabins, and the doors had been smashed in with hideous force.

'You could've showered first,' tutted the Doctor, surveying the damage. 'Although I rather suspect *we've* taken the liberties here.' There was no sign of Vasid in what the Doctor assumed was the man's room. The floor was strewn with data disks, holovids, pornography and dirty clothing, but the Time Lord guessed that, apart from the huge holes in the cupboard doors, this was a fairly normal state of affairs. The room next door had to be Anstaar's, neat and clean-smelling. Every hiding place had been kicked in, every door ripped off.

'Oh, well. Perhaps they're just a little grumpy at being woken up so early.' The Doctor deliberated on what to do next. He had to get Sam back. That was his number-one priority. But he had to find out what was going on here, and that meant talking to whoever had done this damage and left the tracks. That was number-one priority, too. And Hirath wasn't stable, and there was no telling what might happen if he didn't sort that out, so that also was number-one priority. And that ship was on its way. And Vasid of course...

Hmm.

The Doctor stared down at his battered old shoes and clicked his fingers as he headed cautiously back to the control room. He'd had an idea.

Vasid groped his way through the mire of brown sludge sucking and grasping at him from the floors and walls. He looked behind him but it was hard to tell if he was being followed along here.

He stopped still, and strained to see or hear anything in the threatening gloom. His heartbeat sounded ridiculously loud in his ears, his breathing ragged and rasping.

Then he heard something else. A quiet, regular squelching. Something was making its way towards him.

Vasid bit his lip and pulled himself onward down the corridor. There was a faint luminescence ahead to his right, bluish in hue. He didn't know whether to avoid it or head straight for it, but with the creature close behind, doubling back or standing still really didn't seem like much of an option.

He splatted and slid through the thick sticky grease around him until he reached the light, spilling out from a large room which seemed cleaner, cooler than the fetid corridor. A sickbay of some kind?

The room was empty. He walked inside, noticing that the lower temperature had hardened most of the filthy muck. He walked over to the far side of the room, looking for another door, a way out, or a hiding place.

Then he realised the room wasn't empty. Something was there, a figure on a long, black couch in the far corner. He moved towards it with a growing feeling of dread, as if someone else were moving his body.

It was a man, stripped naked. Dozens and dozens of glistening metal blades and pins were slid under the skin on the torso and the arms, tiny wires no thicker than hairs connecting them to a large, glassy sphere glowing with alien energy. The skin from the nape of the neck to the top of the head had been peeled away, and sticking out from the dull grey bone of the skull were hooks and strings and wires leading to small black cubes set into the walls. One eyeball hung out on its stalk, an object like a glass spider squatting over the iris, puncturing the eyeball's base with tiny needles from which oozed a thin grey liquid. A large spike was driven through the flesh beneath the chin, and a taut mesh of steel threads – sewn from inside the lower jaw through to the base of the spike near the drill-holed neck – held the mouth open.

Vost hadn't run anywhere. These creatures had come for him.

Vasid's scream yanked his own mouth open. A tiny voice hiding in the back of his head timidly asked a question of his old employer over the noise of his anguish: what manner of creature could have done this?

When he turned, he saw it, towering above him. The violence and coldness in its huge eyes, the fatty tongue lolling in the black gash of its mouth. The hands, strangely slender with their six fingers, quivering and flexing as the huge balloon head swayed.

One twisted arm reached out and the bony digits held him by the ear. The other hand came up to his face, as if to caress him. He felt the sharp fingertip press against his cheek, then screamed again as he felt the tip slip through it. Other fingers began worming their way into his skull, then the bony foot lashed out and punctured his stomach before skewering him into the mottled surface of the cool blue wall.

You made your own future. Him and Vost, they must've brought this upon themselves. Everything suddenly darkened, but Vasid thought he could see Anstaar in the distance waving coyly at him. She'd been so impressed, really, with the new him, he could see it in her come-to-bed eyes. They burnt so brightly before the blackness swamped them.

The Doctor was driving the Beetle along the base corridors, alternating cries of 'Anyone there?' with long petulant blasts on the horn.

It hadn't taken long before one of the hideous hulking creatures came into view round a bend in the corridor. He stamped hard on the brake and jumped out of the car.

It was huge, but the Doctor suspected it could move quickly if it wanted. The huge, brown, club feet were ragged with curling tongues of amber gum. The legs were glutinous treacle-brown, each calf resembling a bundle of femur bones tied up with thick white string and then wedged into place with sludgy industrial glue. The thighs were fat and wide, dripping with a sweaty liquid slopping down from the creature's midriff. Plastic sheeting was wrapped around the protruding groin, a pale blue, and the stomach was like a huge pile of roasted meat swept into a wet brown tub. Hardened breasts peered out from a bony ridge of muscle stretching from shoulder to pointed shoulder.

The upper arms were like great brute clubs, thick and tuberous, muscles glistening and crunching against the restraining skin in apparently involuntary clenches. The forearms were slimmer, better defined. But the head. It squatted on a burnt brown neck, an enormous ovular skull becoming broader as it stretched to accommodate two huge, rolling saucepan eyes glowing a dull orange, nestling under a thick hood of bone. The jaw was hanging open above the thin pinched collarbone. The ears were like slush icicles drooping down from scab-like mounts at the base of the cranium. The nose was made up of two half-baked pockmarks placed crookedly on the orange-black face, and the tongue sloshed about in the creature's overflowing mouth like a living thing.

Another of the creatures rounded the corner. It looked more or less identical to its fellow, except that the plastic skirt was black. Did they denote differences in rank? Or sex? The faces were hard to read in the bony heads, but the six quivering fingers on each hand caught his attention. They seemed expressive, artistic even, so out of place against the ragged toffee bones of the rest of the body. He raised a hand of his own in greeting.

'Glad to be back in charge?' he called out. 'I'm the Doctor. I apologise on behalf of your squatters for the change in decor but I'm sure you'll soon have it looking really horrible again.' He rubbed a finger down the wall and grimaced as it snagged on some of the slime. 'Something in your lungs reacting with the oxygen in the air I take it. Splendid! Although you do realise the new tenants went to great lengths scraping your secretions off the property. Who are you?'

The creatures kept coming. The Doctor estimated they were maybe fifteen metres away. He held his ground, a pleasant smile on his face.

Suddenly Black Skirt spoke, its voice earthy and low. 'You are the last.'

'The last what?' inquired the Doctor, politely.

'Alive. At least, in any real sense.'

'It's the real sense I've always valued the most.'

Twelve metres.

'You killed Vasid?'

Blue Skirt's turn. Its voice was like rubble falling into a skip. 'You are the last.'

'Does that status confer any special privileges upon my person?'

Black Skirt's treacle lips curled back in an unpleasant smile.

Ten metres.

'Do you know there's a ship headed here? It'll be arriving any minute now.'

'It is the Kusk seeker ship. Our fathers have returned for their ancestors.' Blue Skirt again. Quite the double act.

'So it was you who sent them the guidance signals. Kusks, eh? Never heard of you.'

Eight metres.

'Well.' The Doctor clapped his hands and rubbed them together. 'It's been lovely talking, but I should really be rescuing my young friend, Sam. Goodbye.' He leapt backwards and rolled over the bonnet of the Beetle, landing on his feet facing the advancing Kusks.

With horrifying speed Black Skirt covered the last few metres and lashed out at the Doctor's head. The Time Lord ducked hurriedly into the car as the bony fist dented the metal roof. Blue Skirt punched at the windscreen and again the Doctor ducked, instinctively, but the glass made a fizzing sound and the Kusk pulled its hand back in pain.

'Force field,' said the Doctor, smiling grimly as he slung the car into reverse gear. 'Comes as standard with these later models.'

He reversed at speed down the corridor as the Kusks continued their advance.

* * *

Dwynaar and Sost stood at the front of the assembly hall. Some of the men talked in low tones; some were trying to sleep. It should've been the middle of the night, lamented Sost. But the day outside was as hot and as hard as it had been… well, all day.

'Where are they, then?' muttered Dwynaar.

Sost looked of out the window. 'Some are coming now.'

Dwynaar looked over. 'Felbaac?'

'Yeah, and Yast and a couple of others.'

Shortly after Sost's announcement, the door swung open and Felbaac walked in, smiling encouragingly at the men, and at Dwynaar, who returned his gaze stonily.

'Well,' announced Felbaac, 'here we are.'

'I'll come to the point,' began Dwynaar. 'None of us have any idea what's happening in the sky. Do you?'

'No,' said Felbaac, measuredly.

Sost carried on. 'We think it's that girl who fell here.'

'And we want you to take her away with you in your ship and leave us be.' Dwynaar looked at Sost, who fiercely nodded his agreement.

Felbaac looked at the duo with a strained smile still on his face, ignoring Yast's quivering expression, which he could see through the corner of his eye. 'You can't be serious. We're your rescue party.'

'Being rescued by you is just another kind of slavery,' stated Dwynaar. He folded his arms and some of the men who were still awake murmured in agreement.

'Can you really throw away the freedom of all your fellows here?' Felbaac's voice stirred one or two from their rest and they grumbled. 'Just like that?'

'None of us know what's happening out there with the sun,' reiterated Sost.

'And we've decided we can't spare the bruk rations for you and your men,' continued Dwynaar. 'Or for… her. And there

98

won't be enough water for any of us if that sun doesn't ease up. And frankly, Felbaac, *we* come before *you*. So get off our hell and go to your own.'

Sost began clapping, and succeeded in raising a ragged response from the other prisoners.

'We can take you away from here,' chipped in Yast, nervously. 'Soon, now. Very soon.'

'Soon?' mocked Dwynaar. 'Don't tell me your rocket's not irreparable.'

'Don't be ridiculous. We have transport.' Felbaac looked away.

'Well, good, I'm glad. Because from now on you take her, and your men, and you stay on your rocket and eat your own rations. Understand?'

Felbaac strode to the door, his small entourage in tow. He turned in the doorway. 'The situation will change. You'll have your nights back. And you'll regret this moment throughout every one of them.' He paused. 'If I let you. We'll be back, Dwynaar.'

Dwynaar glowered at the party as they walked through the door.

'Could've closed it behind them,' niggled Sost.

The Doctor yanked hard on the wheel and reversed round one corner of a T-junction in the corridor.

You could turn this on a two-dendeela piece, he thought with pride. Then a third Kusk loomed into view and grabbed the rear bumper, as the Doctor slipped the car into first and tried to speed off. He revved the engine and a cloud of exhaust hit the hideous creature full in the face. It swayed and choked, seeming to weaken a little. Noting the reaction, the Doctor pressed the boot release switch. The small hatch-cover swung up at speed at the back of the car and with a loud clang hit the Kusk in the teeth. Caught by surprise, it let go, and the Doctor sped away, already up to thirty miles an hour.

He swung the car round a sharp corner, misjudged it, and the back of the car slammed into the metal wall with a bone-jarring impact. Thrown to one side, his foot slid off the clutch pedal and the car stalled. Rubbing the back of his neck, he turned the ignition key, but a juddering warble as the engine turned over was the only response he got. 'Come on,' he muttered.

Blue Skirt swayed its head round the corner, and grinned malevolently at the sight of the frantic Doctor at the wheel.

'Come – ON!' he insisted, and the engine finally bit. Squealing away with the smell of burning rubber, the Doctor turned another corner and on to a straight. Another Kusk stepped out from an intersection directly in front of him. The Doctor braked on instinct, but it was too late. The huge biped smashed into the bonnet of the car. The windscreen went dark as the brown twists and nodules of the treacle-bark body slammed into the protective glass, then there were two painfully loud crashes. The next thing he knew he was looking at the body of the flailing Kusk on the metal floor in the rear-view mirror.

'Tut tut,' remarked the Doctor. 'Clearly never heard of SPLINK!'

The image of the Kusk clambering to its feet in the mirror receded as the car sped off once again.

Tanhith was back out in the desert.

He felt curiously calm, staring into the sky. The clouds were frozen in spite of the heat, and the sun sat like a fat bloody eye staring down at the settlement. He thought of Hirath's distant moon, punily stepping into the sun's shoes when the rich darkness of night descended over the landscape, looking so small against the backcloth of stars. He imagined how it must once have looked, huge, majestic and low in the sky before its orbit swept it away, softly and slowly over how many million million years, keeping watch over the troubled planet from so far away. He missed the moon. He missed the coolness of night, and the noise of the nocturnal birds calling to each other, the clattering of their wings in flight.

He coughed again, and rubbed his chest. The birds were still wheeling, but their actions were in real time, like his own. They weren't puppets enacting whatever time of their lives Hirath chose for them. They must know, he thought, they must know it's all going wrong and we're all going to die here.

Then he saw it. A pale flare at first, faint against the pinkness of the sky. Then solidifying, coming into focus. Bright, like an arrow of flame in the sky.

'A burning bird falling to earth…' he breathed, excited and scared at once. He laughed, and it became a hacking cough, one he couldn't stop.

Then the world seemed to rock around him for a split second. He looked up, and the sun had shifted to the east, clouds had changed formation. And the burning bird, the arrow, was a spaceship, suddenly far closer. Dark and sleek, a bird of prey. It would land in front of the cliffs in the middle distance.

Tanhith recognised it and ran.

Felbaac was on the edge of the settlement, attempting to calm down the indignant Yast following their recent dismissal, when Tanhith came running up to them, red-faced, eyelashes hanging down wet with sweat. He coughed violently, spitting a few flecks of blood into the red earth.

Felbaac waited impatiently for the coughing fit to finish. 'What is it, Tanhith?'

'The K'Arme,' he panted. 'Ship just touching down. They've

found us, come for us.'

'A big ship?' Felbaac's eyes were gleaming.

'Yes. A flagship, I think.' Tanhith looked at Yast, who was in turn looking at Felbaac.

'Yes, it would be,' breathed their leader. 'I knew he couldn't resist it. Now it begins.' His voice was suddenly strident, confident.

'What begins? What are you talking about?' Tanhith stared suspiciously at him, then grabbed hold of the fabric of his tunic, pulling him up close to his face. 'What?'

Felbaac pushed him away. He looked at his men, and gestured expansively with his arms. 'This is what we've been waiting for.'

The Doctor screeched to a halt outside the control room, parking the battered Beetle across the entrance. A thought occurred to him, and he pulled out the choke so the revs of the engine increased. Black clouds of exhaust pumped out into the corridor.

'Good job I didn't book that service,' he muttered, getting out of the car and clambering over the bonnet.

'Right. Computer – still online, good. Power still up, now the settings, the settings…' His fingers played over the digitpad as he accessed the destination of recent dispatches from the matter transmitter.

He frowned. There were three or four sets of co-ordinates but only two recent transmissions. Suddenly the screen went black. Then row upon row of alien symbols flickered into being.

'Oh, no! Come on, stay with me, stay with me…' He got up and dashed over to fiddle with his modifications to the matter transmitter. The roof of the small chamber had been removed and welded to the ceiling. Bright multicoloured wiring connected the roof to the walls, and Vost's transmitter spun gently, dangling from a thick cable running from the base of the unit to the ceiling. He inserted the sonic screwdriver into a small hole in the black box and activated it.

Much to the Doctor's relief, a pale glow spread from the floor of the unit to the improvised roof. He marched over to the computer and banged the top of it hard with his fist. The screen cleared, but each transmission still had two sets of co-ordinates.

'Eeny-meeny-miny-mo...' he muttered.

Then he heard the sound of the Kusks advancing, roaring in anger, choking and spluttering on the exhaust fumes. The noise sounded like thunder.

The Doctor closed his eyes and selected the most recent set of co-ordinates. He glanced down at his lapel absent-mindedly for a cat badge to rub. Seeing nothing there, he satisfied himself with shaking his own hand and saying, 'Good luck.'

He looked again at the glowing opacity swirling in the improvised cabinet, then at his small brass fob watch, and walked straight into it. Instantly he began to feel dizzy. He imagined toothless piranhas nipping at his flesh, his bones being stripped, his biodata coiling away into infinity. The control room faded like an old photograph, then his sight was shredded into ribbons. He was left wondering vaguely why unconsciousness couldn't be a rich warm mauve in colour when everything went its usual cold black.

The black ship had settled near the tiny river, and its touchdown jets had scorched a huge basin into the parched earth. There were three white cubes imprinted on the side of the ship in the shape of a basic pyramid, although a ripple of rust had corroded the pristine design. A ramp opened up from the top cube, and soon a dozen grey-suited humanoid guards with the three-cube insignia on their breasts were descending it, each carrying a stubby blaster. They spread out in an arrowhead formation, and after a suitably sinister pause, another figure appeared at the top of the ramp.

He wore the same style of grey uniform but with a long pale-blue cloak that hung down to his ankles in the still air. He was tall, and his white hair was cut extremely short around the chubby oval face, lined with age and responsibility. His big round eyes had their eyelashes cut short, and they flicked around the landscape, left and right. Apparently satisfied, he walked down the ramp slowly, and obviously with some pain. Behind the ramp at the base of the arrowhead pattern, two of the guards swapped glances as they waited.

Behind the old man came a young man and a woman. The man was short and skinny, his face and skin youthful and smooth. He had a wispy moustache that hung down over his thin lips to his pointed chin. His eyes were cold and glassy, and looked out of place in the young face. They were an old man's eyes.

The woman had straight dark hair that was cut above the ears. She should've been beautiful, but there was something about her face that made you look more closely, trying to see what had gone wrong and where. Her eyes were blue, her skin littered with freckles of grey. Her narrow nose turned upward, her lips turned down, and she had no eyelashes – just a fine grey down that stretched over the eyes like a fragile gauze.

Their leader came to a stop at the bottom of the steps. His younger companions stood one at each shoulder.

'Traxes,' the old man murmured, his voice deep and well defined, 'that was a dreadful landing.'

'Pilot reports inconsistencies in the safe-path co-ordinates, Commissioner.'

'Does he indeed?' The commissioner steepled his fingers. 'Break out the land transport.'

The man saluted and disappeared back into the ship,

moving with a speed that dismayed the old man. 'I won't last long on foot in this climate,' he chuckled thinly. The woman looked down at the ground, embarrassed at his admission. He noticed, smiled wryly, and continued: 'Fettal, I'd like you to take five men and circle round. Close in on the encampment from behind.' Fettal nodded smartly. 'Traxes will approach from the front. The direct approach to diplomacy, eh, my dear?' He saw her trying not to squirm. It amused him to make such comments to a woman who was trying so hard to be a man, and these days he was giving in to such little indulgences more readily. 'Oh, and Fettal…'

She looked at him steadily. 'Yes, Commissioner?'

'Leave me two men to guard my person. The two *best* men, please.'

'Of course, Commissioner.'

'Of course,' he said, nodding sagely in return. 'I'm going to wait in the shade, now. Arrange it.'

He felt Fettal's eyes follow him as he walked into the shadow of his big black ship, and made a big display of wiping the sweat from his brow with his ceremonial cloak. He knew it would upset her. Being young, she took it all so seriously. The Code of the K'Arme. The secrecy and the sanctity of the Honourable Houses.

All nonsense and myth, of course – a lot of it perpetuated by himself, he noted, briefly reminiscing on times past. Yet here he was in no official capacity to safeguard its reputation. He glanced down. The colours and symbols emblazoned on his tunic spelled out his name and rank for all to see and fear: Most High Commissioner Sangton of the House of Beckal.

He'd given up on all that rubbish, just as it was ready to give up on him. But the thought of the rebellion's latest figurehead posting the information he claimed to have on the government infonet – the frauds, the abuses of power that he had happily undertaken most of his long life known to all…

The scant information the Outer scum had fenced already was entirely accurate, and he chided himself for becoming less careful with his advancing years. He would be able to evade court martial, he had no doubt, but the damage done to his House would make him a pariah. The young took it all so seriously.

Well, he'd stand down soon enough, make way for the new blood. Just give him this final head on his wall, and that would be that. The suitably bloody end to a suitably long and bloody career. If Felbaac thought he could lure a Most High Commissioner here to make concessions, to barter for an easy life, or even in the vain hope of trapping him here, he and his sorry bunch of forgotten men would regret it.

Sangton looked up into the fleshy-pink sky. 'Looks like we've landed in the middle of the day. Good.' He looked over at the guard next to him. 'I should hate for us to disturb their peaceful slumber.'

Another huge silent ramp started to open under the vast metal wing of the ship, and the land transport carriers began trundling down. Clouds of disturbed red dust were filling the air like swarms of tiny insects as the heavily armoured vehicles pulled up in front of him.

Felbaac marched across the yard with Yast and Tanhith. He was speaking quietly but his eyes betrayed his excitement. 'They won't know we've seen them, so that gives us a little time.'

'How do you know?' twittered Yast, almost tripping over a shrivelling strand of bruk.

'Only a total fool would be out there in the desert in such heat, so far from the shelter. How fortunate we should have one so near to hand.'

Tanhith ignored the gibe. 'Whatever you're planning, it had better be good. That's a flagship. There could be hundreds of troops on board.'

'Against unarmed prisoners left to rot?' retorted Felbaac.

'Against us.' Tanhith looked him directly in the eye. 'They've come for us, haven't they? And you knew, didn't you?'

Felbaac returned the stare, then smiled. 'Of course. I asked them here.'

'You did what?' Yast's face screwed up in incredulity.

'Sangton. Head of one of the major Houses. My contacts unearthed some dirt on him: not much, but enough to get him nervous. I let it be known we had enough to topple his House, desecrate its standing with the "Homeworld" for all time.'

'And you summoned him here.' Tanhith shook his head in weary disbelief.

'Think about it. A major hit like that will boost the rebellion's morale throughout the Outer Worlds. It'll be the push we need!' A fanatical gleam shone in Felbaac's eyes.

'And what's to stop him just blasting this place to smithereens!' said Yast, hands flapping nervously.

'He'll want me alive. He'll want to know how I came by the information, who else knows it, how far it's spread.' Felbaac actually seemed confident.

'There's a lot of supposition in your reasoning,' warned Tanhith.

'We need a victory,' said Felbaac, levelly. 'I've engineered the situation, but you've got to help me finish the job.'

'Isn't that just another way of saying "I got you into this mess, now help me get out"?' asked Yast.

Felbaac fixed him with a stare, still apparently calm and relaxed. 'I always take every opportunity to turn a situation to my advantage. Take… Samantha, for example.'

'What about Samantha?' said Tanhith a little too quickly.

Felbaac came to a halt and looked meaningfully at him. 'She's nothing. Nothing, you understand me?' He paused. 'But we can make *something* of her…'

Felbaac began undoing the chain from the young alien girl's door.

CHAPTER SEVEN

WORDS WITHOUT ACTIONS ARE THE ASSASSINS OF IDEALISM

The misshapen craft cruised into position above the moonbase landing strip, spiralling down through the vacuum like an autumn leaf falling to the ground.

When it was a few hundred metres from impact, huge amounts of slime defied the lack of gravity and fell from the ship to the landing strip, sticking there, heavy treacly strands anchoring the craft and pulling it gently down to land. No retro rockets fired, or gravity jets. The ship simply settled down into the giant pool of slime it had jettisoned, dark and crab-like next to the bare metal of the base.

A sticky tunnel of the viscous fluid began building itself around a wafer-thin force field reaching out to the base airlock.

The Kusk standing in the observation bay of the moonbase swung its great head up and down in satisfaction.

The three Kusks had gathered some distance from the Doctor's car, staring balefully at it, impatiently stamping from foot to foot.

The shorter Kusk that had hunted down and killed Vasid rounded the corner. 'The seeker ship has landed,' it rumbled. 'We must await further instruction.'

The Doctor woke up bewildered, aching and absolutely soaking wet.

'That was some party, Brigadier…' he whispered, hoarsely.

Then abruptly he sat up straight and stared around him with wide blue-green eyes, the long curls on his head shaking and bouncing as his head swung from side to side. 'A cave! Fascinating.'

'Now you're awake, who are you?'

The voice was female, more scared than hostile.

'Company, splendid! Oh dear, you're as wet as I am. High moisture level in the air, by the feel of it.'

'I said, who are you?' The woman moved into view, holding a large rock defensively in front of her. Her hair was dark, her skin smooth and coffee-coloured, an apprehensive frown twisting her features.

'Well, I'm the Doctor and I'm more than a little surprised to find myself actually here, on Hirath, presumably, in one –' he suddenly felt for his legs with a shocked expression that relaxed into a relieved smile – 'piece. So, you must be Anstaar. Delighted to meet you, but tell me, have you seen a young girl called Sam Jones around here anywhere? You can't miss her. She's English and noisy. You know what the young are like –'

Anstaar cut across his babble, her voice a little higher. 'How did you know my name?'

'Vasid told me. Back on the moon base.'

'Vasid? That sewer rat?' She spat at the sodden pink ground.

The Doctor looked at her, gravely. 'That dead sewer rat, I'm afraid.'

Anstaar stared at him, her wide brown eyes unblinking. After a long silence she looked down at the ground. 'What happened?'

'It's a long story. Before I start it, Sam...?'

'There's no one here but me. This is where we came through from the matter transmitter.' She indicated a small platform set into the rocky floor. 'I've been sticking around here in case there was some way of getting back, but I don't know the start-up codes. Didn't have a chance to look them up before I was sent here.'

'It looks like I made the wrong choice.' The Doctor stuck his bottom lip out moodily. 'That power surge – it must've scrambled the systems. Oh, Sam. How am I ever going to find you?'

Anstaar put down the rock and smiled apologetically. Then she sat down in front of him and moistened her lips with her tongues.

'You were going to tell me a long story.'

'We need you to do this, Samantha. Please.'

Sam was getting fed up with this Felbaac. He pronounced her name 'Sam-arn-tha' and obviously fancied himself the big macho leader of the Outer Worlds' rebellion. She looked coolly at him. I could tell you a hundred stories about a thousand rebellions, mate, she thought. Then she thought about her own rebellions, her own crappy little crusades. The Doctor had shown her so much, put her own mundane life into pitiful perspective. Was that why she was being so snooty now? This bloke was a creep, but he was a creep who was putting his life on the line to fight back. His and Tanhith's – and who knew how many others? She should respect that, at least.

Maybe it was because he seemed to enjoy it all so much.

'Samantha?'

'OK, OK, let me get this straight.' She sighed. 'You want *me* to pretend to be *you* for these evil, brutal K'Arme types? Isn't that going to just the teeniest bit unconvincing?'

Felbaac smiled placatingly. 'No one knows who I really am, what I really look like. My name is a rallying cry, not a person.'

Oh please, thought Sam. 'Yeah, but you man, me woman? Christ, you have noticed, haven't you?'

'You have no eye-film.'

'Come again?'

'And you don't speak with the duplicitous tongues of a woman.'

'*What?*' Sam was appalled.

'I mean, you have a man's tongue. Singular. You'll confuse them. In any case, Ipmuss was a mixed labour camp. And I've wiped all records of myself from Central. I don't exist.'

'Oh, God, it's *Knight Rider*,' she muttered.

Felbaac got up and walked about the baking room, seemingly immune to the heat. 'Besides… you don't belong in this camp. The men here, they will back you up. And you're clearly not a seasoned inmate. Your clothes, your skin. And where else could you have come from if not from my ship?'

'I told you, I was sent here from –'

'Yes, yes, I know, but that story is so far-fetched it makes the little pretence I am asking seem quite mundane.'

Smug git, thought Sam. 'So what do you do while I'm risking my life in the name of your cause?'

'I'm afraid I'm not at liberty to reveal my plans to you.'

'I thought you were fighting *for* liberty.'

'The knowledge could prove dangerous for you. The K'Arme already think I know a good deal about their corrupt identities. If they should find out you're aware of any of our plans…'

'I thought you'd be back to save the day long before that could possibly happen.'

'You must understand, Sam*arn*tha –'

Felbaac was raising his voice so Sam raised hers over it. '*Sam*. My name is Sam, OK?'

Felbaac's voice descended to its calmer, more convincing level. 'You must understand, Sam. I am gambling all our lives on this deception fooling the K'Arme long enough for my plan to succeed. And if I die –'

'Oh, I know. The tiny candle of hope dies out in the fascist wind blowing through the Outer Worlds.' Oops. There she

112

went again, sending him up. She may not have had the right to make fun of what he was doing, but God, he was pompous. 'So what would you have done if I hadn't turned up?'

'I'd be forced to show my hand that much earlier. I'd risk a full-pitched battle. Who knows how many would die?'

'Would it be worth it?'

'Now I have an alternative.'

'You want to put me at risk rather than your own men.' Sam shook her head, unsure of what to say.

Felbaac filled in the silence: 'I'm a pragmatist. If a better plan comes along I'll seize it.'

'And I've turned up just in time, ripe for the seizing.' Sam could feel herself flushing. She was feeling scared and confused. How could Felbaac expect her to do this? How dare he lay a guilt trip on her for something she had nothing to do with?

The door swung open, and Tanhith stood framed in the painfully bright rectangle of outside world it revealed. He looked at Felbaac, then at Sam, apparently concerned. 'You all right?'

'Tell her, Tanhith.' Felbaac's cool was finally beginning to falter. 'Tell her she really has no choice if she wants to avoid a bloodbath with herself up front in the firing line. I've got to go.' He took Tanhith aside, and whispered hard in his ear. 'She *must* do it.'

He stalked out, and slammed the door closed behind him. It hit the wooden frame and wobbled back open again. Tanhith walked over and closed it more gently. He smiled. 'I don't think Felbaac's ever made a decent dramatic exit. Pity, really, in his line of work.'

Sam stared at him, levelly. 'So what's this, bad cop, good cop?' But she didn't object when he crouched down in front of her and took her hand.

* * *

The Kusk Leader strode through the white door into the shuttle bay lounge, shaking his head in disgust at the humanoid trappings. He led the others, ten Kusks in total, into the corridor leading to the base.

Waiting for them were the two Kusks from the sealed-off section. Each was embraced by the Leader, before moving back and standing to attention.

'You are lost no longer,' said the Leader quietly. 'Now quickly. Let us proceed to the main control chamber.'

'We will require breathing apparatus to enter it, Leader,' said the blue-skirted Kusk, hesitantly.

'The humanoids?' questioned the Leader.

The Kusk nodded. 'There is a male still inside the control chamber.'

'Then he shall suffer for his interference,' stated the Leader.

'The humanoids have taken many such liberties, Leader,' rumbled the Kusk in the black skirt. 'They have stripped the ship to its bare metal. They have subverted our central computer's functions, seeking to harness our powers for financial gain.'

The Leader paused as he opened the door into the base. 'And you... allowed them to do this?'

'We were in cryogenic suspension, Leader. The computer was monitoring and stabilising the Prize for us,' said the black-skirted Kusk.

'Our suspension system was tampered with,' rejoined its blue-skirted companion. 'It was a freak power failure that reactivated the cryogenic vats.'

The Leader strode on. 'A malfunction in the circuitry?'

The black-skirted Kusk rumbled slowly. 'Our craft is dying.'

'How long since you underwent cryogenic suspension?'

'Two hundred years.'

'Since then,' said the Leader proudly, 'many further advances in our technology have been made.' He paused for effect. 'We stand on the brink of sending living beings back through time.'

The Kusk in the black skirt hissed its appreciation. 'Then we are *so* close.'

The salmon-pink sky stretched over the Doctor and Anstaar like a watery tarpaulin. Ruffled red clouds of wetness draped themselves dreamily around towering spires of sand and rock. Strands of vegetation wormed up from patches of soil, and the Doctor breathed deeply, his eyes gleaming. ' "'Twixt sea and shore",' he muttered. 'Come on. If I've read that indicator display correctly, this is somewhere in the area of temporal leakage I was telling you about.'

'Wonderful,' sighed Anstaar.

'Do you have any idea what this chunk of Hirath is used for?'

'No. There's so many discrete parts. It could be – oh, I don't know. You know I'm finding it hard believing anything you've told me.'

'It was a *long* story,' chided the Doctor, lightly, 'not a tall one. Why would I lie?'

'How should I know?'

The Doctor realised Anstaar wanted to believe him, but the ramifications of what he was saying left her terrified. He placed a sympathetic hand on her shoulder.

'You can stay here if you like, and pretend I never came. But believe me – help isn't going to come from any other quarter. And it won't take the Kusks long to find out where I went or how to operate the matter transmitter.'

'But they'll never fit in it if they're as big as you say.'

The Doctor looked sheepish. 'I had to make one or two minor alterations to get in it myself.'

'Of course. Great. Well, if it comes to a choice between monstrous killer bipeds and a jaunt with you...' She set off up a wide path, her figure soon made indistinct by the fine mist in the air.

'I'm overwhelmed,' commented the Doctor, to no one in particular. 'You haven't asked me what we're looking for yet.'

Anstaar's voice floated back to him. 'Trouble?'

The Doctor set off after her. 'Are you sure we've never met before?'

Fettal led her team of five in one desultory land assault transporter. Her face was impassive, but resentment twisted her guts. As usual, Sangton had detailed the best equipment to Traxes. He did it because he knew it annoyed her. Made her aggressive, and thus more prone to making mistakes. He knew her ambition, and she knew that he scorned it.

She knew also how he looked at her. Not that the old idiot could surely do much with the little he had these days, but if it pleased him to abuse his power over her she'd go along with it. He wouldn't be around much longer. He was an embarrassment.

Still, he and all the old ones in his House, all of them, would die out in the next few years, or be pensioned off to villa worlds. It was a good thing: with their corruption, endless manipulations, diverting of funds and commandeering of craft for secret missions like this one, they had brought disrepute on the sacred Houses and long outlived their time. The old idiot had tried to make it sound exciting to her, but she knew exactly what was going on.

The hunting down of the Outers, and the policing of that rabble of cultures awaiting dispersal around the ever-expanding Thannos system, would be better handled by the young, those who had lived with the issues of rebellion and dissension all their lives. Until then, she had to be grateful for the scraps of information, advice, and command that Sangton gave her. The resentment twisted at her insides again.

She'd been told she had to internalise her anger and her frustrations until a battle situation. Then, as long as her judgement remained clear at all times, she could release it. The pleasure of that release had sustained her for some time. Weeks, a few years back. Not so long now.

Still, the moment was coming, and a tingle of exhilaration was running through her. The camp would be in sight soon, full of pitiful half-dead men. How many of them would she slaughter today to get to the target?

She smiled, the sun catching on tiny beads of moisture on the gossamer covering her eyes. She felt she could be a giant.

'So what's to stop your oppressive army shooting me on sight, then?' Sam was remaining difficult to convince.

'They won't,' cooed Tanhith. 'They've come here to take the information Felbaac carries. He doesn't trust anyone enough to tell them everything. It would diminish his own importance too much. He's probably only so keen for you to help because he told Dwynaar and his lot that you were a part of his plans.'

'Oh, nice one. So they'll put me in a brain drain and then shoot me?' Sam wasn't really sure why she was arguing. She seemed to have few options open to her, and if these troops were really on the way, what would stop them shooting her on sight if she definitely *wasn't* what they were after?

'Sam, Felbaac will have carried out his plan by then. It will be all right.' Tanhith's voice faltered ever so slightly on the last words, but it was enough for Sam to pick up on. She waited for a coughing fit to subside, then spoke softly.

'You're not really so sure, are you?'

'Oh, I'm sure Felbaac will come through for us,' smiled Tanhith weakly. 'His plan may even work out perfectly, although, to be honest, that would be a first.' He coughed again. 'You may have noticed, Sam, that my health is not good.'

Sam looked at him. 'Just a bit of a cough, isn't it?'

Tanhith smiled wryly. 'Probably. I'm sure my body will pull through. I think it's the rest of me that's getting ready to let go.'

'Don't talk like that,' said Sam with a shaky laugh. 'Do I look like a priest?' She took his hand. 'Just shut up, OK?'

'OK.' He straightened up, a little embarrassed. 'You look more like the leader of the glorious rebellion than a priest, that much is true.' His voice was a little colder, and his smile seemed apologetic as if to make up for it. 'Felbaac's going to capture the K'Arme ship, so he says. He'll be able to signal through to your friend on the moonbase.'

'The Doctor!' she said without thinking, a broad smile brightening her face.

'Yes, him.'

Sam looked at Tanhith and stood up, rubbing her legs, which had pins and needles from sitting cross-legged on the bunk. 'All right,' she said at length, 'I'm up for it. It's got to be better than doing nothing. Tell me what I need to do.'

Traxes signalled his two land cruisers to halt. He'd found the rebel ship. It was damaged and abandoned, and none of the information Sangton had requested seemed to be on board. The old man had told him to blow it up as a kind of announcement of their presence, a signal to begin the festivities. It had a certain style, thought Traxes, rubbing beads of sweat from his furry moustache.

The bombs were planted, and they'd moved on. Now, through his optical boosters, he could see the camp, a sorry collection of stone buildings and shacks, a bunch of weedy plants half sheltered by sheets of metal and crates. Nothing moved. The scene shimmered in the blazing heat.

Traxes spoke into his communicator. 'Fettal, are you receiving?'

Her voice came smoothly from his ear implant. 'Receiving.'

'Are you –'

'I'm in position, Traxes. Waiting for your signal.'

Traxes' face twisted in an irritated scowl. 'You'll have it when their ship goes up.'

'Good,' she said lightly, and disconnected.

Traxes looked round to his men. 'When you see the explosion, we roll in together. Understand?'

The men nodded their silent agreement.

The hunter Kusk marched towards the control chamber. A flimsy helmet that looked as if it was made of cellophane coated his long head.

The machine was still chugging away, blocking the entrance. The air was thick with fumes.

Protected by the helmet, the Kusk seized hold of two pieces of thick rubber under the metal frame of the vehicle with its delicate, bony hands and pulled backward. The machine shifted about a metre. The Kusk yanked hold of the metal pipe belching out the choking fumes and pulled it off. The engine noise grew to a throaty roar, as if the vehicle had been angered, and more smoke filled the air. Growling more loudly than the engine, with both hands now under the rear wheel arches, the Kusk lifted the back of the chugging metal carapace into the air and pulled it backward with more success this time. When the entrance to the control chamber was clear, it dropped it, and the suspension creaked and groaned as it landed, still belching out fumes.

The Kusk assessed the instrumentation on the vehicle's control panel, huge rolling eyes eventually settling on a key with a dangling rectangle of blue plastic attached to it. Its delicate bony fingers settling on the key, twisted it experimentally and the engine stopped.

The sudden silence seemed to surprise the Kusk. After a

short pause, it brought both fists down on the vehicle's roof with shattering force, leaving a massive dent behind in the metal. Then it sent a signal to the Leader that the way was clear.

The obstruction removed, the Kusk stomped into the control chamber as aggressively as it could, determined to humble and terrify the humanoid as much as possible before its apprehension and eventual destruction.

But the chamber was empty.

'Doctor, the clouds aren't moving.' Anstaar had started off enthusiastically enough but she was starting to get bored with trudging through the mushy sludge that covered this patch of Hirath. The Doctor, in contrast, was marching ahead as if he did this sort of thing every day. Which, by the manic look in his eye, he probably did.

'Yes, yes,' he enthused. 'It's interesting, isn't it? I would say that, like your computer talking rubbish up on the moon, it's this planet's way of winding down.'

'Winding down?' Anstaar stopped, but the Doctor carried on.

'Yes. It's dying, and it wants to draw out its final moments.'

She couldn't believe the cheery edge to his voice, the satisfaction in his tone as if he'd just solved a particularly tricky crossword puzzle. There was something comforting about his relentless good humour, though. It was distracting, diverting. She wondered if he was trying to distract himself as much as her from his own demons.

'Tell me, are there many planets for your Homeworld to absorb into its empire?'

Anstaar nodded. 'There are fifty-three. The Thannos system is named from the old tongue: *Thenossus*, meaning "bead tapestry". The ancients of the Inner Worlds thought those planets were giant beads in the sky blowing in the space winds.'

'Do you suppose the ancients of the Outer Worlds had a name for them?' asked the Doctor quietly.

Anstaar sighed. 'They just didn't develop as we did.'

'Tut tut,' remarked the Doctor. 'They didn't conform to the Inner ideal.'

It was Anstaar's turn to speak quietly. 'That's just the way it is, Doctor. They're more barbaric than us in many ways. It's because they're further from the sun.'

The Doctor snorted. 'Ridiculous propaganda. Do you believe everything you're told?'

Anstaar looked at him challengingly. 'I'm not sure I believe you.'

'So it depends who's telling you.'

'You're clearly an outsider.'

'True.'

'You don't know the government, Doctor, or the K'Arme. You have to believe what they say.'

'So with the tacit support of the people they remake the Outer Worlds in their image,' said the Doctor, scowling, 'and pack off whatever's left behind to here.'

'A lot of the dangerous pollutants are actually demonstrated to decay faster in the chronally less stable parts of the planet, and as they do so they become incredibly valuable to industry again.' Anstaar was aware she was sounding like TCC's publicity team.

'Their recycling effort does them credit, I'm sure,' said the Doctor, drily. 'Sam would be so proud of them.'

The mention of the girl's name again clouded his features into a sad frown. Anstaar reached out and tugged his sleeve.

'We're a long way out from Thannos here, you know. A lot of us don't sanction the measures the government's employing, but...' She paused. 'It's all I've known all my life. Don't blame me for living with it.'

The Doctor didn't look at her. 'I'm afraid none of us will be living on Hirath with anything much for long.'

'So this whole planet is going to die, with everyone on it.' Anstaar said the words with what she meant to be sarcasm but somehow it sounded more like shocked acceptance.

'Unless we can stop it, somehow.'

'Is that likely?'

'I don't know. But it's from this sector that the temporal leakage is emanating.' He met her gaze at last. 'But leakage from where, eh? That's what we've got to find out.'

'And will that distract you from the guilt you're feeling at losing your friend, do you think?' Anstaar stated the words as a gentle challenge.

The Doctor's face suddenly looked like that of a hurt child, but he said nothing. He turned back round and set off again up a steep incline, shoes squelching in the mud. 'This way,' he mumbled as an afterthought.

Anstaar set off to follow him, feeling a little guilty now herself.

The explosion was so loud that Dwynaar imagined the silent sky would shatter as if it had been painted on glass. He leapt from his bunk in the communal centre stark naked and ran to the door, flinging it open.

It took a few seconds for his eyes to adjust to the bright daylight still outside. By that time, standing in the doorway was a K'Arme guard. Dwynaar almost spluttered in amusement at such a ridiculous idea. Then the guard broke his nose with the butt of his gun and kicked him into the side of the bunks. As the others began to wake, the guard fired several shots up at the ceiling. Patches of clear, bright, pink sky shone through the little holes. The guard walked into the barracks, and two more came in behind him as he pulled people out of their beds, shouting, scared, furious, or disbelieving what was happening.

'Felbaac, you stupid crusading bastard,' muttered Dwynaar, swallowing thick mouthfuls of blood. Sost, pale and sweaty, helped him stand, and the two of them were pushed with the others to the side of the room.

Tanhith looked at Sam, who seemed both scared and excited.

'What the hell was that bang?' she asked him.

'Our ship, I think. It's… OK. It wasn't going anywhere.'

She looked at him worriedly. 'Are you going out?'

'No. I think they'll know me. I used to be quite a famous activist myself before they had me mineral crunching on Ipmuss, helping their terraform effort. My escape was big news.' He smiled, wryly. 'Felbaac wasn't much back then. My being here may help convince them you're Felbaac, fresh from some mission of liberty.'

'Fresh? Very likely,' said Sam, looking down at herself, at her stained clothes.

'It'll confuse them,' soothed Tanhith. 'Just like you confuse me.'

'Meaning?' Sam looked at him, kept looking at him as his face moved towards hers.

The door was abruptly smashed open and a chubby-faced man with an Artist-formerly-known-as-Prince moustache charged in with a drawn pistol and a guard in tow.

'Down!' he ordered, and Tanhith and Sam complied. There was a long silence as Sam gritted her teeth and waited for death to hit them, wondering what form it might take.

Eventually she heard Prince give an order to the guard. 'Get hold of Commissioner Sangton.'

One side of her face pressed flat to the ground, she saw Tanhith's eyelashes doing their Mexican wave.

The Kusk Leader entered the control chamber, hissing angrily when he saw the modifications undertaken. 'Barely recognisable,' he rumbled, his jaw drooping in a curiously pathetic manner. 'Where is the humanoid responsible for the poison gas? He must be crushed.'

'He has gone,' said the Kusk technician dismissively, already busying itself checking circuitry.

'His life trace is not present,' confirmed the hunter Kusk.

'Then there must be some kind of transporter device in this area.'

The technician trudged over to the cannibalised transmission booth. 'This would appear to be a crude attempt at matter teleportation,' it rasped.

'Is it still functional?'

'Apparently.'

'Then that is how the humanoid has vanished. We shall use it ourselves to retrieve the Prize.' The Leader's gleeful smile abruptly dropped. 'Wait. The humanoids have added... this.' He gestured disdainfully at the digitpad. 'We shall be unable to interface with our computer.'

'Not so, Leader,' said the technician, delicate fingers flicking over the digitpad as it restored basic life-support to the areas sabotaged by the dangerous humanoid. 'We have assimilated the cranial functions and physiognomy of the humanoid leader. We *can* operate the systems, but the interface is not as effective.'

'It will suffice,' muttered the Leader, slightly aggrieved at the technician's sudden authority in this situation. His voice became lower, barely more than a gurgling moan.

'Locate the Prize.'

Most of the men in the settlement had been rounded up and made to stand among the brukweed. Grey-suited guards were firing a few shots above the heads of some of those trying to run away, bringing them down with the threat of brute force.

Chasing them, catching them. The years of enforced idleness made the men easy prey. Yast was saddened to see a couple of the men try to employ some of the techniques his crewmates had been teaching them so recently. Unconfident, hesitant, they were made to feel their final beating down and defeat all the more painfully.

Yast averted his eyes. He'd never been one for heroics. He'd fallen in with Felbaac and Tanhith on Ipmuss, sent there because his father had spoken out one time too many against the government and the K'Arme's atrocities. Father had died shortly after sentence of exile was carried out. Yast had kept his head down, and soon worked out that the best way to stay alive was to ingratiate himself with Felbaac, whose reputation was growing in the camp. A reputation Yast himself helped to spread. A rumour here, a blatant lie or exaggeration there. And he'd made sure Felbaac knew exactly what he was doing. His own status, son of a rebel agitator, made him the ideal mouthpiece for propaganda.

Yast had barely been on Ipmuss half a season before he'd joined Felbaac's and Tanhith's escape with Somaath. Felbaac had noticed Yast's talent for calming down a rabble, recognised that patience was occasionally more effective than shouting or losing your temper. Yast had made a virtue of that fact, and worked hard to make himself indispensable. He'd grown used to Felbaac's limited palette of reactions and interceded accordingly, always stepping in at the right time. His contribution to rebellion was small and safe, but prized above the more obvious talent of a lot of Felbaac's cannon fodder. In return, he never questioned Felbaac's motives or decisions, and helped maintain the myth of invulnerability.

And right now he was painfully aware that the myth was being put unpleasantly to the test. Another man was brought down, smacked, shot in the arm, kicked again. Yast knew the K'Arme troops were probably bored and unoccupied for much of the time. Events like this were an opportunity to vent their frustrations and let off steam. They made the most of them.

He saw the woman. Harsh-looking, smiling coldly at the frightened men, staring with disgust at their naked or semi-naked bodies. She scared him – all the more because he was so obviously not a part of the settlement. He looked around, and noticed with resentment that Elb, Maadip, Yattle, and Caft, all that was left of Felbaac's small advance guard, had stripped naked to blend in. It was something he just hadn't thought of until it was suddenly too late, and the realisation that he would be instantly spotted made him feel sick.

He was jolted back to attention as the woman spoke, her voice imperious and clear. 'Which of you is the spokesperson for this rabble?'

Dwynaar, his nose inflamed and crusted with dried blood, walked forward without hesitation, unconsciously trying not to trample the brukweed as he did so.

'I am,' he said simply.

'Then tell me, where is Felbaac?'

'Who?' He looked round in mock bewilderment at his men. 'Sorry, name don't ring a bell. Been a bit out of modern politics, I'm afraid. So leave us alone.'

The woman shot at the ground near Dwynaar's feet. Yast flinched, and tried to hide himself a little further back in the crowd.

'I'll ask one more time,' she said, coolly and clearly. 'Where is Felbaac?'

Dwynaar stared at her, then spat into the dusty earth and brukweed.

Raising her pistol, the woman fired at Dwynaar's hip. His screech of agony rang around the yard in the hot still air, and a low murmur of pained voices started up. Yast saw the woman smile.

The quiet rumbling of a motor rose above the noise of

Dwynaar's agony. A shiver ran through Yast as he took in the sight of a K'Arme commissioner in his land transporter, flanked by two guards. Behind the transporter were Tanhith and the girl-thing, Samantha, being pushed along by a young K'Arme officer and several troops. The transporter stopped.

The old commissioner rose and addressed the woman. 'Be patient, my dear Fettal, none of them must die yet,' he began. Relief washed over Yast and he wondered for a brief moment if it was worth his offering his services to the K'Arme in any way. If they valued patience…

'Bundle them away, Fettal. Send them back inside for a time. Once they're in there…' He smiled. 'Shoot each of them in the foot. I don't want any more running away, and I don't want any more defiance. Am I clear, you men?'

Yast looked around, feeling sick to his stomach. The men said nothing, but their faces spoke volumes. Fear, anger, resignation even. Their shadows were thrown down thick and black by the unmoving sun as they shambled off into the sleeping dorm. He looked at the woman – this Fettal – and shivered despite the cloying heat. She was staring straight ahead, unblinking, in the sunlight, a smile spreading over her pale face.

Yast felt like a beast entering the charnel house as he shuffled through the door into the room, his heart racing, the sound of tears and anxious mutterings rising in his ears. A rush of horribly vivid memories, something that had plagued him since their arrival here, hit him, and he felt the combined fear and tension of the last half-hour in one hit. He almost began to gibber in the confined space.

He closed his eyes and held his breath, shivering as the door quietly closed behind them.

Commissioner Sangton looked at Tanhith and the skinny wretch next to him. 'Can it really be Felbaac with his number two, left all alone and unguarded?' Both remained silent. 'Hmm, Mr Tanhith? Is this strange creature meant to impress me, or delay me?' Again, Tanhith and the girl-thing said nothing. She stared dead ahead, while Tanhith burst into another coughing fit.

Sangton climbed gingerly down from the transporter, and hobbled over to the blonde creature. He decided it was more female than male, some kind of Outer freak.

Taking hold of her chin in his frail fingers, fixing her with his watery grey eyes, he spoke, his voice low and soft. 'Felbaac? The latest, greatest figurehead for the rebellion?' He rubbed a hand over his sweating forehead. 'Well I'm here, as you wanted. We found your friend Vost most co-operative in giving me the safe-path co-ordinates here, just as you suggested he'd be. Do you know –' Sangton's eyes were cold – 'I really do think he may be afraid of me.'

The thing that wished to be known as Felbaac stared at the ground and said nothing.

Sangton tightened his grip on her chin. 'I don't believe a stripling creature like you could be my target. Not for one moment.' He jerked his hand upward, making her look at him.

Tanhith spoke without looking up. 'That's Felbaac's greatest strength. Hadn't you heard?'

Sangton ignored him. 'Nevertheless I am keen to discover your origin, and why you should wish to mislead me so.' He let go of her skin, and turned to Traxes. 'Take her to their meeting room.' He straightened up, painfully. 'There we shall discover the truth.'

The Doctor had become quieter as they travelled. He trudged on, lost in thought, hands deep in his pockets. Anstaar thought of a hundred things to say, but couldn't find the right words to articulate any of them. They walked on in silence.

The Doctor peered out between two walls of rock, wiping

his soaking-wet hair from his brow. Suddenly he turned to her. 'Look.' She came to join him.

They appeared to be at the edge of a large natural arena, with walls that edged rockily down to a flat squelching plain littered with spongy red boulders. A few birds with mauve plumage circled and swooped between vantage points overlooking the plain and their nests in the bubbly rock that housed scraps of food and sheltered the young. As Anstaar followed the flight of one of the birds into the arena, she realised that way below her, through the vaporous haze, two figures were visible, humanoid as far as she could make out. 'What are they doing?' she asked.

'Sitting down, by the look of it. Funny place for a picnic, though, don't you think?' As she was about to answer he shushed her, shaking his head, his face suddenly intent. 'Listen.'

Anstaar did as she was bidden. 'It's just the birds, isn't it?'

The Doctor shook his head almost imperceptibly, but the caws and shrieks of the birds continued despite his dismissal of them. 'A slightly lower pitch.'

Anstaar's face whitened a fraction in realisation. 'It's one of them down there. Screaming.'

Describing a sludgy circle, one of the figures was screeching and shaking, writhing in the thick alien soil. The other remained perfectly still.

Anstaar was frightened. Now she had identified the terrible noise, it seemed louder than ever. 'It's like an animal,' she whispered.

Without another word the Doctor had leapt over the edge of the precipice and was scrambling down the steep incline, his fine velvet coat becoming spattered with the thick mud, his shoes disappearing under layers of orange clay.

Anstaar took a deep breath of warm wet air and followed him down.

* * *

The Kusk Leader stood trembling with impotent rage in the control chamber. The computer was not responding properly to their manipulations.

'We cannot trace the exact location,' said the engineer, a younger Kusk than the others, falteringly. His voice had a high-pitched twist to it that made him sound constantly nervous. 'The information has become confused. The computer has become one with the Prize. The two have merged.'

The Kusk Leader was outraged. 'The computer was designed to stabilise the artefact. Not to become it!'

There was an uncomfortable silence, during which the Leader glared at the technician, who was tampering with the connections the humanoid had made earlier. The other Kusks looked down at the floor, a little embarrassed.

'How many Kusks do you still have in cryogenic suspension?' the Leader asked the black-skirted Kusk.

'Ten, Leader.'

'Prepare them.'

He swiped his heavy fist through the air and slammed it down on the console. 'We shall send Kusk forces to every area on the planet to locate our goal. Anyone who stands in our way must be destroyed.'

'We have not sufficient numbers to achieve that in the time allowed. I suggest we send small parties to the zones surrounding the chronic leakage on the planet.'

The Leader clenched his fist. The other Kusks in the room were looking at him, more with interest than respect, he felt. Finally he nodded. 'It is most likely the Prize will be at its epicentre.'

'Or on its periphery, Leader,' said the technician. 'There is no way of accounting for the directional patterning of the chronal infection.'

The Leader narrowed his huge eyes. He had the

uncomfortable feeling he was being mocked. 'I shall arrange the detail of our troops.' He paused. 'In consultation with yourself, Technician.'

The Kusk nodded.

Sam was sitting at the head of the camp meeting table, determined not to cry. She was flanked by two grim-looking guards, that Prince lookalike git, whose name she now knew to be Traxes, was pointing a gun straight at her, and directly in front of her was the evil smile of the elderly commissioner. She could hear blaster fire and the muffled screams and cries of each and every man as he was shot. It was a ghastly image; even focusing on the dark malevolent boss-eyes of her interrogator was a little better.

'I don't know what manner of creature you are, she-male, but you are most certainly not the rebel leader I've spent these last few years pursuing and who presumes to make my private affairs public knowledge. I confess I find you a disappointment after I've chased Felbaac so –' he looked with an ironic smile at his shaking hands as he placed them on the rough wood of the table – 'vigorously.'

'Don't believe me, then. Doesn't matter to me. You can let me go, can't you?'

The commissioner smiled again, displaying his yellowing teeth. 'How do you come to be here? Felbaac picked you up somewhere?'

'I suppose that would follow if you believed I wasn't Felbaac, wouldn't it?' Sam was trying so hard to think what the Doctor would say, but could feel any illusions of cool fading fast. Another gunshot from the next building. A scream that was high, almost theatrical, replaced by a noisy sobbing and a further warning from that bitch Fettal. It sounded like the last victim was Yast. She'd rarely felt so helpless.

'Yes,' announced the old man. 'You're some inbred freak

from an Outer World Felbaac has picked up to lend sympathy to his cause. You know nothing. I have no use for you.'

Traxes tightened his grip on the weapon and Sam let slip an involuntary moan of fear. Her hand moved to her mouth as if she was afraid she would be sick.

'However,' interceded Sangton, waving Traxes' arm away, 'you clearly must know who the real Felbaac is.' He leaned closer to her, and it took all her willpower not to recoil. 'And I hope you will lead me to him sensibly. I'm going to arrange a little show for my men. After all, we have travelled far through difficult and dangerous terrain, and we have not yet had enough entertainment to warrant such a journey.'

He slapped Sam hard around the face, licking his lips, as she felt a sting and then a glow fill her right cheek.

'Not nearly enough.'

The Doctor helped Anstaar down to the bottom of the steep slope, then motioned her to stay back while he advanced on the strange pair. The screaming man was clutching mindlessly at the stony soil with bleeding fingers. His skin was a pale blue and covered in scratches and sores; a thick metal nail was hammered through each arm above the elbow; and his eyes rolled in his head as he yelled out in agony. His legs, emaciated and bent into shaking, angular shapes, were gradually burying themselves in the mud.

The Doctor wasted no more time and ran to the screaming man's side, cradling his head in his arms. Anstaar stared angrily at the man's silent companion. He was old, with a balding head, a little ridge of stubbly pale-blue flesh forming a helmet over the jug ears. A patchy beard sprouted from scarred flesh, and bushy white eyebrows threatened to obscure the eyes themselves. There was a terrible stench in the air, but Anstaar could not decide which of them it was coming from.

'I don't think these people are from Thannos,' she announced.

'Really?' said the Doctor uninterestedly. He was looking at the old man, who was apparently deep in contemplation of his companion's suffering.

'What does he think he's doing?' cried Anstaar angrily.

'Why don't you ask him yourself?'

Anstaar watched the thick mud slopping over the terrible wounds in the injured man's arms like a mucky poultice. She ignored the Doctor's suggestion and crouched down in front of the tortured man to try to soothe him. But his injured arms flailed out at her, beating her back. Fearing he would inflict further damage on himself, she moved away. Impotently, she shook the old man by his skinny legs instead.

'Let me be,' he whined. His voice was high-pitched and reedy, and he swallowed hard between each barely recognisable word.

Anstaar instantly softened a little. 'Are you deaf?' she said, as he looked at her with wet, blank eyes.

'No,' he said. 'Nor am I blind. I see this man.'

'Then how can you just *sit* there –'

'There is something of the demon in you too, I fear.' The old man looked her up and down, and she turned to the Doctor, bewildered. He was wiping a handkerchief over the man's forehead, muttering soothing words that sounded like a lullaby. The old man moved slightly, slapping at the Doctor with ineffectual swipes of his hand.

'No! Leave him alone!'

The Doctor's blue-green eyes flashed angrily at him. 'It's not in my nature.'

'But the demon!' The old man sounded pathetic and desperate. 'He is purging himself. You must not interfere!'

Anstaar straightened up in disbelief. 'You're saying this man put himself in this condition?'

The old man swung up his head on its wizened cockerel neck to look at her. 'There is no alternative. We come out here, to the wilderness, the mentor and the child.'

'And then you push nails into him?' The Doctor's voice was quiet.

The old man with his bent little head looked alarmed at the questioning, his fingers drumming on his bare blue knees. 'Keep evil away. A self-written mantra through the screams of our suffering. We *all* have the demon.' He looked from the Doctor to the ground, mumbling some kind of guttural rhyme with his eyes shut tight.

'He must be mad, Doctor. What's he talking about?' Anstaar held her hands up to her ears as another wail of suffering rose from the injured man.

'Anstaar, can you remember if any religious extremists rented space on Hirath?' The Doctor looked sadly down at the whimpering body in his arms. 'People endure much for their beliefs.'

Anstaar looked appalled. 'Are you condoning this?'

'Of course not! But we're only observers, passing through.' His eyes sought her understanding. 'Can we impose our own code on them, in this place?'

'But this could've happened against his will.'

The Doctor looked helplessly down at the suffering man's bulging eyes, scanning them intently as a low penetrating moan died away into the frightened, fragile whimpers of a thing close to death. 'His mind's gone,' whispered the Doctor, softly, stroking the thick, black, muddied hair. Anstaar moved round to join him.

The man gave a sudden roaring shout of pain that shocked both the Doctor and Anstaar. They looked up; the old man still held the bloodied rock he had just cracked through the bruised ribs of his helpless victim. He toppled over with a squeal of laughter on top of the mutilated body. The Doctor was knocked backward on to his behind, staring, incredulous and hurt, in silence. Anstaar jumped behind the wizened attacker and tried to pin his skinny arms behind his back.

The old man giggled helplessly in Anstaar's grip. 'You're nice, you are!' he chortled, rubbing the bristly back of his head against her chest, enjoying her shuddering against him. 'I'll keep you!' With a grunt of horrified distaste, she let him go and went to help up the Doctor, but he waved her back. 'No no no no no no no,' he muttered, staring at the terrible gaping wound in the man's chest. Anstaar reluctantly looked too, feeling her stomach heave, and then she realised what the Doctor had noticed.

There were hundreds of tiny electrical components spilling about in the man's insides. Small implants shone out of the fractured ribs through the watery blood.

'What in the deity's name is going on here?' whispered Anstaar. A sudden breeze ruffled her thick black hair. 'Is it a cyborg?'

'Half man, half machine? No, I don't think so.' He reached gingerly into the cavity in the man's chest and fished out one of the tiny implants, simultaneously pulling a jeweller's glass from his pocket.

It seemed that only a few moments had passed before the Doctor gave his diagnosis. 'I would say these implants were turning his blood into a synthetic fuel, an alternative energy source to power his organs. They're also showing signs of severe decay, as if exposed to some vast temporal embolism.' He looked up at her blank face. 'Time disturbance, in other words.' The old man was still laughing hysterically on the muddy floor. The Doctor passed the implant and glass to Anstaar. 'What would you say?'

She didn't bother to look. 'I would say you were scaring the absolute hell out of me, Doctor.'

* * *

Sam looked around her, biting at her nails. The entire camp had gathered out in the yard, some two hundred men, and none of them jogging very far in the near future. She thought of her own love of running, imagined trying it with a big scorched hole in the middle of one foot. She thought she could see the blood still flowing from some of the wounds, but the red soil made it hard to tell. Fettal was making the men stand, whatever.

Sam was being held some way away from them. They were facing her, staring at her as though she was some exhibit, a freak. Suspicious, mistrustful. Behind her, Sangton stood next to Fettal, the old man now leaning on a walking stick that looked as if it had been crafted from ebony or machonite. Very suave. Evil little Hitler.

To her right, and scaring her rigid, were Tanhith and Yast. Yast was holding his ankle where the laser bolt had taken half of it off, still whimpering to himself and rocking like a baby. Tanhith had been badly beaten. He'd been stripped half naked and his chest was a mass of bruises, and small bloody welts peppered his eyelids where most of his eyelashes had been yanked out. A thin trickle of blood ran from the corner of his mouth, the flow increasing every time he coughed.

Over to the left, Traxes stood with the grey-suited troops, arms folded, expectant. A small smirk played about his chubby features, and Sam's blood ran cold despite the overwhelming heat.

'Now,' began Sangton in his crisp, refined voice, stepping forward a little painfully and addressing the injured camp dwellers, 'you've had a small taste of the *terrible* injustices we can inflict on a person –' he smiled a jackal's smile – 'but really, as I'm sure you're aware, that's nothing. Is it, my dear?' He patted Fettal's backside, and seemed vaguely disappointed by the lack of any response. 'So listen to me. Some would have me believe that this –' he gestured distastefully at her – 'is

Felbaac, inspired rebel genius of the Outer Worlds.'

He lashed out at the back of her knees with his walking stick and Sam found herself falling involuntarily to the ground, the impact stinging her hands as she instinctively put them out in front of her. There was no noise, no reaction, and she heard Sangton bark, 'At ease, men, you are at liberty to laugh.' The guards looked at each other uncertainly, but Traxes raised his voice and managed quite a good guffaw.

'Very amusing,' muttered Sam, rising to her feet and turning to face Sangton. 'But you're just too funny really. I mean –' she looked him up and down, as if assessing a potential pull – 'just look at yourself.'

She smirked at him cheekily, and Fettal grabbed a length of her hair and yanked back her head. Sangton walked stiffly over to her and dug his index finger into the front of her throat. Her blue eyes bulged slightly, and she heard what she assumed was Tanhith struggling somewhat uselessly to his feet and getting knocked down again.

Sangton's dry, low voice jolted her back to her predicament. 'Spirited, certainly. Oh, yes, very spirited, fine qualities in a hopeless rebel.' He took his finger away and she found she could swallow again, although it felt as if a half-brick was lodged in her throat.

She noticed that some of the guards had put their helmets back on, perhaps protecting themselves from the sun. It reflected in their face visors like a fat red eye, transforming them into evil mute Cyclops watching her every move. She wished she was wearing magic red slippers instead of her battered Converses, or could hear the sound of the materialising TARDIS cutting through the hot heavy air like cavalry trumpets. But there was nothing but silence as Sangton moved around her to stand next to Yast and Tanhith as he addressed the injured men of the camp.

'I know Felbaac is among you. This is his associate and

these two – Mr Tanhith and his well-dressed associate – are known rebel accomplices.' He rapped his stick down on Yast's injured ankle, and paused with a small smile as the cry of pain rang out. 'Now. I'm a fair man. We of the House of Beckal are notoriously generous of spirit, despite what the slanders of scum like Felbaac would have you believe. So I ask you – stand forward, whichever of you is Felbaac. You have sought to summon me here, have you not? Why cower away?'

A low murmur of disbelief rose among the men, but nobody moved.

'We have equipment back on my ship that can detect electromagnetic particles in the blood unique to the planet Ipmuss where Felbaac was incarcerated.' Yast screwed up his eyes and tried not to whimper any louder. 'But that will be a tedious and, if I choose, quite a painful process.'

He said the words apparently regretfully, and looked without interest at the motley assortment of men in front of him. He did not wait long before continuing.

'Very well.' He turned to Sam with a small flourish of his cane. 'My spirited rebel,' he smiled, 'I'm going to place things in your hands. A little dilemma for you. All good rebels cut their teeth on such quandaries.'

Sam was surly in reply. 'What are you talking about?' She wanted to add 'boss-eyes' but didn't dare.

'It's really down to you. A clear choice.' He paused, theatrically, for effect, then took a weapon like a small rifle out from under his cloak. 'If I give you this gun,' he said, smiling coldly, 'you must use it to kill those two worthless individuals whose pathetic rebellion has forced me to expend such energy.' He pointed at Tanhith and Yast. 'If you do that for me, I shall take a humane sample from each of these men for testing, and leave them in peace.'

Sam gaped at him, struggling for words that stayed resolutely out of reach.

'If you do not kill them, I shall have my men take something else for testing. I shall have them take the head from every man here. All two hundred of them.' Ragged laughter came from a few of the K'Arme troops. 'I'll make sure the long-distance life-scanners are disconnected or faked, just in case there's a soul in the government that remembers you. No one will ever know.'

Sost struggled forwards to the front of the terrified throng. 'Felbaac's not here. He went away!'

Sangton was outraged at the interruption. 'Be silent! A pathetic attempt to deceive us. Fettal!'

'Yes, Commissioner.' Her eyes never left the inmates.

'You will first remove an arm and a leg from that one if our spirited creature here does not comply.'

Sost's jaw trembled and he sank back into the crowd as if seeking to hide.

Sam's world was spinning. She felt sick as she turned to face Tanhith, who was looking at the hot dry ground, and Yast, who was staring at her with beseeching eyes.

'Please,' he whispered, hoarsely. 'Please, please, please.'

Sam swung round to Sangton but could barely find the words to hurl at him. 'You evil, sick –'

'Yes, I am sick.' Sangton's pale face was growing crimson as anger contorted his features. 'Sick of scum like you assuming you have any rights to do as you please. We govern you. That is our sworn duty. We can protect or we can persecute, and when you anger us, when you provoke our wrath –'

'These people weren't provoking anything at all!' She was aware that her words were catching in her throat, aware that she sounded totally helpless, was losing it. She couldn't stop. 'How can you do this?'

Sangton had recovered his composure, and was smiling his cold bright smile. 'Like this.' He offered the gun to her. Immediately Fettal's own pistol swung up to cover her.

Traxes motioned to his men and they did the same.

Sam felt like a rabbit caught in headlights – no, like a diva expected to perform under a hot red spotlight. It was all a trick, anyway, she told herself. She wouldn't have to play out this sick little charade. The second she took the gun she'd be dead, blown apart by twenty or thirty blasts. Her head spun and throbbed, as though a tide was rising behind her ears. Just reach out, take the gun. It won't hurt much, not for long. It's not like you've never been about to die before, is it? That's part of making a difference. It can't go on for ever, it just can't.

She began to reach out for the gun, hesitantly.

The Doctor would find her in the end, he wouldn't give up on her. He'd find the bits of her, and what would he say then? What would he do?

She thought of her parents, relatives, the people she used to know at school. Wondered if her vanishing would ever make headlines. How quickly would she be forgotten? No funeral, no last respects, and no imagination in the world would guess how Samantha Jones had ended up as dogmeat on a big pink planet light years from anywhere.

But in spite of her mind trying to distract her with these pointless questions, despite the freezing fists of fear pummelling the inside of her stomach and her head, Sangton's rifle was still being presented to her, the guns were on her, it was all going to be over, all over, all over…

Sam took the gun offered to her and nothing happened. The day was as still and hot as ever, and her spectators were as still as statues. She realised she was crying.

Then Sangton smiled at her again. 'You kill two men and all these poor, browbeaten penitents get to keep their heads. It's up to you. I shall of course kill those two misfits myself if you do not, but those poor men. Can you imagine how each of them feels, waiting in line for the protracted end? Oh, it will be a long, bloodthirsty business, and you'll be made to watch, my dear.'

Sam felt her arms move as if of their own accord. The rifle she'd been given had turned in her hands, and she realised she was pointing it at Sangton. The silence went on. She waited for the gunfire to hit her, to tear her apart, but it didn't, and she found herself shouting as hot tears poured down her face.

'You can tell your men to shoot if you like. But I'll bloody well take you with me.' She sneered, and took a step towards him. 'Come on then!' she bawled at the guards. 'What are you waiting for?' She turned her head briefly to check on Fettal. 'Move round here where I can see you.' The adrenalin was surging through her now – it was almost as if someone else was acting for her. 'Come on, do it!' she yelled, shaking the rifle in Sangton's direction.

Then she realised he was smiling at her again, a smile shared by Fettal, the woman's grey freckles beginning to turn black like little melanomas in the sunshine.

Sangton chuckled. 'The reason you haven't been shot like the dirty little animal you are is because I know, and my men know, that that weapon –' he pushed a bony finger into the end of the barrel of Sam's rifle – 'is not loaded.'

Sam felt her heroic self-sacrificial high evaporating. The sickness returned, cold and tight in her stomach. She sniffed noisily, and her voice was small and fragile when she spoke. 'What?'

'It's not loaded.'

She turned round to look at the sobbing Yast and at Tanhith, stony-faced, still staring at the ground. Sangton's words sounded behind her but her senses were almost too numbed to fully understand their meaning.

'You must use the weapon to bludgeon them to death.'

CHAPTER EIGHT
THE SKY COULD FALL IN

The newly revived Kusks shambled and ambled down the corridors of the base. The clean metal of the walls, floor and ceiling of the areas appropriated by Temporal Commercial Concerns were already beginning to show signs of the brown deposits that caked all Kusk vessels.

Each of these recently thawed Kusks wore the yellow sash of combat duty, and each six-fingered hand held a tiny, delicate weapon. They kept up their loping march all the way into the control chamber.

The Leader stared at his troops with large, proud eyes. The information assimilated from the humanoid ruling here showed the habitable areas of Hirath to be occupied by puny creatures. Old people, the sick, the insane. Easy targets.

His troops would not distinguish between the humanoids. Humanoids were all the same.

The first Kusk in line saluted with both arms and stepped eagerly into the pale luminescence of the modified matter transmitter.

Having recovered from the shock of the violence in the rocky plain, Anstaar was brimming with questions. The Doctor walked a little way ahead of her, but the deepening mystery seemed almost to be a stimulus to his good humour, so she decided to play on it.

'So you think those people were mad? Insane?'

'Yes,' said the Doctor, sadly. 'I think so.'

'Well, it's more than possible there's an area set aside for psychotically insane criminals from some race I've never heard of, if it's any help.'

'That's very helpful, Anstaar,' said the Doctor, solemnly.

'But was that man a self-made lunatic or were the implants responsible?'

The Doctor looked at her as if to ask her to show more respect. She remembered the way he had cradled the dying man. The same way she'd seen her father cradle her as a newborn on her mother's holovids.

'I would say the implant came after. The laughing fellow, did you get a good look at his back? His backbone looked like it had been strengthened by some kind of alloy. And the scar left behind looked comparatively recent.' He thrust his hands deep in his pockets. 'A good supply of uncomprehending guinea pigs, handily isolated from prying eyes. It's obscene.'

'You think whoever put these people here sees them as nothing but test subjects for new technology?'

'I have that most unpleasant thought in my mind, yes.'

'So what we really need to prove your hypothesis,' said Anstaar, pulling a face, 'is another violently insane psychotic.'

'Wait,' said the Doctor abruptly, pushing her against a wall. She felt its soft surface sliding against her weight. 'I think we might have found one.'

Ahead, through the mist on a turn in the narrow mountain path they were on, was a figure. The Doctor peered at it intently. 'Another man, I think,' he muttered.

'Well, off you go then. Put your theory to the test.'

'All right.' The Doctor smiled a little nervously, then walked up to the vague figure in the haze.

The platform in the pink cave suddenly flared with a brilliant white light. As it faded to a milky glow, the huge brute shape of a Kusk gained corporeal form. As it lumbered off, disorientated, into the wet air of this part of the planet, another pattern of light began to form behind it.

* * *

'Hello! I'm the Doctor.'

He cringed inside. Not the way to gain the trust of a sick man with a psychotic nature. He carried on quickly.

'Which is not to suggest you need a doctor or any such nonsense. It just happens to be what people call me. I've thought of changing it lots of times, but what's in a name, eh? What's yours, for example?'

The figure didn't speak, so the Doctor carried on advancing, warily. 'I wonder, have you noticed anything odd around here lately? Or perhaps anything remotely normal? That would probably stand out a little more.'

The man was close enough for the Doctor to make out his features. The eyes were blue, the face bored. He was wearing a uniform, he was someone in authority. But there was someone standing behind him.

The same someone in authority. And the same someone behind him.

The Doctor rounded the corner and saw a procession of the same man, fifty times over and more, fading away out of sight in the hazy air. On each version, the expression on the face varied ever so slightly from the one before and after, the pose shifting subtly by gradations. The more the Doctor looked, the less real each personification of the man seemed, as if each were some kind of projection. The Time Lord gingerly touched the man's shoulder, then gave a small cry of alarm and snatched his hand away. His fingernails had grown by about a centimetre.

He chewed them thoughtfully on the way back to Anstaar, and thought of Sam. 'Terrible habit,' he murmured, pulling at a hangnail with his teeth.

'You got the proof you were looking for?' she asked him, nervously.

'No. Not exactly.' He held out his hand for her to take. 'But cheer up. I've found us some company for the journey onwards.'

Anstaar allowed herself to be led towards the shape in the mist. 'You've what?'

'Yes,' replied the Doctor, airily. 'You may find him a little repetitive after a while, but trust me – stand too close to him and you just won't know where the time goes.'

'We have no contact with our warriors when they are on the planet's surface?' The Kusk Leader looked questioningly at the technician with his huge eyes.

'No, Leader. But the tracer units should allow us to monitor their life signs. Each must return to the matter transmitter terminals as soon as they are able to, in order to move on to the next possible area.'

'Have you no more troops, Leader?' rumbled the black-skirted Kusk, concerned.

'No,' said the Leader, shaking his great head. 'No more could be spared on an interstellar journey of such hazard.'

The engineer broke in. 'Preliminary readings and forecasts suggest the planet Hirath will no longer be stable enough to support any life outside a time span of twenty units.' The engineer continued in a gravelly whisper. 'The Prize is dying, and with it our control computer dies also.'

The Leader snarled quietly to himself, a sound almost lost under the constant humming of the matter transmitter as it dispatched more Kusks to the surface of Hirath. 'We have not traversed the gulfs between stars to be frustrated by time now. Our troops will find the Prize within the allotted time, and retrieve the information we need.'

'I too will go, Leader,' announced the black-skirted Kusk.

'You are not combat-trained, but that should scarcely be necessary here.' The Kusk Leader suddenly rose up and pointed to the engineer. 'You also will go.'

The technician opened his slash of a mouth to protest. 'The engineer is needed here to –'

'You will have to work harder alone to complete preparations here. Locating the Prize must be our first priority.' He paused as the technician's eyes glared into his own. 'Must it not?'

The technician backed down and turned to the engineer. 'You will be sent to one of the most likely areas. Your skills may be of great value if you find the Prize.'

The Leader smiled at the pair, lips drawn back as far as they would go. 'This shall be excellent experience for you, Engineer.'

The Kusk saluted, uneasily.

The fragments of the man flickered in silence all the way down the path. Anstaar had watched the legs move gradually from figure to figure, the eyes close and open again, the lips open little by little, a yawn stretch itself lazily across fifty or sixty faces before leaving. It was nightmarish, unsettling. She saw the way the feet sometimes disappeared into the ground, or into rock, the legs almost merge into the legs in front. The Doctor had clearly sensed her unease. He had christened the man George, and once on their seemingly endless walk, he had glanced up and done a double take before exclaiming, 'Hello, George! Fancy seeing you!' Anstaar remembered almost smiling.

Now the Doctor was marching on ahead. Having named their ever-present companion, he was now seemingly oblivious to him. Periodically he checked his fingernails, scrutinising them up close and tutting occasionally.

Overhead the sky was like a giant painting, the canvas still pulled taut above them, keeping in the warm wet air. There was a tension in the atmosphere as if the world was waiting for a thunderstorm, an outburst from nature that would cleanse, relieve, liberate all around them. But the same clouds sat in the sky, and around them was nothing but the spongy rock and the distant cries of lonely birds calling to each other.

Dizziness dogged her as they walked. On one occasion she'd pulled abruptly on the Doctor's coat, making him slip a little, almost reaching out to the uniformed man for support before realising, arms windmilling back as he tried to right himself. But when he had finally balanced himself and looked at her, the concern in his eyes alone made her feel much better.

She realised how grateful she was to have someone to talk to. She'd spent too long cooped up in the base on the moon with Vost and Vasid, desperately rationing out her use of the comm-link to talk to friends, or her parents. She could see Vost now, staring at her through his narrow watery eyes, instructing her in how important it was that the base's location be kept secret, that only poor-quality, well-bounced signals could be sent, and even then not very often for security's sake. She saw herself hunched over the receiver, straining to hear familiar, well-loved voices over the static and cross-talk.

Now the Doctor told her the base was overrun by monsters, that Vost and Vasid were dead. But all that seemed so distant now, like an old, half-remembered dream that seemed more and more unreal in the face of this sudden, uncertain reality she was facing now. The events in the arena repeated themselves through her mind. She was scared, her legs ached, and that wretched dizziness kept spinning her round and round...

She stumbled and fell to her knees. She could see them sinking into the mud as if she was being sucked into quicksand. She tried to look up, but her head felt heavy – no, it was as if someone was holding her head down. She strained against it. Her eyes darted to her right – and to her horror she saw the projections of George begin to meld together, begin to move, slowly along the path. The whole world seemed to be shifting around her, and she called out to the Doctor.

But her voice was slurred. With terror she realised it was as if a recording of her voice was played at an absurdly slow speed. Her tongue was like lead in her mouth, it didn't want to move, it hurt to move, and now she could see the Doctor's legs moving in front of her, but so quickly, too quickly, he couldn't be moving that fast, he was playing about, what a time to be clowning, what a time –

Then it was if a roaring wind was filling her ears as she was grabbed by the Doctor and held up against his body. George was a million statues again, the Doctor was breathing hard, and now she could feel herself breathing, her chest heaving up and down as if the air didn't want to stay in her lungs. She could talk again, but a choking sob came out and then tears followed in their place. The Doctor held her, very tightly, and she clutched hold of him until the panic went away.

Gently, she felt the Doctor pulling himself away from her. He spoke low and urgently, and it took her a time to work out what he was telling her.

'Time is unsettled here, Anstaar. We're in great danger, and we've got to move quickly. The distortion effect is increasing, and this zone is getting more and more unstable.'

'You mean we're going to end up preserved for ever, trotting all the way along this path?' Anstaar looked at him, and felt tears rising once again. 'Doctor, what happened to me?'

'You were caught up in a time eddy. Don't worry, it was very minor. But it's not something you want to happen to you too often.'

Anstaar almost laughed. 'You don't say.'

The Doctor looked puzzled. 'I do say! Come on. We'll move quickly.'

'But where are we going?'

'To the centre of all this. I'd leave you here, but I'm not

convinced it's a lot safer.' The Doctor looked sympathetically at her. 'I'm sorry, Anstaar. But there's nothing else to do.'

She looked at the form of the uniformed George stretching away over the uneven track. 'No. I don't suppose there is, is there?'

In the watery pink cave, the platform glowed white once again and another of the creatures began to materialise.

In her panic Sam's eyes flickered over the whole crazy tableau before her. In what felt like a split second she took in the men, Tanhith, Yast, Sangton, Fettal, the troops.

Tanhith's eyes rose to meet hers. They were calm. He seemed at ease – then she realised. He was imploring her to do it. His eyes were hard, focused on hers. His eyebrow lifted a fraction, like a lover having asked for a small, trivial but much-appreciated favour.

He wants me to do it, he really wants me to.

Then she looked up at the sun, still sitting unchallenged in the pink sky, blazing and burning down on all of them. She didn't shield her eyes, and the sun burnt down into them.

She grabbed the gun, held it over her head like a club, then brought it down hard on her forehead. The pain yanked at her but it wasn't enough, she could still think. She hit herself again, hard on the side of her head. Then again, as an almost triumphant gasp escaped her lips. Another crack on the forehead, another at the back of her head, and she was on her knees, senseless, before she became vaguely aware of the gun being pulled from her numb hands.

Sangton looked at her in surprise, his eyes wide. Then suddenly he began to laugh. A low guffaw rising to an incredulous peal of laughter, as if at a wildly unexpected but perfectly fitting joke. The troops too began to laugh, following his lead. He saw Fettal smiling tightly – the bitch couldn't be seen to laugh, but her eyes were shining darkly with pleasure. For a second his laughter died away before he turned to look at the hysterical Traxes and burst out laughing again.

But suddenly Traxes was screaming, not laughing. A gout of red splashed out from a hole in his chest and he stared wildly around, a look of paralysed amusement stubbornly on his face as if he was trying to catch the perpetrator of this latest stunt to give them a good-humoured caution. But his eyes went glassy and the smile finally faded as his body keeled over, hands desperately scrabbling to hold in the blood that was pouring out.

Sangton's head spun round over those of the prisoners gathered before him, but he could see nothing. Then a scream from another of his guards rang out, dying in a strangulated gargle as most of the man's neck was turned to molten putty. He saw another guard fire a shot automatically in the direction his comrade had been facing, but the guard next to *him* was already being cut down by a silent bolt of energy fired seemingly from near Sangton himself. He turned in confusion, reaching for his pistol, his grip on his weapon hard and cold. 'Protect me!' he roared, his voice loud and angry, his face furious and twisted in outrage.

His men ran towards him. He turned to see Fettal being grabbed round the neck by Tanhith, then her elbow slamming back into his ribs, Tanhith coughing, shouting at Yast to help him. He turned back to his men. Two had fallen, one quite still in a cloud of red dust, the other lying on his side and screaming. He turned once more to Fettal, and saw Tanhith delivering a blow to her neck that sent her sprawling unconscious to the ground.

Sangton suddenly reached forward past his guard and grabbed hold of the blonde creature's collar where she knelt in the heat, head lolling downward. He felt a muscle pull in his side as he yanked her towards him and cursed his old body while realising how desperate he was to preserve it.

Sinking to his knees behind her, he shouted out. 'Stop it! Stop it now, or I kill this one.' There was silence. 'Is that you, Felbaac?' he yelled, gasping for breath. 'I mean it. Show yourself or I'll kill your pathetic attempt at a stand-in.'

There was still silence, and Sangton could feel his heart pounding away against his ribs, so hard and fast he wondered if it might break through the fragile old bones. Why had he risen to the bait laid by this piece of scum? 'I mean it! And I'll fire into your crowd of believers, indiscriminately. I'll kill all of them if you don't come out now.' Still silence. He felt the warmth of the creature's body against his side, even in the wretched heat. Then two more of his troops ran over to join him, flanking his armed escort. 'Damn you, Felbaac, these are prime K'Arme troops you're facing! You really think you stand a chance?' But he knew the fear hung heavy in his voice. How could this be happening?

A hole suddenly appeared in the back of the head of one of his guards, and Sangton felt a shower of blood spatter his silver hair and yelped like a wounded animal. The man slumped to the parched earth, his arm catching Sangton's shoulder a glancing blow.

'And this is a prime K'Arme high-fusion tool I took from the dead body of one of your flight engineers.' The voice was triumphant. 'I hold your flight matrix in my hand. I'll crush it unless you surrender your weapons immediately.'

Sangton raised himself arthritically to his feet once again. 'Fool! You'll never escape here yourself if you do. I've blown up your antique rocket ship!' He looked around for the source of the voice but the echoes in the hot still air disguised the actual location of the sound.

'You think that's the only antique in my possession? I have

another ship on the way, and I've stolen your entry codes and your safe-path co-ordinates.' Laughter. 'Perhaps I'll let the Homeworld send a rescue mission here to find you. I'm sure they'll be interested in picking you up when the truth of your depraved life story is out in the public domain.'

The scum was enjoying himself. Sangton stared around himself more wildly. 'You're bluffing.' He saw two of his men crouching behind one of the ramshackle shelters the inmates had built to protect the precious bruk from the glare of the sun. Fettal still lay unconscious to his right, but Tanhith and Yast had vanished into the crowd of prisoners.

Of course. While the girl-thing had provided spectacle, Felbaac had slipped round and joined the throng of men, moving about in it whilst fighting to fool the guards. He watched grains of red dust begin to settle of the glossy black of his boots as he tried to decide what to do. Surrender was not an option. Even one such as himself who had abused the vows of the sacred Houses time and again would not stoop to that – besides, he would surely be killed, the honour of his House stripped bare. His only chance was to bargain. Making sure the two guards were between him and the seemingly bewildered prisoners, he reached his long bony arm between the two guards and pointed his pistol at Sam's head as it lay face down. 'I can kill this wretched creature before you can destroy my flight matrix, Felbaac,' he called, his voice collected and calm. 'Consider your next move very carefully.'

'Go ahead. That creature means nothing to me.'

There was a sudden murmuring from the crowd of men as a figure forced it way through. Sangton cowered back still further behind his guards, but his finger tightened on the trigger of his pistol.

'No!' It was Tanhith, standing with his arms up in surrender. 'Why kill her?'

Sangton stared at him, an icy amusement suddenly in his

eyes. 'Rebelling against the rebellion?'

But suddenly Tanhith jerked, and a puddle of blood began to form at his feet. His mouth opened as if he were about to speak, but he only pitched forward on to the prone body of the girl-thing.

Felbaac's voice rang out over the astonished whispers rustling between the men. 'No, he isn't.'

Felbaac cursed. The idiot! Just as everything was going well, his words coming out clear and in the right order and everything working like a dream. Sangton down to his last men, the camp back in his hands, the K'Arme ship theirs for the taking, his ship and its cargo coming into land. The work of a true hero. He'd taken some time to enjoy the moment and now Tanhith had spoilt everything. He felt the faces of the terrified, desperate men around him now turning to him in angry disbelief.

'I had to shoot him: he was going to get us all killed,' he hissed, hoping Sangton and the K'Arme wouldn't hear, but his voice was so quiet that only those close by stood a chance of hearing, and their shock was such that it seemed they couldn't take in his reason anyway. 'He was surrendering our advantage. Look, it's all right, it was a low-level blast, I had to do something –'

One of the men – it was Elb, the idiot – was reaching out for Felbaac's weapon, trying to wrest it from his grasp.

'I'll get us out of this,' said Elb, gruffly.

'Get off!' hissed Felbaac in indignant surprise. Elb wouldn't. Felbaac felt a surge of anger and ingratitude, and fired. The man spun backwards with a surprised cry, his stomach suddenly melting. He knocked down two men beside him, and left Felbaac staring in disbelief. He realised the men around him were outraged, angrier than ever.

'It went off in my hands!' he protested, pleadingly. Damn

Tanhith. Everything was going wrong, the moment slipping away. The situation was beyond him now – he had to get back the initiative. Someone else went for the weapon, and this time it did seem to go off by itself. A man fell shrieking to his knees as his hands erupted into liquid and a babble of further angry voices started up.

As he tried to move away from the arms reaching out for him, he heard Sangton's voice, a roar of hatred. 'Forget taking him alive. Open fire. Kill them all!'

They'd been walking for ages now. Or it felt like ages, but she was aware time had little meaning round here. Eventually, a collection of buildings had come into sight. 'Look,' she'd heard the Doctor say ahead of her. 'That must be the headquarters.'

And now here she stood surveying it. The buildings were made of the same crumbly stone as they'd found everywhere else in the area, pressed into square holes inset on metal girders. The roofs were flat. Narrow windows held panes of clear plastic looking out on the mountainous landscape they'd travelled over. One building was obviously for staff quarters. Another was probably a playroom of some kind, judging by the way childish scrawls had been painted over it. Probably by the inmates, thought Anstaar, a little unkindly. Badly drawn birds and people, standing in front of a big sun sitting on top of a hill.

The Georges had finally come to an end at this place. The real George, the living, breathing uniformed body, was leaning back against a wall a little way away. She'd seen the terror in his eyes, moved forwards to try to help, but the Doctor had stopped her. Now he was pacing in a careful semicircle around the terrified man.

'Can you hear me?'

A slow, ponderous 'yes' seemed to pull itself out from his lips. 'Recorded at seventy-eight, played at thirty-three and a third,' muttered the Doctor, cryptically. 'I'm going to reach out to you, now. Don't be scared. Try to stay calm.'

Even from here Anstaar could see the eyes bulging with fear. 'Be careful, Doctor.' she shouted, coming closer. 'And don't even *think* about dying and leaving me here by myself.'

The Doctor turned and smiled wanly. 'I never think about dying. Or death in general, really.' He turned back to George, his voice low and quiet like that of a sombre child. 'I mustn't.'

Then he moved forward and embraced George with a low moan of pain. There was a brief flare of light, and suddenly George was draped over the Doctor's arms. A look of grim triumph flickered over the Doctor's features, but Anstaar felt her jaw drop.

'Praise the deity, protect us,' she murmured.

George had aged dramatically, shrinking into a wizened old man in seconds. Liver spots formed and bled into the wrinkled skin as she watched. He looked at her in pained confusion.

'Tell us,' said the Doctor, sinking to one knee and cradling the frail form in his arms. 'Tell us what this place is for.'

The man opened his mouth, but Anstaar could see the bafflement in his cloudy eyes. 'The shock. It's too much for him.'

But the Doctor shushed her as George began to speak, trying to put a happy tone in his voice. 'You know what it's for. It's home!'

'Listen to me, it's desperately important,' implored the Doctor, squeezing the old man's hand. '*Is* this some kind of asylum?'

George smiled faintly. 'They said *I* was mad to want to work here.' Suddenly he tried to sit up straight. 'They never came back for us. They never came!'

'Who?' urged the Doctor.

'Relief guards?' asked Anstaar, but the old man stared round in confusion.

'I – I –' he began, but then sank back into the Doctor's arms. He tapped the side of his head. 'I.' It was said like a statement of fact. Then he brightened, smiling. 'I can hear for ages. See for ages. Things are coming.'

'How can he know?' demanded Anstaar, straightening up with a chill.

'He could well be feeling echoes of the senses of those thousands of temporal projections along the track.' He turned back to the frail old man in his arms and whispered, helplessly, 'Please, stay with us.'

The man shook his head. 'I hear well now. Since I…' His voice died away into a solemn muttering, but he kept tapping the side of his head wearily, poking a finger in his large pink ear. Anstaar crouched back down and peered inside. Stifling a gasp, she noticed something inside. She looked at the Doctor for reassurance, she reached into the ear canal a little way and grasped a metal clip. As she pulled gently, a lengthy implant came out of George's ear, its long tip soft and covered in residue.

She stared at him. 'Not just the inmates, then.'

The old man suddenly sank back further into the dark green velvet of the Doctor's coat sleeves. 'They're coming,' he said, very plaintively, before slipping into a deep sleep.

A couple of minutes later he was dead. 'RIP, George,' said the Doctor solemnly. He stood up, and gently picked up the body from the ground. 'Let's get him inside, away from all this.'

Anstaar shook her head, as if trying to clear it of all the fear and the questions. Glancing behind her, she could see that George still lived, hundreds of him in a long line. His warning…

She followed the Doctor inside.

When Sam regained consciousness she realised something

heavy and sweaty was on top of her. It smelled a bit, but not horrible. Then she realised her mouth was full of thick soil, clay-like and heavy with the moisture in her mouth. Suddenly she began to panic. She could hear voices, shouting, gunfire. She was buried, she thought to herself, buried under something and they were going to dig her out, she'd be safe if she just held on.

Then events flooded back into her mind, painfully vivid, and she froze. What the hell was happening now?

'Damn you, Felbaac!' It was Sangton's voice, quivering with age and indignation. 'Shoot him. Kill him!'

Anger twisted Sam's face into determination, and she was about to struggle against the weight holding her down, when she recognised the musky smell and realised it had to be Tanhith. What had happened? She could hear his breathing, shallow and fast. God, he smelled good, but she felt guilty for even thinking it in this situation, and she pictured the Doctor wagging a finger at her. Just her luck to stumble upon an alien humanoid male whose body odour didn't gross you out even when he was half dead in never-ending sunshine and she wasn't allowed to do anything about it and –

The Doctor, wagging a finger at her.

Yeah, well, come and get me out of all this if you're that bothered.

She stayed still, ears straining, thinking hard what to do next.

Felbaac was running from his own would-be private army, from the K'Arme troops, from the whole sorry situation. Damn Tanhith, damn him, damn him, damn him. He needed to get away, come back when things had died down. No, how could he? The main things dying down would be the men when Sangton rounded them back up. It was a good job they were hampered by the pain of their injuries, he thought, then flushed with shame; Felbaac the fearless rebel running from fellow revolutionaries who had only one good foot. Damn Tanhith! Where was his back-up – Maadip, Yattle and Caft – and where the hell was Yast when he needed him?

He had to win back the respect of the men. And to do that, he had to kill Sangton and his troops. Take the men off this planet for good. Let them rest up, then carry on fighting the good fight. Somaath's name would be eclipsed by his own, the glory of Felbaac shining brighter than the sun up there.

But right now glory was nowhere, and the sun beat down so hard he felt he could just lie down and fry. Behind him a few of the prisoners were limping at a half-run after him, about five or six of them. He scrambled up a small rise. A guard was approaching fast from behind. He waited until the guard had shot one of the running men, then fired the fusion device. Silently it took off the guard's shoulder, and he screamed in agony. The men chasing Felbaac stopped, turned to see.

'You see?' panted Felbaac, struggling for breath. 'I can save you all. But I must *lead* you to victory.' The men looked at the guard thrashing about on the floor in a dust cloud, then back at Felbaac. A few of them glanced at each other, but Felbaac knew he was getting them back onside. 'We can make it – together. We can win!'

The men turned away from him and back to the guard. They began hitting him, savagely. Then one of them picked up the guard's gun and shot him with it.

At least they were firing it at the K'Arme, thought Felbaac. 'That's right! Well done!' he cried.

But the men were running back at a fast limp in the direction of the camp, led by the man holding the gun, who was firing it wildly. 'That's right!' bellowed Felbaac. 'Let's take the fight to *them*!' But the men were out of earshot. 'Wait for me!' he muttered, steeling himself for the run back. He had to protect this bunch. They'd have to confirm his bravery to the others.

Sangton was cowering on the back seat of one of the land transports. The one guard left was driving. One guard. Traxes was dead, and most of his general guards had followed him that way. Fettal was still unconscious in the dust. He hadn't had the time or the strength to get her aboard and frankly he didn't fancy her chances with two hundred maimed men – put in their condition by her trigger finger – milling about.

His counterattack had begun quite well, but the sheer weight of numbers against them had forced retreat. He'd pushed the prisoners too far, from fear into anger. It was a fine line, and being an old man losing his judgement, he had crossed it. Now, this was a mess.

He had to get away, never mind the information Felbaac had over him, never mind the information that could surely bring a vital part of the rebellion to heel. The coup of Felbaac's execution could perhaps offset the misdemeanours of the past. But how could he explain this expedition at all? It really was a mess, but staying alive was the imperative now.

If there wasn't anyone in his flight crew left alive, well then, he had one man. He'd help to fly the ship himself if he had to. And then he'd rake the whole settlement with enough blaster fire to destroy a city.

His final mission, and there he was: an old man taking back his youth, the hands-on approach, hands steeped in rebel blood till the end. Until the end of public service, anyway.

He permitted a tiny smile to flicker across his face, thin lips stretched tight. 'Faster, man. Do you want them to catch us and kill us both?'

The vehicle was already going flat out, but just giving the order made him feel better. They would reach the ship way ahead of the rebels. The sound of the commotion was ebbing away. He snorted at the thought of the whole ill-disciplined mass, fighting and bickering among themselves. But that had typified rebels from time immemorial. No order.

As the vehicle sped away from the outer boundary of the penal settlement, Sangton slowly pushed himself into a sitting position and looked back. The settlement seemed quiet, at peace, as if nothing had happened.

He thought of Fettal again, and the ghost of a smile played about his lips once more.

Tanhith coughed violently, the noise thick and hacking. It seemed to stir him into consciousness, and Sam took the opportunity to roll him off her with one almighty heave, hoping that the distraction would surprise whoever was around her long enough for her to decide what to do next. To run away bloody quickly sounded like a good idea.

But as she heaved him off, the deep gasp of profound pain that came from Tanhith made her turn back instantly to look at him. His body rolled over in the dirt, and as he landed back on his front, she saw the gaping wound in his lower back, his tunic covered with mud and blood. She held a hand up to her mouth, afraid she would be sick. 'No!' she bawled at him.

'Yes,' came a smug voice behind her. Turning slowly, she saw Fettal pointing a gun at her, the silky threads over her eyes doing little to disguise the hatred burning within. 'And now it's your turn.'

The Doctor rifled through cabinets full of disks and datacubes. 'Why is nothing written down on paper any more?' he cried with theatrical anguish, before kicking a swivel chair across the room, then clutching his toe in mock agony.

Anstaar appreciated his levity. She watched him, dextrous fingers skimming through reams of information he couldn't possibly be taking in (could he?), face gripped by fierce concentration. It was clear that the staff headquarters were proving a disappointment to him. She doubted they would find any answers here, and told him so.

'There must be some clue... some reason for all this.'

'You're getting distracted, Doctor,' sighed Anstaar. 'Maybe there just *isn't* a reason.'

' "The universe is nothing but a functional chain of causality at every level, governed by the oldest and simplest laws." I was taught that when I was young,' he said, and smiled wistfully, his eyes looking into the distant past. 'My tutor was the most attractive person I've ever seen, but just didn't get it.'

'Get what?' asked Anstaar, a little uncertainly.

'That however much people try to take the mystery out of things, they can't diminish wonder –' he plonked a black box on a large desk – 'beauty –' he slipped a datacube into place – 'and discovery.' With a flourish, he activated the file, and a small icon glowed into life on the cube. He smiled at Anstaar, and she smiled back. Then he sat down and began to read, scrolling down through page after page of documentation. 'It's a kind of log, a diary, kept by the director's assistant. His face became grim. 'Judging by the dates of these records, I'd say this asylum was founded around thirteen years ago. The patients here were psychotic, but not all that many were criminals. It would seem that this race considered anyone not functional in society to be substandard and they were deported. Apparently the atmosphere on Hirath is stimulating to certain areas of the mind in some subjects –'

'Is that why I keep remembering everything of late in such detail?' Anstaar stared quizzically at him.

'Do you? Quite probably, then,' confirmed the Doctor. 'Anyway, this was to be the first of many such insane settlements on Hirath if there was any proven gain in the patients to be had.'

'And was there?' It was weird, she realised, looking at the patch of sunshine in the dingy room behind the Doctor, never moving, frozen as if painted on...

'Unproven. I'm afraid the nature of this settlement changed somewhat. The director's assistant was a miserable soul by all accounts, and that's not mentioning his appalling grasp of grammar –'

'Yes, Doctor,' interrupted Anstaar, 'but moving on...'

'Moving on, his entries suddenly stop. Just like that. Not on any great discovery, or revelation, they simply stop, around five years ago. They recommence months later, but the tone is different... more euphoric sometimes, then completely flat.' He looked around him. 'Lifeless.'

Anstaar came and squatted on the floor, looking up at him. 'Some sort of narcotic control, do you think?'

'Or an implant. During the gap in records, I think it's fair to say something pretty monumental happened. Wait a moment.'

Anstaar felt her heart beat faster. 'What?' she breathed, bracing herself for yet more impossible news.

'The patients found something during excavation work to build more facilities.' The Doctor seemed almost sinister, his stern face illuminated in the gentle blue of the datacube screen. 'They found it some distance over there.' He waved a hand in the opposite direction to which they had arrived. 'Could that be the source of the leakage, I wonder?'

'What does the last entry say?' Anstaar got up and looked over the Doctor's shoulder. Her coarse dark hair tickled against his nose, and he sneezed noisily, making her jump.

'Hold on,' he muttered, looking at her a little reproachfully. He found the end of the document, and read blankly: '"Nashaad has metal legs."'

Anstaar giggled despite herself. 'What?'

'Simply that, at the end of a long description about the odd dreams he's been having.' He turned to her. 'How would

163

supplies, new patients, new staff arrive here?'

Anstaar shrugged. 'There are safe flight paths leading through the time striations.'

'Yes, I know, Vost supplied them – legitimately on this occasion.'

'Of course,' said Anstaar a little defensively. 'Most of the zones were operated like that. A spaceship takes you in, and back out again if you need it.'

'And you're collected by TCC ships, to maintain control over who goes in and out?' the Doctor had leapt to his feet and was pacing about the echoing room.

'Yes. *Hirath's* location is no real secret, but if just anyone could get in they couldn't charge for entry, could they?'

'Exactly. So, do you know what I think?' The Doctor marched up to her. 'I think someone took a look at this little settlement and decided that a low-maintenance colony with a lot of defenceless patients would make an ideal testing ground for a whole range of implants and AI technology designed to interact with the humanoid physiognomy.'

Anstaar got what he was driving at. 'With the tacit consent of Temporal Commercial Concerns?' She shivered. 'How could they?'

The Doctor misunderstood her. 'A small, unimportant, tucked-away little unit like this one… doctor a couple of files and there's no evidence it ever even existed. Just the management popping in every now and then to keep an eye on how their new investments are getting along.'

Anstaar turned away and looked out of the window. 'Better hearing, strengthened bones…'

The Doctor picked up her thread: 'A new improved formula for blood, and possibly some kind of cerebral dampener on the director's assistant. Perhaps attempting to modulate mood patterns…' He banged his fist down on the desk, and Anstaar could see that his mild words had belied his true feelings – he was trembling with fury. When he spoke, it was in a hoarse whisper. 'How could anyone take these people apart and do this to them?'

Anstaar looked at him as if he had accused her personally. 'It's like I said, it could be any government. The company deals with many worlds from all over…' Her voice trailed off. The look on the Doctor's face reminded her of a petulant child. She sighed. 'This isn't helping us find out what's going on, Doctor,' ventured Anstaar, nervously. 'What about the director?'

'She left her assistant in full control some time before the records stop. I imagine something affected this area very badly, necessitating a withdrawal of valued staff.'

'That thing they discovered?'

The Doctor stared at her with dull eyes. Then she saw them widen and almost sparkle in the dim light. 'You're right. This isn't helping things. Let's go.'

'But Doctor, if the staff have been left altered or killed, or split up like George, are the patients here looking after themselves?'

'Those who have clung on to life, evidently. Remember our laughing friend?'

The Doctor was out the door in seconds. Anstaar followed him.

The skinny old man in the rocky arena was still sitting by the side of his dead companion, his face sombre and composed. He noticed the two huge figures coming towards him only vaguely, but reached out and shook the dead man as if to rouse him.

The figures continued their dead march towards him. He shook the corpse a little harder. 'Big men with big eyes coming,' he whispered conspiratorially. 'Pretend they're not there and they'll go away.'

The two massive figures paused in front of the tiny old man.

He was still pretending they weren't there as they killed him.

Sangton was surprised when the guard actually spoke to him: 'What's that, Commissioner?'

A simple question. Sangton looked in the direction in which the guard was pointing. A small dark speck was visible in the distance. No, two dark specks.

'Ignore them. Head for the ship.'

'But –' the guard was obviously pained at having to have this conversation – 'whatever they are, they're heading for the ship too.'

Sam looked up into Fettal's eyes. Cold, calculating malice was staring her out.

Sam looked down at Tanhith and waited for the inevitable, putting her hand in his.

The shot came.

Fettal fell to the ground next to her, eyes wide open in surprise. Blood dribbled from a small hole in her shoulder.

One of the prisoners was standing above her, his face red, eyes that could've looked mischievous now looking dull and blank. He shot Fettal once again, in the hip this time. The crack of the laser discharge echoed round the camp.

'I'm going to leave you there to die, you K'Arme bitch. I'm going to watch your blood boil in the heat. How does it feel?'

Sam stared up at him in confused elation at her escape. 'Help me with Tanhith!' she cried.

Tanhith stirred at his name, and twisted himself round with a grunt of pain. His eyes focused on the man with the gun. 'Sost – is Dwynaar all right?' he muttered.

Sost looked back, dispassionately. 'Not very.'

Sam tried to ease Tanhith back. Fettal's breathing was

ragged and with an edge to it that rubbed Sam up the wrong way. The woman was clearly in agony, but Sam couldn't bring herself to feel any pity. She concentrated on Sost. 'I said, help me with him!'

Sost's eyes were stone-cold in his hot face. 'Help him yourself, you freak. You made all this happen. I'm going to fetch Dwynaar. Show him this dying bitch. Show him I got her. Then we'll decide what to do with you.'

Suddenly Sam clutched her head in dizziness. The world seemed to swim around her, her vision blurred and deadened; then a crackle of energy seemed to jump-start her senses. The first thing she noticed was that the sun had moved round in the sky, the clouds were different. Even some of the men she'd seen milling round in the background had moved, vanished, as if into nothing. Again, recent events overcrowded her mind in a series of freeze frames, and a terrible pressure built up behind her ears. Tanhith was clutching his head. Was it affecting him in the same way?

Suddenly she realised Sost was screaming in rage. He was looking at Fettal. The blood that had dribbled through her uniform in a spot was suddenly an enormous stain, and her breathing had stopped.

'No! You're not allowed to die yet! Dwynaar...'

Sam watched as Sost stumbled off towards the meeting hall, calling his friend's name, thankfully without another glance in her direction. She turned anxiously to Tanhith to see if his body had suffered in the same way. But his wound seemed to have begun to heal. The damage to his back still looked awful, but it was a better kind of awful than before. 'Time...' she breathed to herself.

Then the ragged breathing started up again. Sam spun round to see Fettal's eyelids fluttering, her face contorted in pain. She gasped in surprise, then thought hard. 'Frozen in time for a few seconds?'

This place was breaking down. Time was running out, running amok as it left. Pushing Tanhith forward, holding on to Fettal...

With a twist of fear, she wondered how it was affecting her, looking at her sunburnt hands, checking for wrinkles rubbing her fingers along her face.

Then she heard Tanhith stirring again and helped him to his feet. As he paused to catch his breath and deal with the pain, she looked at the helpless eyes pleading up from Fettal's sweaty face.

She wouldn't tell Sost that the woman still lived, she decided, her mouth set in grim determination. That was all. That was all she could do.

Gently, she helped Tanhith to stumble away from the blood-soaked ground towards shelter.

Sangton gasped as the dizzying wave of nausea broke over him and the world speeding along outside the land transporter seemed to slow down, to twist and undulate around him. His senses seemed shrouded in grey, punctuated with flashes of brilliant colour, colours so vivid and intense he couldn't even think of names to describe them.

When it passed, he realised the sun was now glaring down from a new vantage point. The clouds had changed, their feathery mass shifting round towards the west, stretching up for miles into the pink sky.

And the two specks in the distance were now directly in front of them. Huge, powerful-looking alien creatures, dark brown, the sunlight glittering on – Surely that had to be armour, not skin? The huge heads of the beasts swung to look at each other, as if they themselves were surprised.

The driver swerved hard to avoid them. For a sickening moment, Sangton knew he was going to be thrown from the transporter. He gripped on tight but it was no use: the driver had swung the controls in the opposite direction in an attempt to rebalance the vehicle, and Sangton's frail body shot out like a wiry projectile, hitting the dusty earth and rolling over and over.

Blinded by dust and frozen with shock, Sangton felt pain start biting at his body. He heard the transporter screech to a halt. He waited for the sound of it slipping into reverse to come back and pick him up.

He waited for quite some time but the only noise was a scream from the guard that ended in an unpleasant splitting noise.

Sangton slowly pulled his cloak more closely round his battered body, lifting his head a fraction, then burying it in the soft, dark folds of his cloak. He closed his eyes against the sting of the dust, nuzzled up against the thick, dark fabric. Perhaps they would think he was dead anyway and leave him be.

His reports had told him there were no indigenous bipedal life forms here, but the information was clearly wrong. That was typical of the way things were going. Everything was so different now, and if he made it back, if he held on to his honour, his retirement speech would be to warn the Houses of the dangers of sitting back and allowing the young their turn and command unfettered by the ruthless discipline of procedure. Had he not lived by the scared vows of his House all his life, with relentless devotion? How they would applaud his final sentiments...

When the huge foot stamped down on his spine, Sangton was glad he couldn't see what was happening any more.

CHAPTER NINE
FALLEN APART

'Look!'

The Doctor was grimly marvelling at yet another display of time's elegant torturing of this region. Anstaar had already passed enough sights to haunt her for the rest of her life, but apparently the Doctor seemed to feel her scientific curiosity should be rearoused by every fresh horror.

She'd already stared at two patients attacking each other again and again as if preserved for ever on a looping holovid, watching the same pained expressions on their faces reappear every few seconds. She'd seen a young boy whose arms had withered away to little more than ancient bones, his face frozen in a mask of terror. There'd been another officer walking along in slow motion on patrol. They'd tried talking to her but the Doctor had decided she was caught in a bubble of time drifting backward. She couldn't answer them because she was moving back through her own past, and so the present had no meaning.

Now a patch of odd-looking plants were growing – well, backward and forward, shrinking into the earth, then bursting back out into pale yellow flower. Tendril-like vines being sucked into the soil then spat violently back out.

Anstaar sighed. 'Life in a loop. Are we going to go the same way if we keep going?'

The Doctor smiled half-heartedly at her. 'Brings a whole new meaning to "watch what you step in". Stay close to me. I'm a Time Lord.'

'Well, I think you should exercise your responsibilities with a bit more care!' she retorted, but he continued regardless.

'I'm usually more or less immune to this kind of temporal embolism. Hopefully my biofield will help protect you too.' He placed an arm round her, held her close as they walked awkwardly along, but she wasn't complaining now. The Doctor still seemed confident they would find a way out of this nightmare. The closer she was to him, the better her chances of some of that optimism rubbing off on her.

They walked through an area where a bird remained frozen low in the sky, mid-flight, where the water in the air seemed heavier and harder. Then the nausea hit her.

'Anstaar! Are you all right? What's happening?' It seemed to be taking him hours to say the words. She clung on to him until the sickness passed. Then with a loud screech the bird resumed its flight; moisture in the air returned to its normal level. The sun had moved round in the sky, but gradually they realised they had merely swapped one painting for another. The sky was still warm and still.

'Wait, Doctor – we're not where we were!'

Wiping more thick brown hair off his forehead, he looked around. They were at the foot of a slope. 'We probably would've reached here in a few minutes.' He looked at her meaningfully. 'If you hadn't been with me you might have become a part of that landscape.'

'Perhaps.' She nodded. 'But at least I wouldn't know what was happening to me. That's got something going for it.'

'Well, I hope that's true. But given the mental state of poor George…'

'You mean these people are aware of everything that's happening to them, over and over again?'

The Doctor smiled bleakly. 'Like I say, I hope not.'

He held her close as they went up the steep incline. Soon they realised the path was coming to an end. When they reached the edge, and stared through the thin mist, Anstaar gasped.

There was a steep drop into a smaller version of the natural arena they'd come across earlier, but this one seemed impossible to clamber down into. A huge excavation machine – or what was left of it – lay rusting and ancient against the far cliff wall. There was more of the strange spongy vegetation covering a lot of the floor of the basin, but one area was bare and blackened, the rock more like powder, the air itself seeming to spark all around it. In the centre of the charred ground was a metal object, roughly spherical and about half the size she was. It looked as if it was tarnished with age, pitted with tiny goosebumps on its pale silvery skin. Telescopic legs curled round in sections into the air, as if it was a huge metal insect lying on its back. Looking through a pair of strange glasses she'd taken from the Doctor's proffered hand, she could discern banks of instrumentation in the sphere's upper hemisphere. She didn't know why, but it frightened her.

The Doctor was peering above and beyond the far side of the arena's rim. 'Wait a moment,' he breathed. 'Look! That must be the neighbouring zone.'

A softly crackling haze of pale light reached up from the lip of the crater. Flecks of light danced about it and the sky seemed darker above it.

'Doctor, surely it's dangerous to be so close to one of the time dividers?' Anstaar's voice was timid.

'Undoubtedly,' he whispered. 'But fascinating nonetheless. Wait.'

The lights flickering in the haze died down, sporadically, and they could discern more of what lay beyond. It was a bizarre kind of forest with huge trees stretching into the distance. The trunks had an almost metallic sheen to them, and while some of the trees were clearly saplings, others were thick and gnarled. Fat, thick leaves fanned out over branches covered in huge clusters of berries, strange fruit glowing with a dark powerful light.

The Doctor gave a short, hollow laugh. 'Time trees.' His eyes became distant.

'I'm sorry?' Anstaar looked over at the sinister forest swathed in the warm, pale, crackling light and shuddered instinctively.

'So am I. I've only ever seen one before. You pull on the berries. Spatially you remain in the same location, but you and the tree move back through time.'

'That's ridiculous.'

'Possibly. Who was it that said "The universe is ridiculous to someone who thinks, but tragic to someone who feels"?'

'I have no idea. Do we really need more questions, Doctor?'

'Here's one answered, for me. The waste product from your terraforming, the heavy metals dissolving into the soil, the time disturbance... Of course! Perfect conditions. Oh, your Homeworld have a lot to answer for.'

'They wouldn't know about that,' protested Anstaar automatically.

'Maybe not. But it's another profitable enterprise for TCC, no doubt.' The Doctor's lip had curled in disgust.

'Look, Doctor, what about that thing down there? Surely that's more important to us right now?' Anstaar found herself looking into the Doctor's eyes, now. They were blue – no, grey-green. Or were they –

'You're right.' He glanced up at the static sky and took another long look at the forest of time trees before looking down into the crater. 'The next question we don't need is: How do we get down there?'

'Wait!'

The two Kusks turned in surprise to hear the voice of a comrade.

'Why are you here?' asked one, looking pointedly at the

brown skirt of the engineer class.

'You may need my skills in safely handling the device.' The engineer was aware that its voice was higher than theirs, and took pains to speak more gruffly.

'We are only retrieving the datacore, are we not?' The trooper looked at its fellow.

'That is what *I* will supervise.'

The two troopers turned without answering and moved onward. The engineer found itself following on more nervously behind.

Tanhith was pale and clammy, lying on the table in the deserted meeting area to which Sam had managed to manhandle him. She sat on a chair, waiting for him to come back round. The sun shone through gaps in the shutters, glaring into her eyes. She closed them and shook her head sadly, barely believing what had been happening. Her face and head were covered with cuts and bruises, her forehead in particular so swollen she felt like the elephant man. Not a pretty sight, she told herself. But then neither was Tanhith, so he couldn't talk. But she wished he would.

Things had quietened down outside. The camp doctor was trying to treat the survivors as effectively as he could with rationed supplies. She'd been told that she and Tanhith didn't qualify for aid or attention, and her protests had been ignored. She supposed she couldn't really blame them. They'd all been cooped up here for so long with nowhere to go, and nothing happening except the daily struggle to remain alive in this heat. Then strangers come along and before you know it everyone's maimed, or dead, and destruction's all around. That was the kind of apocalyptic effect the Doctor usually had on places. Perhaps his jinx had rubbed off on her, too.

The camp doctor had said they'd been given enough medical supplies allegedly for fifty years, but that figure had been optimistic at best and didn't allow for the kind of horror that had happened today. She'd thought it better not to push her luck in case they decided to kill her in retribution. She was keeping well out of Sost's way, and wondered vaguely what had happened to Felbaac.

Tanhith stirred at last, and Sam started anxiously forward. 'Don't try to move any more, you stupid sod. Just stay still. I'll get you some water.'

Tanhith exhaled a heavy, painful breath. 'Let me die.'

'I refuse to let you be so melodramatic,' said Sam, ignoring the tightness at the back of her head that told her tears were impatient to come. 'So drink this and get better.'

Tanhith wasn't looking at anything as he stared blankly upward. 'I saw the birds circling, flying up into the sun. They were wheeling like carrion in the sky, waiting for me to die.'

'Well, I got fed up waiting so I thought I might actually try to do something about it,' snapped Sam. 'You saved my life out there in the desert, but I came from the moonbase. There's got to be a terminal out there, the other end of that matter transmitter. We can use it to get back to the moon.'

'The moon...' echoed Tanhith. 'It's so far away...'

'It's still there, Tanhith. Things make a bit more sense there than they do here. You'll see –' she wiped his forehead with a piece of damp material ripped from her T-shirt – 'because you're coming with me.'

The Doctor had found no way to reach the strange device. 'We do appear to be rather stuck,' he muttered.

Suddenly a frightened face appeared at their feet, clinging on to the edge of the precipice. Anstaar screamed, and even the Doctor took a step back. The bluish face screamed back at her, dirty teeth jagged and yellow, big black eyes wide with fear, thick fingers digging into the earth at her feet.

The Doctor shushed at the man, and the screaming

stopped. The man shushed back at him. Anstaar looked at the Doctor to gauge his reaction. He shrugged and smiled, then took another step back as the man pulled himself over the ledge, ignoring the Doctor's outstretched hand. Anstaar gasped as the rest of his body came into view, but the Doctor grinned widely.

'Nashaad, I presume.' He reached out a hand and this time the man took it and shook it.

'Nashaad!' beamed the strange man, proudly waving an arm below his waist. 'I've got metal legs!'

The Kusk Leader walked through the ancient corridors of the section of ship sealed off from the humanoids. He felt more at ease among the smell and texture of this place. He hated the alien atmosphere in the control chamber, felt almost sick with the indignity of it.

He had been puzzled at first by how the humanoids had managed to subvert the Kusk ship to a different function, how they had conquered the technology that was so different from their own. But now he had sifted through the captured mind of the one called Vost, he realised that a third party had capitalised on the sleeping Kusks, and on the strange new abilities the artificial intelligence in the ship's computer had developed.

He wandered into a darkened recess of the ship. In certain parts, life-support had been shut down to maintain power to the control chamber. These areas were cold and icy, airless. They disturbed the Leader but did not deter him from his inspection.

A door slid away to reveal a warmly glowing area, the crew briefing room. The communications screen sat on a crusty plinth. Since the maenus chip was discovered among the jetsam of the stellar war that had devastated Kuskas, all technology could be linked to varying degrees. It enabled the long-unused comms screen here, for example, to patch into his ship computer as it sifted through endless subspace transmissions for fragments of newscasts and information from far-distant home. But why then was the control chamber's computer system so totally unresponsive, so unreachable? It reinforced the Leader's belief in the dangers of trusting too much in technology. And his instinctive fear of the technician.

Gradually he'd compiled a picture of how life on his home was developing. The news of the success of the time-travel experiments had filtered through only months ago, and the impact of that discovery had fuelled the technician's ego still further.

The screen idled into life under the commands of his delicate fingers:

THE TECHNOCRACY HAVE STATED THAT THE RECENTLY GRANTED ENTERTAINMENT RESOURCES ARE TO BE COMMANDEERED FOR FURTHER RESEARCH INTO THE CLONING AND TIME-TRAVEL EXPERIMENTATION SERIES. FURTHER LOSSES TO THE ARMED DIVISIONS ARE LIKELY. ENFORCED BREEDING PROGRAMME IS SHOWING ONLY 1% INCREASE IN GROWTH.

The Leader turned away from the screen, remembering the years he'd lived through as a child before the outer universe was discovered. Then, there had been only Kuskas and its sun. One large planet alone in space. They must have stood out like a beacon for the warring aliens.

The whole planet had been used as a tactical front. Caught in the crossfire of layers upon layers of lethal weaponry, the Kusks' own missiles had had no effect on the mighty fleets as they battled. They were ignored, microbes at the feet of giants. Before long the giants had moved on, and Kuskas was nearly dead.

Then the wreckage. Then the new technology. The quest to

rebuild. The armed divisions had been most important then, their discipline and knowledge vital in saving the survivors, restoring order. He himself had played no small part in the restructuring of Kusk society during those long years that followed.

A society changed beyond measure. Scores of proud cities turned to rubble. Insufficient populace to resume industry. New ideals formed from despair. The need to survive, to protect Kuskas from similar attack. No strength of numbers, but the will to grow stronger seizing the survivors. Influx into the armed divisions. New technology ravaged and haltingly understood. Military technological divisions becoming a technocracy, the will to survive and grow stronger increasing with that knowledge.

But they were too few to stand a chance of survival by military means. Other avenues needed to be taken. Technology was stronger than brute force. The armed divisions began to lessen in importance, a historical power only. When the ability to move through history itself came little by little, the military were not much more than a reminder of past glory, a resource easy to bypass until the time was right. At least then armed might would be useful to the Kusk race.

He was leader of this mission, the most important the Kusks had ever known. But it was technology that was leading him, and what further changes would sweep Kuskas in the decades it would take to return?

He touched the screen and it dissolved into internal communications mode. 'Report,' he hissed, his body squelching into the slime-covered hard chair.

The technician's voice rasped over the speaker-sensors. 'Computer holding the Prize stable. Hirath responding well to weakened manipulation signal, but fluctuations are frequent.'

'Are our troops safe?'

'All life signs registering, Leader.'

The Leader paused for a moment, his huge bubble eyes scanning the darkened chamber, thinking back once more to that better time long ago. He roused himself, and his bellowing grumble filled the room once more. 'Have you retrieved a detailed account of the operational areas on Hirath?'

'Yes, Leader. There are fifteen areas pending, life-free. There are several hundred toxic dumps, waste ground held far in the planet's future for chemical products inimical to life. Many sites for the old and infirm to live in exile, thirty-seven penal settlements held in the planet's mid-history – we feel it unlikely the Prize will be located in these places, Leader.'

The Leader scowled. Clearly the technician regarded his command as irrelevant and foolish. 'And the areas near that… disturbance you mentioned?'

'There was only one still to be explored. Upon Unit Two's return from the disused Area Four, I dispatched them there.'

The Leader nodded, sadly. 'Excellent.'

Nashaad was an amenable soul. He seemed pathetically eager to please, and happy to be in company. He kept looking at Anstaar shyly, which was beginning to irritate her – although she realised this was more due to the amusement it afforded the Doctor than any other reason. Punctuating every stilted conversation was his apparent war cry of 'I've got metal legs!' He had demonstrated them by leaping high into the air and scrabbling up the sheer mountain face behind them, before leaping back down again with a look begging for approval or admiration.

'How come he's not affected?' Anstaar had whispered.

'Perhaps he was an old man, once.'

Now she watched, bemused, as the Doctor tried to scramble on the back of the funny little man who swayed about under his weight. 'Right the way down, Nashaad, we need to go right the way down into there.'

'I've got metal legs,' said Nashaad, cheerily nodding.

With a wink at Anstaar, the Doctor had found himself yelling out as Nashaad bounced down into the arena, the impact sending the Doctor hurtling off into a confused acrobatic roll. Miraculously, he jumped to his feet at the end of it like a prize gymnast – then slipped into a patch of vegetation. Anstaar found herself laughing, something she hadn't imagined happening for some time.

'Stay there!' the Doctor called to her as he set about freeing Nashaad's famous legs from the soft soil.

'I will!' She waved back, and watched the two figures turn away from her and towards the sinister device in its charred crater.

From this angle the Doctor could tell the spheroid had impacted quite heavily – a lot of debris had been chucked up around the site of collision.

'Do you come here often, Nashaad?' asked the Doctor brightly.

'I'm always round here. Got nothing else to do except watch the colours there.'

The Doctor nodded. 'Pretty, aren't they? But you never go near them?'

Nashaad lifted up his shirt to show a terribly scarred stomach. 'Never do no more.'

'And is that why they gave you metal legs?'

'I do my jumping here,' enthused Nashaad. 'Got to use them, they told me to use them.'

' "They", Nashaad?' the Doctor's voice lowered and became conspiratorial. 'The director and her friends? When was this?'

Nashaad looked down at the ground. 'Don't know, can't remember, don't know, can't remember, don't know –' He repeated the words like a mantra, and the Doctor soothed him.

'It's all right, Nashaad, don't worry. Probably a result of playing in the confines of this thing. Memory displacement, perhaps.'

He gestured at the alien machine they were nearing, but Nashaad wasn't looking. 'I've got metal legs!' he announced, staring at them proudly.

'Or perhaps you're just mad, of course,' smiled the Doctor, brightly.

Suddenly the Doctor found himself putting a hand to his own head, his legs threatening to buckle under him. He leaned on Nashaad, who almost collapsed under the unexpected weight. 'I'm sorry,' he muttered, composing himself. 'I'm clearly more sensitive to this sort of temporal emission than I thought.'

Nashaad cheerily ignored him and went off bouncing about in Anstaar's direction the other side of the arena.

The Doctor surveyed the metal artefact. 'Here we are, then. What are you? I wonder.'

He began to examine the banks of instrumentation that lined the sphere.

Anstaar had watched the incongruous pair walking towards the probe for a while, then looked around her, feeling a little isolated at the top of the basin by herself. Through the dense watery air, she thought she could make out a great dark shape some way in the distance. Just a glimpse... but there it was again, and in the same place. She racked her brains, trying to remember that part of the route, and how far away it was. Then she realised she remembered looking through a gap in the rock to her side at this view as they had made their way here. The path doubled back round and led on to this causeway.

She'd glimpsed the shadows passing the gap, which in turn meant two dark shapes were on their way.

There was a sudden scuffle of stones and Anstaar cried out involuntarily. Looking down, she was first irritated, then pleased, to see Nashaad beaming shyly up at her.

'Take me down there, Nashaad. Come on, quick.' She held tightly on to his neck and hoped he wasn't enjoying this close proximity to her person as much as she thought he was. 'Try to jump into those bushes, all right? And take care, won't you?'

'Don't worry, I've –'

'I know. *Jump*.'

The Doctor looked up in surprise at the sound of Anstaar's indignant yelp as she landed heavily in the patch of plant life that had seemed so much denser from above.

'See?' said Nashaad, proudly.

'The Doctor ran across to help her up. 'Are you all right? No bones broken? Where did you land?'

Anstaar gratefully accepted his helping hand. 'On my dignity.'

'Oh, good. Much better than landing on your backside. Come and look at this.'

'What? Doctor, wait, up there I saw –'

'No time now, Anstaar!' he cried, racing back to the machine, muddied coat flapping behind him in the breeze.

She followed him, thanking the deity she could still walk. 'I think we've got company coming.'

The Doctor turned away from his study of the spheroid, tutting at his lack of tools. 'Large, nasty bipedal company?'

She nodded, grimly. 'I think so.' Behind her, Nashaad suddenly landed with a small excited whoop, making her jump before leaping off again himself. 'Where does he get his energy from?'

'That's the wonderful thing about Tiggers,' muttered the Doctor, ignoring her puzzled look.

'They're just rounding that bend in the track.'

The Doctor looked at her sharply, then slapped a palm down on the metal surface of the machine, a dull clang resounding heavily around them. 'That's it!' He cried. 'A hairpin bend!' He reached to the back of his head, and with evident relief pulled a small piece of kinked, dark wire. 'Hairpin,' he explained. 'Picked it up earlier. Never know when something may come in handy.' He unbent it and stuck it into a barely visible indentation under the control panel. Keeping another button depressed, he passed his sonic screwdriver to Anstaar. 'Pull down on the central shaft when I say now, all right? Pointing at this bit here.' He waved a finger in the general direction. 'Now!'

She depressed the sonic mechanism, and the Doctor snatched his finger back from the hairpin as it glowed red-hot. 'That's enough!'

She stopped. Nashaad was staring in wonder at them. The Doctor gave a small smile, then clicked his fingers. A gap began to open and widen in the structure of the sphere below the control operating unit.

'Now we can get to the bottom of things. Provided of course that *this* didn't land on its bottom as well.' He smiled at her and she felt herself blushing.

She turned to Nashaad. 'Jump up to the top again, Nashaad. Tell us if anything's coming. You understand me? Tell us quickly, come straight down.'

He smiled at her, and opened his mouth. She put a hand across it to stop him speaking, and smiled encouragingly. He slowly smiled back, and bounded off to the lip of the basin.

'Well, well…' breathed the Doctor. 'Well, well, well, well, well, well.'

Anstaar looked helplessly at him as he delved inside the dark gap in the machine. 'Well?'

'Yes, very, thank you,' he answered vaguely, before bolting

his gaze on to her. 'It's a probe.'

'A probe? You mean, like a space probe?'

'Yes. Except I'm afraid this has travelled through more than just space.'

Anstaar stared at him, her voice an incredulous whisper. 'Through space and *time*?'

The Doctor kept her fixed by his gaze, and nodded slightly. 'The technology is fairly basic but rather elegant.'

'Is it damaged?' she began, cautiously.

'Crippled. It's been sitting here, phasing in and out of the present, sending out a signal to be found, reclaimed, to share all the knowledge it's acquired on its way through this part of time and space.'

'And it's seepage from that that is causing the time problems round here?'

'Must be.' The Doctor suddenly clicked his fingers. 'Wait. These circuits match some of those back in the moonbase computer.'

'What?' Anstaar stared at him.

'That's it! The Kusks created this probe as well!'

'But it malfunctioned in some way and crashed here?'

'Phasing in and out of the past...' muttered the Doctor. 'You know, back on the moon I thought the main computer had been attempting to cure some kind of embolism in time that was affecting the regulation of the time fields, and in so doing had somehow formed a bond with it.'

'Really,' said Anstaar, blankly.

'Now I know why!' He held her shoulders, a delighted expression on his face. 'Temporal pollution from this damaged probe must've caused Hirath's condition in the first place! The Kusks sent out a ship to trace the probe and reclaim it.'

'But if it was phasing in and out of the past, how could they?'

'Precisely! They had to wait while the artificial intelligence in their computer insinuated some level of control over the intelligence in the probe. It attempted to stabilise the shifting timelines by regulating them, channelling them over different parts of the planet, creating these different zones. They went to sleep ready to wake up when it was ready –'

'And TCC came across it and decided to help themselves,' breathed Anstaar.

'A unique business opportunity,' said the Doctor, darkly.

'So why was the base breaking down?' asked Anstaar, struggling to take it all in.

'What if, while the computer was distracted trying to contain the time pollution that threatened to destroy the entire planet along with the probe itself, the probe's intelligence became too strong for it, swamped it, *infected* it? It's malfunctioning, and has made the base computer malfunction too. That would explain why everything's been breaking down.'

'And meanwhile another group of Kusks has been sent to find out what happened to the last lot,' stated Anstaar.

'Persistent, aren't they?'

The heavy silence following the Doctor's words was broken by the sudden landing of Nashaad in front of them. His face was flushed with excitement. 'Did just what you said. They're coming, they're coming!'

Anstaar looked over to the ridge, a panic-stricken look on her face.

'Oh dear,' said the Doctor.

Felbaac poked about in as many dark corners as he could find, and his suspicion that Yast was hiding in one of them was proved correct.

'Come on. Out.'

Yast was reluctant. 'You made a mess of that, didn't you?'

'Shut up. Come on. I need your help to get them back on my side.'

Yast stared at him. 'What? After all this? You're the only man who can walk, Felbaac. You're responsible for the destruction of this entire camp, and all because you wanted a K'Arme head on your wall.'

'But now we're safe. I saved everyone! And I've got us safe passage off this dump! We've got to get ready to get out of here.'

Yast climbed painfully to his feet from under the bruk shelter and grabbed hold of Felbaac's tunic. 'Then come on, let's go. Forget everything here. We can just go, recover our strength –'

'Yast...' Felbaac turned away, as if from an overwrought child he was losing patience with. 'Sangton got away. He'll be heading for his ship. But I was clever – too clever for him!' Felbaac assumed a smug expression. 'I got the safe-path signalling frequency *and* the safe-path co-ordinates in and out!'

'I know that, I heard,' muttered Yast, but he looked suitably impressed at Felbaac's daring.

'Then I took out communications once I signalled through to our cargo thruster, and that's coming down soon.'

'You had the cargo thruster up there all the time?' Yast's eyes were wide open with sudden hope, but Felbaac ignored him.

'There's no flight crew left alive on the K'Arme ship but Sangton will still be trying to stop us. So we've got to round up the men, and get them ready to leave as soon as our cargo's taken their place.'

Yast shook his head. 'What cargo?' But the Fearless Rebel Leader, who had almost lost everything for them, was already moving quickly away.

'Come on then,' Yast muttered to himself, wincing with pain as he set off. 'Let's be quick.'

* * *

The Doctor was scrabbling for bits of the probe's workings, the scraping of metal against metal putting Anstaar's nerves further on edge. Every now and then the Doctor would threaten to topple over, clutching at his head as energy from the probe assaulted his senses.

No other sound could be heard in the dead, damp air save for the steady plopping of Nashaad's landings in the soft wet mud and the unearthly rustling of the time barrier above. She saw the look of intense concentration on Nashaad's face. How long had he survived here, all alone, his friends and comrades dead or dying? How long before he joined them?

She glanced up at the lip over the huge basin they stood in, scared to imagine what monstrous shapes would soon be standing there staring back at her.

'Tanhith! Tanhith, wait!'

Sam kept the injured man moving. 'Ignore him. Come on, ignore him.'

Felbaac caught them up. 'Wait! Wait! Didn't you hear me?'

'Yes, we heard you,' snapped Sam. 'We just chose to ignore you.'

'But I don't understand –'

'Drop dead, Felbaac.' It was hardly a sophisticated riposte but Sam was feeling too frazzled for pithy repartee.

'It looks like Tanhith might do so first,' said Felbaac, gravely. She spun round to glare at him, eyes flashing. Tanhith leaned heavily on her.

Felbaac looked at her, as if sizing her up. 'Now listen, Sam, you did a good job stalling the K'Arme, but I'm back now, and I'm taking command.'

Sam stared at him, and at Yast beside him in all his pallid splendour, in disbelief. 'Command of what, for Christ's sake?' She groped around incredulously for the right words. 'Look around you!' She gestured at the walls of the settlement, cracked and still smoking from blaster fire, the ragged queue for medical attention, the bodies still lying pink and blistering in the heat. 'It's over. Leave us alone.'

'And where will you go?' Felbaac's voice betrayed his impatience with her. She knew he thought her nothing but a tool, a useful diversion that could now be discarded. A freak to be rid of. For a moment she felt guilty at not wanting to tell him about the matter-transmitter terminal she felt sure must exist out there in the desert, even though with more of them searching it would be easier to find. She looked over at the plain at the end of the dusty street, the wide, wide-open area. Easier. Right.

Yast spoke up, nervously. Beads of sweat stood out over his pained face, white despite the great heat. 'We can give Tanhith medical attention if he comes with us. Our ship's on its way. We can get away from here.'

'Away?' Sam looked at him. 'Could you take me back to the moonbase?'

Felbaac looked as if he was about to object, but Yast butted in. 'We could take you anywhere.'

Felbaac looked at him, then back at Sam. 'Yes. You're brave, you could be useful to us.'

Sam's shoulders slumped. 'I'm not necessarily on your side, you know. I'm sick of this. Sick of it all.' She realised her eyes were filling with tears but she didn't care now. 'If I could trust you to get us off this planet I would happily let you. But you scare me, Felbaac. You don't know what the bloody hell you're doing.'

'Do I not?'

She saw Felbaac's face contort with rage, then he shoved her backwards and she fell heavily against a bruk shelter, banging her already bruised head noisily on the corrugated iron. She vaguely heard Tanhith falling to the ground with a low yelp, and Felbaac's angry voice. 'Help me with him. If they see I've got *him* back on my side, they'll realise they can trust me again.'

Sam tried to use her elbows to prop herself back up, to call out, to do something. But the sun was so hot and she hurt so much that the temptation to lie there was too great. She found herself sobbing again, but this time no tears would come.

'Right!' said the Doctor, putting the pieces in a plastic bag and wrapping the whole lot up in his velvet coat. 'Time for us to move on –'

Suddenly the whole area seemed to fragment and swim around him. This time he recognised it as another time break, and his muscles tensed involuntarily as he wondered if this would be the shift that tore the planet apart.

Things stabilised once more, and suddenly the air was drier and the sun much lower in the sky. Clouds bathed pink and orange in the twilight had gathered menacingly over the horizon, stretching out from an epicentre somewhere in the west.

Nashaad was whimpering in fear, and the Doctor went over to him, looking into his frightened eyes. Softly, he began singing a soothing Venusian lullaby. Nashaad cocked his head, as if listening intently but actually focusing on something far, far away. The noises died down in the back of his throat, and a faint smile twitched on his lips.

Anstaar came over. 'Another time slip?' she began. The Doctor turned to look at her, and an expression of concern flickered across his face before he composed himself and attempted a watery smile.

'What is it?' she asked him.

'Nothing. Nothing at all. Now come on –'

'What is it?' Anstaar suddenly felt very scared. She ran a hand through her hair, but a few strands came out with the sudden movement. She looked at them, and saw they were grey.

She looked at the Doctor, but he couldn't meet her gaze, and turned back to check on Nashaad. She pulled frantically at her hair now, moving it down in front of her eyes. Grey, lank hair. 'No,' she stated simply. Then louder, panic in her voice. '*No!*'

The Doctor's face was anguished when he turned back round to her. He reached out and held her by both shoulders. 'It's an effect of the time –'

'*I know what it is!*' she bawled, angrily. 'I know!' The Doctor backed away as if stung. Then her anger went and her face crumpled. 'Is it permanent?'

'I –'

'Can it be reversed?'

Her eyes were pleading at him. He looked back down at the ground, his face shadowy in the fading light. 'I just don't know.' He brightened. 'Maybe. Maybe with the help of the TARDIS. I'll –'

She felt her face, feverishly. 'How old am I? How old do I look?'

'Hardly different,' said the Doctor, blushing. 'I'm never very good at guessing people's ages. A few years?'

She looked at him and wanted to believe it. The probe was made of dull metal, but she would see something of her appearance in its surface if she only dared look.

The Doctor took her gently by the arm. 'Looks aren't everything. They won't be anything at all if we don't get out of here.'

'Great,' muttered Anstaar bitterly. 'Like I need a lecture right now.'

The Doctor moved on quickly, clearly desperate to change the subject. 'What we really need is a good way out. Or a giant to give us a bunk up, of course.'

'Giants!' Nashaad's voice was high-pitched and scared. The Doctor and Anstaar followed the way he was pointing.

Two huge figures were standing way above them at the far side of the basin, heads swaying about, seemingly searching out scents on the snatches of breeze that blew about them. Small, stubby guns gleamed in the orange sunlight.

'Behind the probe!' hissed the Doctor to his companions, bundling up his coat and squelching through the mud as quietly as he could. Nashaad bounced lightly and beat Anstaar to the hiding place. The Doctor hushed him furiously as he landed noisily in some undergrowth.

One of the massive figures brought a funnel-like device up to its huge head.

'What's that?' whispered Anstaar, nervously.

'That's a Kusk,' replied the Doctor, his eyes never leaving the creatures.

Anstaar rolled her eyes. 'No, I mean, what's that it's holding?'

A low, rasping swell of a voice boomed around the rocky walls of the basin. 'Creatures below. Surrender immediately. Allow us access to the Prize, or face a lingering death.'

The Doctor smiled a little apologetically. 'It's a loudspeaker for delivering somewhat predictable threats, I'm afraid.'

Felbaac stood facing the small crowd of men he had dragged back out into the heat of the day. The halls were full of injured men, and their moans of pain and the stench of their sweat was, Felbaac had decided, a little too distracting for proper speech-making. Besides, Sost was asleep and he didn't need that idiot poking his nose in.

'You've seen the evil of the K'Arme in action once again, you've felt it. It wasn't enough to leave you here to die. They had to hound you even here!' He surveyed the rows of withering bruk, the dust and the broken shelters.

'You invited them here! They told us!' came a voice from

the back of the small crowd, and a few angry assents started up.

Yast signalled them be quiet. 'They were coming for you anyway. Why else do you think we came here, to you? We wanted to free you, to take you away before this slaughter began.'

Felbaac resisted the temptation to raise an eyebrow at this outrageous lie. The men seemed to be listening. He saw Yast catch his eye, but there was no cunning or knowing in the look. Just a tired anger, directed at Felbaac, at himself perhaps; at who knew what? And who cared, as long as the lies worked?

'That's right. Things are often not how they appear. Remember, I had to seem prepared to kill poor Tanhith here.' He gestured at the body of Tanhith, slumped at his feet, supported by his own hands, looking down at the ground and breathing heavily. 'But Tanhith knew it was subterfuge. And now my ship – *our escape* – is coming, and with it supplies, to make Tanhith well again, to make you *all* well again, and to give you freedom. Freedom to fight back against those that would have you die in this filthy heat! I will give you vengeance. And –' he paused, looking each of the small crowd in the eyes – 'I will give you victory.'

The men looked at each other, and Felbaac could recognise just enough baffled hope in their eyes to know he had won them over. 'Go, tell your comrades. Tell them to meet me at the west plain beyond the settlement within the hour. We must strike out now to escape – to be *free*.'

There was a pause. If Felbaac had been expecting any kind of applause, he was to be disappointed. The men dispersed sullenly, and Felbaac watched them go before turning to Yast, who was looking at him with a disgust Felbaac chose to ignore.

'The old magic still working then?' Yast snorted.

'No magic, Yast,' began Felbaac, po-faced. 'Just simple hope and inspiration.'

'And my lies.' Yast smiled, tightly, looking at the ground. 'Go to hell, Felbaac.'

Felbaac hauled Tanhith to his feet. 'Come there with me, Yast.' He paused, meaningfully. 'Or be left behind.'

Yast took Tanhith's other arm and the three of them staggered towards the west plain.

Sam had crawled to her feet, her consciousness returned in full. She saw men milling about in the square, heard angry conversations. Some of the inmates were pulling at the few brukweeds still half green, arguing with others who wanted them to leave the plants where they were. A fistfight broke out between two more over provisions. She winced as she saw one man bang a box of medicine against the injured foot of a fellow to make him give up the tools he had just taken from a pile built up outside the dwelling that had been her prison. Some of the men were obviously clearing out. Some had decided to stay, and were locked in pathetic disputes over distribution of supplies.

It's the end for this place, she thought. She saw the men shouting and protesting under the horrible heat burning down on them. The dead plants, the half-empty water tanks in the scraps of shade afforded by the bruk shelters. It was the end of this world.

Something made her look past the milling men and across the square. Dwynaar, bandages swathed round his groin and his foot, was slumped heavily against the door frame of the sleeping area. Sost stood behind him in the gloom of the building, a pale spectre in the shadow. Both were looking through the confusion, through the panic, straight at her.

She shivered. This isn't my fault, it can't be my fault.

But she could feel two shattered pairs of eyes on her back

as she turned and made her way west out of the settlement.

The Doctor popped up from behind the probe like a jack-in-the-box, but if the Kusks were surprised at the speed of his moments, they didn't show it.

'I need to speak with you!' he cried. 'Don't shoot. There isn't time to ask questions later. We need answers now.'

The creatures stared at him. He could see the sun refracting through the menisci of their huge bubble eyes.

'They'll kill you, Doctor!' hissed Anstaar behind him. He turned to face her and took in the physical damage of the time slip more subtly this time. Her skin had aged visibly – in Earth terms, perhaps twenty years. He had no idea of the life span of Anstaar's species but theorised she was in no immediate danger. What was important was to get her – and Nashaad, who seemed unaffected by the sudden time acceleration, perhaps thanks to his extended proximity to the time barrier – away from here to somewhere comparatively safe. Wherever that might be.

The Kusk's voice blasted across his musings. 'Move away from the Prize.'

'What, this?' called the Doctor airily, waving at the probe. 'Did you *win* this? Splendid. What a competition that must've been.'

'Move away.' The voice, distorted and even more sinister crackling through the loudspeaker, seemed to roll round and round the arena.

The Doctor ignored the interruption. 'Only they're terribly useful things, space-time probes.' He saw the two huge heads swing to look at each other. 'All sorts of things you can do with them. Study and record extinct flora and fauna throughout the cosmos. Understand ancient cataclysms and their effect on the biospheres of this galaxy's many planets, in order to guard against similar catastrophes in the future –'

'Move away.' The voice was angrier now, more impatient. The Doctor saw the smaller of the two giants wrestle the loudspeaker off its fellow.

'You cannot understand the complexity of our technology,' came the higher-pitched voice.

'Oh, can't I?' challenged the Doctor. 'Why have you sent this machine back through time and space? What are you planning to – *Don't shoot!*'

Anstaar had peeked warily at the Kusks above her in the distance and had seen the gun suddenly raised in the Doctor's direction, as the other Kusk presumably became bored with the Doctor's tirade. She'd frozen as the Doctor had suddenly held out the bundled-up ball of his coat. She heard his voice, angry and defiant.

'I'm holding here the memory banks and central computer of the prize you've come so far to find. Shoot me and you risk destroying it for ever.' Anstaar saw him holding it above his head, then in front of his face, down in front of his body. She saw the Kusks look at each other once again, and found herself smiling. So that was why they were so insistent the Doctor move away from the probe.

The voice rang out once again. 'Your lives will be spared if you give us the Prize.'

'Spared?' the Doctor challenged. 'Spared to do what? To die here when time runs out for all of us on this poor tortured planet? No, I'm afraid I need something a little more tangible from you – otherwise, no deal.'

'Explain.'

'No, you explain. Tell me what this obscene device is really for.'

'The intelligence in the probe has not only recorded historical events throughout this part of the galaxy, but interpreted them,' came the slithering rattle of the voice from the loudspeaker. 'It is a master strategist, able to plan for us while taking into account everything that has ever transpired throughout recent history.'

'Planning for what? I wonder,' said the Doctor, his voice growing louder, angrier. 'For war, perhaps? Conquest? Send something back through time to assess the weakest points in the history of every planet in the galaxy, the point where you creatures can walk right in and seize control of an empire with only a minimum of force?'

Suddenly, Anstaar caught a glimpse of movement above her and away from the rocky ledge supporting the Kusk creatures: a dark-brown chitinous shape in a black skirt, the setting sunlight reflecting off its body as it moved stealthily down through a narrow fissure she hadn't seen before in the cliff face towering above the arena. A third Kusk, moving round to get a clear shot at the Doctor's back.

'Our numbers are few,' the high-pitched rattle from the loudspeaker informed them. 'Our race was left for dead long ago during a war not of our making. We *have* to become stronger.'

'Why?' stormed the Doctor. 'So you can inflict your suffering on somebody else?'

It's keeping him talking, she thought, her heart sinking. But if she spoke up, the thing would see her and surely kill both her and Nashaad. The idea of dying still terrified her, but the Doctor was holding the one thing that stopped these creatures obliterating them all. Was she meant to sacrifice herself for him?

Above her, the third Kusk moved with a sinister grace across the narrow lip of rock above the basin, searching for the best vantage point from which to kill the Doctor and regain the Prize intact.

* * *

Sam followed a large ragged rabble of men limping through the outer limits of the settlement, about seventy or eighty of them, clearly with a destination in mind. She had thought of looking for the matter-transmitter platform by herself. Well, she would do that once she'd checked Tanhith was OK. If he didn't want to go with her, well, fine, but she still had to check up on him. She owed him that much for saving her life out in that red desert, didn't she?

The men were tired and in pain, but fear was the overriding feeling she sensed in the air. Fear of being left behind now their options were dwindling with the water supply and the withered bruk. Fear of having passed up the chance to stave off death by falling in with Felbaac. Turd though he was, he now had the easiest route off this planet, and at this stage she doubted if these men cared about anything much other than that.

Cautiously keeping her distance, Sam scrambled up a dusty rise of land that the men, with their injured feet, were hobbling the long way around. She could see Felbaac, Yast, a few other men – and yes, there was Tanhith. She could see a narrow strip of bandage round his midriff, and felt relieved he was getting even the most basic care.

Felbaac was looking at his wrist, then up at the sky, then back at his wrist. Some sort of monitoring device? wondered Sam, vaguely. She looked around her. Could she move to somewhere a bit closer, somewhere with a bit more shade? She couldn't see anywhere likely – or much at all, really. She guessed Sangton's ship must be somewhere to the east. Felbaac wouldn't have wanted the men to contemplate any other form of transport, knackered though it undoubtedly had to be.

Suddenly she grabbed at her ears, wincing as she pressed a hand against a bruise. A pressure was building in her head, her jaw ached all the more. Then a noise like wind filled the air, a screaming noise, gradually lowering in pitch. A huge shadow fell over her as the sun was blotted out.

It was a spaceship, large and ugly, boxy and graceless. She saw the men pulling their tunics over their faces to keep the dust from blowing into their faces, and pulled up her own T-shirt to do the same, feeling tiny grains of sand peppering against and stinging her naked torso.

Through the white cotton fabric she saw the shadow of events taking place before her. Felbaac – she assumed it was him – seemed to be waving frantically at the craft as it descended uncertainly towards the huddled men below. She heard its huge engines roaring, retros thrusting indecisively in small bursts – or were they just failing to ignite, properly? She heard a voice yelling over the shriek of the engines. 'Back! Get back!'

She pulled her T-shirt back down to see more clearly what was going on, but sand was blasting into her hair, her eyes, her mouth, and she turned away, eyes streaming.

There was a sudden heat against the back of her legs. Twisting round, she discerned through the sandstorm part of the ship almost directly above her.

I'll be fried, I'll be crushed, I'll be roasted alive.

She staggered off through the blinding chaos of dust and sand, slipping down the other side of the rise she had climbed, stumbling blind, her ears splitting with the noise.

CHAPTER TEN
HOPELESS AND HELPLESS

There was a sudden change in pitch of the craft's engines, a low rumbling noise that sounded ominously loud in her ears. Then with an angry whine she felt the shadow lift off her, the sun back at her skin through the dust cloud. Turning once again, she saw the craft pitching back suddenly away from her, and away from Felbaac and his group of men crouched in fear in the dust, as the storm subsided. And with a horribly loud thud the ship landed heavily against the rocky outcrop standing behind them, bringing an avalanche of debris down on top of the rear end of the vessel.

'What in the name of the deity was that meant to be, Felbaac?' snarled one voice. Sam recognised it as belonging to Crichter, a burly man who'd been complaining loudly in the queue for medical supplies earlier, although she could see nothing with half a sandpit seemingly lodged up her eyelids. Her eyes stung and watered, and as she rubbed them she realised just how badly burnt her eyelids had to be for them to be hurting quite that much.

'You could've killed us all!' came another voice she didn't know.

Then Yast: 'Look! Look at the state of it. Felbaac, what's happened?'

In the eerie stillness after the landing of the ship, Felbaac's voice sounded louder than usual, deliberately so, Sam reckoned.

'Nothing. There's nothing wrong. Just some minor malfunction of the drive unit.'

'But look at the state of it, Felbaac!'

Sam was desperate to clear her vision to see what Yast meant, her curiosity increased further by the astonished rumblings of the men taking the sight in.

'Never mind that,' came Felbaac's voice, followed by the noise of a mechanism being activated. 'Let's get them off and get them on.'

'What do you mean?' came Crichter, warily. 'Who's on there?'

Sam heard Felbaac again, weary. 'You know your numbers are monitored by the government randomly, just to make sure you're all still rotting here. If I take you all away with me they're going to notice, aren't they? Send in the ships to check up on you.'

Patronising git. Sam imagined him looking at Yast for support, wondered if the little man would speak up. Nothing. Her eyes felt like pin cushions, and she realised jealously there were advantages to having thick long eyelashes beyond the merely cosmetic.

Felbaac was continuing: 'So I simply arranged for a few K'Arme supporters to have a taste of their own medicine. Some of my men took a group of them hostage to take your places. No one will ever even know you left until *we* choose to strike!'

There was silence. Sam tried to take in this latest act of ruthlessness, while Yast chipped in, 'But they'll die here anyway, won't they? There's nothing left, not enough food, water, supplies –'

'How was I to know that?'

'And you really think anyone cares enough about this dump to check whether they're still alive?'

'We were serious offenders, Yast,' came Crichter's voice, protestingly. Sam shook her head in sad disbelief at Crichter's ego, smarting even at a time like this.

'So you're going to leave those people to die here?'

'Them or us, Yast. It's not our problem, is it?' said Felbaac dismissively. 'Anyway, there isn't room for us all. Would you rather I took miserable Inner Worlders with me instead of you?'

Just when she had thought Felbaac couldn't fall any further in her estimation he had proved her wrong. Sam could finally focus a bit more clearly, although blinking was agony. She tried to stay calm, breathing deeply, waiting for her vision to improve as she squinted into the dry, bright sunlight. She heard the whirring of the protesting mechanism stop with a clang, and reasoned that perhaps it was a door opening. What should she do? What *could* she do? Help the people on board fight back against the prisoners? Try to get everyone to live in peace? Nothing seemed feasible, or even desirable. Sam cursed Felbaac for turning her life into little more than a cosmic game of Scruples.

She heard footsteps clanging up the metal steps, saw a watery vision of what was presumably Felbaac and Yast going inside the spaceship. She wondered if anyone had seen her, if Tanhith was all right in the aftermath of the landing. There was an expectant hush about the men, standing in the eerie silence that had followed the terrible noise of the landing. Sam realised her ears were ringing. God, I'm a mess, she thought. Please, get me out of here.

With her eyes finally clearing, Sam could see she was looking at a fair-sized cargo thruster. But it looked so old, as they had said. The metal was scorched and pockmarked, the markings on the side of the ship faded and scratched. It seemed a museum piece. She straightened up as the shouting got louder, looking about for Tanhith and noting with relief he was still breathing strongly under the shade of a stolen tunic draped over two sticks. Then a muffled shout of anger came from somewhere inside the ship.

It was Felbaac's voice, and he sounded furious as he

suddenly emerged back into the light. He was pulling something behind him, and Sam gasped as she realised it was an old man, protesting weakly at the rough treatment he was receiving. Felbaac threw the frail figure off the side of the ramp to the dusty floor below.

'Answer me!' he raged. 'How the hell did you get on board and what have you done with my pilot?'

The old man looked up at Felbaac, the harsh sunlight blinding him, but said nothing. Sam pushed her way forward to help him, and took his head into her hands.

'You again!' cried Felbaac in exasperation. 'Leave him alone. I want answers.'

'You want a smack,' Sam snapped back. 'Look at the state of him.'

Felbaac glared at her. 'Then perhaps *you'd* like to ask him, you little freak, why the men, women and children I had circling in orbit waiting for this moment have become gibbering idiots like him or else so many old bones?'

Yast came out behind Felbaac, knocking into him in his haste to reach the doorway before retching. 'It's like a charnel house in there,' he muttered, terrified. 'Most of them are dead and rotting.'

'Including my pilot,' said Felbaac coldly. 'So what's going on, old man? What in hell's name happened in there?'

Crichter spoke up. 'Wait a minute, Felbaac, why don't *you* tell us just what's going on?'

'Seems to me you can't do anything without messing it up,' said another voice in the crowd.

Sam lowered the poor old man's head to the floor and got up, a thin smile on her face. 'They've got a point, Felbaac, don't you think?'

'Shut up, you freak,' yelled another voice. Sam turned to answer back, then assessed the mood of the crowd and decided maybe that wasn't such a good idea.

'But this wasn't my doing!' implored Felbaac.

Sam thought he was about to burst into tears.

Yast turned to him. 'The safe path. It must've been wrong. You can see the state of our ship as well as I can.'

'Impossible,' said Felbaac in a low voice. 'Those were the K'Arme co-ordinates. You think they'd risk the life of a Most High Commissioner of the House?'

'This whole planet's going wrong,' shouted Sam, suddenly. 'Look at the sun. Time's done a bunk, and it must've taken your ship with it.'

Felbaac glared angrily at his hecklers and turned to Yast. 'Have you got the medijab? Tanhith's the best pilot here. He'll have to fly us out.'

'All right,' said Yast, quietly, his face still pale.

'You're not serious,' said Sam, outraged. 'He can barely walk. How's he going to fly?'

'We said "shut it", you freak!' cried an unpleasant voice from the crowd. Sam spun about and saw hard, angry eyes staring at her. 'Just trying to help,' she ventured, in what she hoped was a placating manner. 'Surely you can see he's crazy –'

'Crazy to want to help us? Is that what you think?' came another voice.

Sam lost patience. 'Oh, for God's sake, grow up. You think that thing's going to get you out of here?' She pointed at the blistered hulk of the ship, backing away up the rise as some of the men began to advance. She saw Yast administer a weird kind of injection to Tanhith, saw Tanhith's body writhe as a result. Heard Felbaac telling some of the nearby men to empty the hold of all the old people and the bodies. She realised she was already forgotten by Felbaac, by the bulk of the crowd. Only these few limping along towards her seemed to care about her presence at all, and as far as they were concerned, she'd brought these terrible changes about. Sam realised she'd finally pushed her luck with them too far.

As she reached the top of the rise, she turned about, ready to outrun them – then froze. Her bruised jaw dropped in disbelief.

There were two of them, walking steadily towards her, heading for the rise. Easily eight foot tall, each was big, brown and glutinous – like giant Mars Bars squeezed and welded into nightmarish sculptures. Huge eyes caught the sun, but the massive mouth on each of them took her attention, sharp bony teeth sunk into dark gums. They were holding guns in delicate six-fingered hands, and pointing them straight at her.

If she'd been given to screaming, Sam would've done so then. As it was, the men advancing on her were more than willing to scream on her behalf as they hopped, limped and staggered back down the rise to get away.

Sam followed them.

'Nashaad,' whispered Anstaar, 'I'm going to have to ask you to do something very dangerous.'

'I've got metal legs,' whispered Nashaad back to her, uncertainly.

'I know,' said Anstaar, smiling, 'and they're very special.' He smiled at her, and she felt a twinge of guilt. 'How fast can you bounce about on your metal legs, Nashaad?' she asked, slowly, not meeting his shy, confused gaze. Behind him she could see the Kusk was cautiously moving round into position.

'Fast. Really fast. Really, really fast.' He touched her arm. 'Shall I show you?'

She looked at the ground, smiling sadly. 'Yes, show me. But go the fastest you've ever gone, all right? You're not allowed to stop or slow down.'

She saw the Kusk raise its gun.

'Now, Nashaad!' As the little man bounced out of hiding she screamed at the Doctor, '*Get down!*'

The energy bolt flew past the Doctor's surprised face as he turned, and it was swiftly followed by Nashaad, whooping with laughter. 'Look at me!' he shouted as he bounced through the air. 'Look at me!'

The Doctor flattened himself against the earth as another bolt impacted into the ground at his feet. He held out the probe in the direction the shots had come from, shouting, 'No, Nashaad! Stop it, come back!'

Anstaar saw the energy bolts flying from the Kusk's gun at the crazy figure of the jumping man, wincing, waiting for the impact she knew must come as the other Kusk fired as well. 'Doctor, this way, quickly!'

The Doctor made his way through the deadly crossfire, his long brown curls flying behind him as he ran in short, sharp bursts, weaving and dodging as he managed to keep one step ahead of the deadly bolts. 'Nashaad, come down!' he yelled as he ran, and Anstaar joined in.

'Cease firing!' came the anguished voice of the Kusk with the loudspeaker. 'You may damage the Prize.'

To Anstaar's disbelief, both the Doctor and Nashaad were suddenly both back by her side, panting and out of breath.

'Told you I could move really really fast,' beamed Nashaad. 'I've got metal legs!'

The Doctor looked pointedly at her, and she felt suddenly ashamed, then angry. 'Well, that Kusk up there would've killed you, and both of us, too, from that angle.' A bolt whizzed over their heads. 'And it looks like it still will.'

The Doctor shook his head, his breath returning. 'That was just a warning shot. They won't fire for risk of damaging this.' He patted the bundle wrapped up in his coat. 'You know,' he ventured, 'I think it's time for an exchange.'

'What makes you think they'll listen?' demanded Anstaar, a little peeved at the Doctor's lack of gratitude.

'Time's running out,' he muttered. 'For all of us.'

* * *

The Kusk Leader returned to the control chamber to meet two of his returning troops. He had almost expected them to come back empty-handed, but was irritated to be proved right.

'Trooper eight, report!' he barked.

'Our sensors gave no readings. Reconnaissance confirmed this,' came the low, respectful rumble.

'Did you meet with any resistance?'

'Yes. It was a humanoid colony for the old and infirm. We eradicated all life.'

'Good,' whispered the Leader. 'Connect your mindlink to the experiential processor on the crew-room screen.' He clapped his hand together, and began to stroke the tough skin of his palms with quivering fingers. 'I will enjoy the actions you have taken today at a later, calmer time.'

'When the Prize is ours, Leader,' hissed the technician, almost as if reminding him to keep to the task in hand. 'Troopers three and four and the engineer have spent some time stationary in their area. Perhaps they have located our target.'

'Perhaps,' concurred the Leader in a grumbling bellow, saluting troopers seven and eight, and praying for the swift successful return of that party.

You had to admire his nerve, decided Anstaar. These creatures were hideous crusty great giants, and the Doctor talked to them as if they were children. He'd told them to drop their weapons or have Nashaad drop on to their precious components – from a great height. Anstaar felt a little justified in her actions now as the Kusks were well aware of the little man's abilities. The creatures had done so, and she'd felt a surge of relief so strong she'd had to sit down, tears welling in her eyes. Now as she sat in the wet earth, feeling the new wrinkles round her eyes, the tears fell freely.

The Doctor had insisted the two Kusks move round to join their fellow on the precarious ledge far above. She'd collected all three of the guns while Nashaad sat around and waited, clearly bored. She looked at the guns now. Sleek, smooth metal. The delicacy of the craftsmanship was at odds with the brute physical appearance of the creatures. Watching these Kusks shuffle round the ledge, she felt a shudder run through her once again. They scared her to death.

'All right, Nashaad, this time you've got to get *us* out of here,' said the Doctor, patting him encouragingly on the shoulder with a broad smile.

'I can do that! I can do that!' whooped Nashaad, starting to bounce up and down in delight.

'Not now!' urged Anstaar. 'In a moment.' She squeezed his hand and saw him blush. She let go, embarrassed.

'You go first, I think, Anstaar.' The Doctor spoke over his shoulder, watching as the last of the Kusks moved into position at the other side of the arena.

Anstaar wrapped her arms round Nashaad's neck and held her legs round his waist. The little man tottered slightly, then bent his legs. She wondered if he had hinges rather than knees under his tattered trousers, then suddenly her stomach was in her throat, her greying hair was tight against her face. Then she was grimly scrambling for a handhold as Nashaad hit the side of the wall some way from the top. She heard the Doctor's voice floating up, warning them to be careful.

She pulled at a handful of vegetation, and shrieked in alarm as it came away from the spongy cliff face, but Nashaad had a strong grip on the rock, and by climbing up him and standing on his shoulders, she could just reach up to the lip. He reached up a hand and she trod on his upturned palm to lever herself up the last few inches. Scrabbling in the dirt, she was seized by a sudden panic-fuelled desperation, and she hauled herself up, working muscles she barely knew she had, digging in with her knees, her feet, anything to get herself over the edge. I can't be that infirm, she thought with a measure of relief.

When she finally reached safe ground she caught a crazy sideways glimpse of the three sinister figures watching her in the distance with their hideous eyes. With a short involuntary cry she rolled over and away from the edge. Nashaad clambered up behind her, clearly hoping for some kind of praise. Anstaar offered him a weak smile and it seemed to suffice.

It was a weird sight, the Doctor all alone in the arena, wreathed in mist under the setting sun, with the charred black of the crater around the circular probe almost like a huge Kusk eye staring back at her. The three dark shapes were standing the other side of the rim, watching him. She could see defiance in the Doctor's face even from here. He wasn't scared, not even in this predicament. She shook her head in a kind of silent wonder.

Nashaad walked up the edge of the rim, but the Doctor seemed to sense his movement. He spun round, his voice ringing out, 'No, Nashaad, stay there. You'll never take the weight of me and all this.' He shook his coat at Nashaad. 'Look after Anstaar.' Anstaar moved forward to protest, but the Doctor immediately went on, 'And Anstaar, you look after Nashaad.'

Nashaad turned to Anstaar, confused. 'Who looks after him?'

'I was wondering that myself,' she replied, her eyes fixed on his small shape in the rocky basin.

'Hey!' yelled the Doctor. 'Does your elementary Kusk boy-scout kit include some kind of climbing equipment?'

The creatures were ripping through the crowd of desperate men.

Yast couldn't run any more. When he'd seen the hideous

creatures lurching towards them over the rise, it had been almost a moment of release. The fear, the pain, it all seemed to melt away. He stood there as the crowd dissolved in panic around him, their cries and shouts echoing away in his head. There was just silence, silence and the huge brute heads of the alien creatures bobbing towards him at the top of the burnt, brown, gristly bodies. It seemed so ridiculous, so stupid, to have survived all he had just to face death in this form in this ridiculous place. So he sat down heavily on the ramp of the ship and looked at his foot and laughed giddily among the dusty bones and carcasses they'd pulled out from inside.

'Get out of the way!' Someone was trying to hobble past him, pushing at him.

'You're blocking the doorway! Quickly, man!' Felbaac's voice. Yast felt a hand pulling at his collar, and allowed himself to be hauled up and thrown through the closing doorway of the craft.

Only once he was inside did the fear suddenly ebb back into his body. Now he had to start panicking again, worrying again, wondering whether he would get through this after all. And, slumped against the brown rust, breathing shallowly, his stomach a tight knot of pain, he really wasn't sure he even wanted to.

Sam had dragged Tanhith to his feet. He was stronger now: the effects of the drug Yast had administered, clearly. He seemed confused at the chaos and the slaughter as the aliens – they'd called themselves Kusks – either shot or pulled apart the terrified men.

'Where's Felbaac?' he muttered, allowing Sam to pull him away out of sight.

'He's on there,' replied Sam, hollowly, indicating the ship. The ramp door was closing up. The old man she'd tried to help had been trampled by one of the terrible creatures. 'He ran like a rabbit as soon as those things showed up.' Sam sighed. 'I don't know. I just don't know. Have you ever had a nightmare, one that just goes on, and on, and on?'

'Yes.' Tanhith looked at her, his eyes bleary.

She put a hand on his shoulder. 'Why can't we just wake up?' she whispered.

Felbaac thumped a hand on the control pad in the shuttle and swore. Only two of the other men had made it into the ship behind him. All this planning, this time and effort, this *risk*, for two new converts at the expense of almost his entire original crew. No Tanhith, Yattle and the rest of his team doubtless lying slaughtered outside… He'd called to them but they'd been screaming too loudly to hear. Only Yast had made it. Well, that was typical. And those disgusting things… some kind of K'Arme secret weapon? Whatever, it was a disaster. A total, stupid disaster.

He hit the console again, and looked at Yast, slumped miserably in the corridor outside. Then his attention turned to his two new recruits, who were staring mournfully down at the pitted and scarred metal floor. Some exchange. Both were in their forties or fifties, one skinny and emaciated, the other dour-looking and grey.

'What are your names?' snapped Felbaac.

'I'm Furstican,' said the grey-haired man, 'and this is Mortayne. He's deaf.'

'I'm not,' snapped the skinny man.

'Nearly deaf,' apologised Furstican.

Felbaac punched the console one more time, then sneered at them. 'Listen to me, you two. You're my crew. You're going to do exactly what I say, when I say it, understand?'

'Pardon?' asked Mortayne, grumpily turning his ear towards Felbaac.

Felbaac attempted to keep a hold on his rapidly disappearing patience. 'We *are* going to get out of this. Understand me? And if either of you so much as breathes a word about *anything* that happened here today...'

It was steel flex. It would be painful, but it was possible.

The Doctor grabbed the flex and gave an experimental tug. The Kusk holding the other end didn't move, and the rope stayed taut.

'Doctor, you're mad!' Anstaar's voice floated across the arena.

'It comes with the territory,' he cried back, with a smile. 'Sorry, Nashaad.' But Nashaad just waved, perplexed.

Shirt sleeves rolled up, the Doctor flexed his muscles experimentally. 'Here we go, then.'

Holding on with one hand, the Doctor swung both feet against the cliff wall. He grasped his bundled-up coat in the other hand, and balanced it on his chest, so that, when he took the flex into his other hand, his forearms formed a kind of cradle for it.

He pulled on the rope, got a firm grip and yanked himself slowly, painstakingly up the rock. Straight above him, he could see the huge impassive face of the Kusk holding the rope staring down at him.

The Doctor continued his ascent.

Their instinct had been to get back to the settlement as fast as possible – why, they didn't know. They had slipped away while the aliens had busied themselves with the screaming targets about them, but Sam was sure she'd seen the bulbous eyes of one of them regarding her, coldly, as she hustled Tanhith away and over the rise. 'Why are you doing this?' she'd screamed at it. That look had haunted her on the journey back to the camp.

Sam liked to think she was going there because she wanted

to warn everyone, to tell them all to get away while they could. But there was a suspicion deep down that she was seeking safety in numbers. Whatever, the bodies they passed on the way were a clear and horrible reminder that the creatures had already been here. Sam's stomach started to tense up at the thought of what they might find.

The sight that awaited them was worse than she could've imagined. Bodies were piled high in bloody pools. Clearly, the men had been forced to fight or die. From the look of the corpses, they had managed both.

Sam found herself resting her head on Tanhith's shoulder. She felt his hand cradle the back of her head, and it was all the sympathy she needed to let herself give in to tears.

'You've cried a lot since you met me,' mused Tanhith in her ear.

'I suppose I have,' she agreed. 'I'm pig sick of it too, if you're interested. Some date you turned out to be.'

Tanhith sadly heaved a sigh that turned into a long bubbling cough that hacked through the air like gunfire. She shushed him, rubbing his back, and they looked around them at the carnage in the heat, in the dreadful silence.

'Yast got away, didn't he?' asked Tanhith.

'I think so. He was near the doorway. Didn't take Felbaac long to shut everyone out, did it?'

'They're survivors, those two.'

'I can think of better words for them.'

Tanhith paused. 'Why didn't you just let me die, Sam?'

Sam closed her eyes. 'I told you. You saved my life. I'm grateful.'

'Well, I'm not.' He sounded weary, and in pain. 'Why did you want to bring me back to *this*?'

She pulled herself away from him. 'What is all this?' she began angrily. 'Stop it. Stop it, will you? Look around, at all these people. You think they wanted to die? You think there hasn't been enough death round here already?'

Tanhith just looked at her.'It was my destiny to –'

'That is such *crap*!' Sam spat at him. But she thought of her own travels with the Doctor, thought of how much was preordained, wondered how much of a difference they were allowed to make. But then she thought of the dreams she'd had of being someone else, a dark-haired girl holed up in a King's Cross bedsit, with nothing special in her life, just endless days of being ordinary. The Doctor had cheated her of that life. And if she shared his jinx for accompanying cataclysms wherever he went, well, maybe it followed that she could cheat this death for Tanhith.

'Anyway,' she murmured, looking at the ground, trying to shut out the horror around her, 'Yast gave you the injection that brought you round.' She paused. 'How long will it last?'

'I don't know.' He smiled, faintly, then coughed some more. 'I'm quite a wreck, Sam, really.'

'Well, we're going to get away from those creatures. We're going to find the transmitter platform and work out how to use it, and we're going to get back to the moon.'

'Right,' said Tanhith, his face nodding mock-seriously as if taking an order.

'Then we're going to find the Doctor and get you to the TARDIS – his ship – and make you well.'

'Right,' concurred Tanhith again.

'Forget all about burning birds and all that, OK? The only burning bird you've got is me. People with fair hair shouldn't stay out in the sun for too long, and frankly I think my complexion is ruined for ever.'

Tanhith smiled a bit more fully, and Sam felt a small tingle of relief. Or something.

'So we'd better get you out of the sun then and start looking,' said Tanhith. 'Before those creatures come back.'

Sam clapped her hands together, and the sound echoed like

a pistol crack around the deserted camp. 'That's it! Those creatures!' Tanhith just looked at her, trying to stifle another coughing fit, which Sam ignored. 'They're not indigenous, are they? They can't be.'

Tanhith nodded, slowly. 'The men would surely have mentioned them if they were.'

'And they were carrying guns – laser guns or whatever. So they must've come from somewhere else.'

'Another ship?' ventured Tanhith, leaning against one of the outbuildings as Sam continued her train of thought.

'Maybe – although if Felbaac's ship was anything to go by, that could cause ageing problems. They didn't look ready to draw their pensions, did they?'

'They seemed unaffected,' concurred Tanhith, less colourfully.

'So maybe they came some other way… Before I left the moon, there was a ship approaching that knew where the control base was. It was coming straight for it!'

'So?' asked Tanhith.

Sam knew he was patronising her a little but didn't want to break off her chain of thought. The Doctor never did that, no matter what the provocation. 'So what if those monsters came here from the moonbase?'

'Why would they?'

'I don't know. Maybe they like easy targets.'

'Could they have come the same way you did?'

'No, it was too small.' Sam looked downcast, but suddenly brightened again. 'But there might be another, bigger transmitter there! No, then the Doctor would've come looking for me. Unless he couldn't 'cause those creatures got him…'

Tanhith looked on somewhat bemused as Sam had the conversation with herself. Then she stared at him, her blue eyes clear, her voice low and urgent. 'Tanhith, we've got to get back to the moon. I know how! We can follow those monsters back - they're organised, like soldiers. They *must* know the way back.'

Tanhith smiled broadly at her. 'I'm impressed,' he said, and Sam guessed that if her face hadn't been so red anyway her blushes would be clearly visible.

A voice spoke: 'You've got to take me too.'

Sam froze, and Tanhith's happy face creased into concern in a second. She spun round to see what he was looking at, and her mouth gaped in disbelief.

CHAPTER ELEVEN
DAYS DIE OUT IN DREAMS

'Fettal!'

The woman was swaying before them. She held her gun, but loosely, pointing it down at the ground. A huge crimson stain had spread over her stomach and her face was red and crispy from the sun, the gossamer threads over her eyes singed black, or broken. She'd discarded the military jacket and in her dishevelled uniform she looked more like a helpless schoolgirl than a Nazi wannabe. 'Please help me,' she croaked.

'Didn't expect to see *you* walking about,' breathed Sam when she found her voice again.

'I don't know what happened,' Fettal groaned. 'Everything was swimming around me, then the world just seemed to stop, stop dead.'

'You should've stayed dead,' sneered Tanhith.

'Yeah, why should we help you?' challenged Sam. 'You're evil. An evil little sadist.'

Fettal fired her gun into the ground. The mud spat up from the floor under the impact and Sam kicked the weapon out of her grasp. 'You reckon that's going to make us take you? You sad cow.'

Fettal kept looking at the floor, swaying uncertainly. 'I was just discharging the gun to show you I mean you no harm,' she pleaded.

'Only because you're too hurt to inflict any on us,' said Sam, disbelief in her voice.

'You can't just leave me to die,' wailed Fettal. 'Those creatures will come back. They'll destroy me. They destroyed everyone here. Don't leave me for them. You can't.'

Sam turned away, and looked at Tanhith. A long silent look passed between them, until she kicked a foot against the wall. 'I am so *sick* of choices.'

The Doctor was halfway up the cliff face now. Anstaar watched him make his painfully slow progress, like a bizarre yo-yo inching its way up a string. She realised she'd been holding her breath.

'Hurry up, Doctor,' she muttered.

Suspended from the creaking metal rope against the rocky wall, the Doctor felt the sweat warm on his brow. The Kusk's face was still staring down dispassionately at his struggles. He was close enough now to see the small fingers gripping the cord, the crackling skin hanging down in ragged amber around the thick feet protruding over the edge of the rise.

Every step against the soft rock, every blistered handhold on the rope, and the creature jerked closer in his vision. Once again he was surprised at the incongruity between the bulk of the alien and its obvious sensitivity. 'Fascinating!' he announced, blowing a drop of sweat from the end of his nose. 'What are conditions like on your planet, then, hmm?' The Kusk did not respond. 'Quite harsh I'd guess. You've evolved over a long, hard period, haven't you? You should really take a rest when you've hoisted me up.'

Another two handholds, deep breaths, the creature drawing nearer. 'Changing concentration of gases in the atmosphere back home? A result of that war you mentioned, perhaps? That would certainly explain your lungs' unusual filtration system, and that –' another handhold – 'charming little by-product you produce as a result of your –' deep breath in, breath out – 'exhalations!'

Still silence. Must be a beautiful sunset behind him. The dusky rose glow of the sun was reflected on the glutinous skin of the creature. Nearly there. Another handhold. Nearly…

Anstaar wanted to move closer to the Kusks and to where the Doctor would arrive, but fear kept her back. She'd heard that sharing near-death experiences bonded people, drew them together. She certainly felt something for the Doctor, but somehow she felt he shared near-death experiences with people every day. Still, she'd never known a day as long as this one. No wonder she looked so old.

She repressed a bitter laugh and kept her eye on the Doctor, now getting dangerously close to the group of creatures watching him so closely.

As the Doctor neared the end of his climb, he wondered what he could do to stop one of the other Kusks reaching down and snatching the bundle in his coat from his chest, enabling the other simply to let him go and plummet to his death. It occurred to him that this was something he should perhaps have thought about on the long way up, rather than time trees, the apparent ubiquity of time travel these days and how planetary conditions can fashion race development.

Just as the toe of his battered shoe cleared the edge of the rise, the Kusk nearby lunged with awful speed and precision at his chest. With the last of his strength the Doctor swung himself in a short tight arc away from the grasp of the monster. He felt the fingers grab at the fabric of his grey waistcoat, scraping against his side. He let go of the rope and folded his arms in around his chest, landing on top of the bundle in his coat squarely on the narrow ledge.

'I did think you might try something like that but told myself I was being paranoid,' he began, speaking quickly, face down in the mud a few metres from the creatures. 'But one must never overestimate the predictability of a military mind and – please – don't come closer, because if you do I shall –'

he broke off the chatter, and spoke slowly and clearly – 'throw your precious "Prize" right back down where it came from!'

He felt rather than saw the three Kusks standing like statues. Rolling over slightly on to his back, he saw they'd stopped, and smiled. 'Very good.' He scrambled to his feet. Already he seemed to have recovered his breath. 'Now, gentlemen, I'm going to leave this present for you here.' He backed away from them a few metres before carefully placing the green velvet bundle at his feet. 'Enjoy your Prize, won't you?' He could sense the loathing in their huge saucepan eyes, and after a small bow he ran away as fast as he could.

Anstaar saw the Kusks move like giant locusts on to the bundle of fabric, and the figure of the Doctor tearing towards her, his face manic, curls bobbing about in the breeze of his flight. 'Run, everybody!' he cried.

She didn't need telling twice. She grabbed Nashaad's hand and pelted away through the soft mud and back the way she and the Doctor had come. The Doctor soon caught them up, then overtook them.

'I'd better go first – there may be others,' he explained, simply. They ran on for a short while, Nashaad treating it a bit like a race but not wanting to get so far ahead of Anstaar that she'd have to stop holding his hand. At a turn in the pathway the Doctor motioned them to stop, peering carefully round the corner.

'Wait, Doctor,' she panted. 'What exactly have we achieved here except holding on to our skins for a while longer? I thought you wanted to figure out what was –' Her eyes widened and she felt her cheeks redden. 'Doctor, what is *that* in your trousers?'

'Hmm?' said the Doctor, puzzled, looking down. 'Oh, that!' He reached into the waistline of his grey trousers, and pulled out a plastic bag filled with odd-shaped bulges.

Anstaar shook her head in disbelief. 'But…'

'Oh, yes, this! I couldn't just give it back to them, could I? Far too interesting to throw away the second we've laid our hands on it.' He beamed at her, and rummaged in his plastic bag with glee.

'But what did you give those monsters?' asked Nashaad, a silly smile on his face.

'A rock! Plenty of them lying around behind that probe –'

'– while we were clambering up the side of the valley.' Anstaar interrupted. 'Right. But putting it down your *trousers*, well…'

'What?' asked the Doctor, blankly.

She stuck out her tongues at him. 'You're lucky those Kusks didn't get the wrong impression!'

The Doctor still seemed puzzled. 'What, that there was a rock in my trousers?'

Anstaar decided to end the conversation right there.

The images of George weren't there any more. They'd passed the room containing his body, but his visual echoes had finally subsided. Anstaar was wary of walking where they'd been, however, just in case any side effects were lurking around.

Nashaad had seemed disturbed as they had entered the grounds of the abandoned camp, but it was not until they'd passed through most of it that the fit came. He'd screamed and fallen to the floor, his legs kicking out dangerously, ploughing up earth and stones as he frothed at the mouth and convulsed. The Doctor had soothed him as well as he could while staying clear of the metal flurry below Nashaad's waist.

Now, at last, the poor man was calm again, one fist holding on tightly to the Doctor's cravat, so tightly he had to loosen it with the other hand and take it off.

'I'll be naked at this rate,' he grumbled good-humouredly.

'Nice day for it,' Anstaar flirted, then realised she was probably too old for him now. A sick feeling washed over her.

Just then something happened. It happened too quickly for Anstaar even to work out how she'd felt during it.

The ground beneath her seemed to blur, to wash away like paint in the bottom of a wet bucket. Then she realised that it was the planet itself changing, and not, thank the deity, her with it. Anstaar saw more plants retracting into the squashy surface, saw huge splits rip open in the mountainside above them. The Doctor dragged Nashaad away from a vast chasm that had suddenly opened up, but then everything had shifted so fast she couldn't keep up. The ground trembled and shook like a jelly; a sound of collapsing buildings echoed around like endless gunfire or explosions. The moisture in the air became so heavy she almost felt she was drowning, and would've panicked if it hadn't happened so fast.

Abruptly, it was over. A strange silence settled, and she opened her wet eyes.

The world had changed. The settlement was nothing but wreckage, and the land above it was smeared with bits of the debris, nestling in the rocks like bizarre plant life. She looked for the Doctor, but he and Nashaad were nowhere to be seen.

'Doctor!' she called out.

'Could you come here a moment please?' came the polite reply from some distance away. She followed the voice round a newly formed rise of land and saw Nashaad lying apparently unconscious, perilously close to the edge of a precipice under which the world just fell away. It was the largest chasm she had ever seen, and in the setting sun it was a sight almost too beautiful and tranquil to be believable.

And there was the Doctor, hanging on to a thick tendril of root at the edge, his legs dangling above what appeared to be precisely nothing.

'Do you mind lending me a hand?' he asked apologetically. 'Only my legs *aren't* metal and I think I'd end up a little squashed.'

She moved forward, but the Doctor shook his head. 'Roll Nashaad away first, would you?' She did as she was told, then tried to help him back up over the ledge.

'What happened?' she asked, gritting her teeth as he pulled on her arm.

'I think it was one of the dam gates bursting open.' He rested his elbow on the lip of the precipice and it almost crumbled away under his weight. He held on more firmly to her arm and the plant root and tried again. 'Geological re-formation. We were lucky our own time streams weren't caught up in the time–mass equation.'

'I'm sorry?'

With a final heave, he was up and by her side, dusting off his muddy palms. 'By some fluke, our patch of the planet has regressed countless centuries in time while we've stayed put.'

Anstaar could think of nothing to say. 'That's freaky.'

The Doctor grinned. 'One word for it, certainly. I had hoped that now I've isolated and incapacitated the faulty circuitry the temporal anomalies would stop. But perhaps the damage already inflicted is too severe.' He punched his fist into his palm. 'I've got to get this circuitry off the planet.'

'Is it having an effect on you?' asked Anstaar, suddenly concerned.

'Perhaps,' he nodded. 'I hope not.'

'Hey, wait,' breathed Anstaar excitedly. 'We could be a little safer, now. The Kusks behind us might have been wiped out by all that!'

The Doctor looked a little crestfallen. 'Indeed. So you can throw away those guns, can't you?'

Anstaar stared at him as if he was mad, then looked at them

lying by her side.

'Please,' he said simply, but she almost felt it was an order. She found herself throwing them into the chasm. No noise floated up to confirm their landing, and she shivered.

'There's something else I've just thought of.' The Doctor's voice was grave once more, and Anstaar looked at him with a familiar sinking feeling. 'Go on.'

'If the landscape has rolled back, there's a good chance the transmitter platform has been blocked off, buried, or completely destroyed.'

Anstaar stared at him. 'We could be trapped?'

He looked round at the unrecognisable landscape and nodded, sadly. 'We could be trapped.'

Another thought hit Anstaar. 'Always provided we find our way back there, of course.'

'Oh, well, now there we are lucky,' beamed the Doctor, climbing to his feet and checking on Nashaad, who was beginning to revive. 'I'm blessed with a wonderful sense of direction. Come on, it's this way.' He pointed ahead of him.

'But Doctor, I just came from round there. Surely it must be this way?'

The Doctor frowned. 'Ah, well, if you want to take the *boring* route...'

It took them a little time, but eventually they worked out their bearings. The pathway round the mountain had practically vanished, but the mountain itself remained. Nashaad had bounced them over particularly inaccessible passages, and Anstaar was doubly grateful to him for taking her further from the possibility of the Kusks catching them up. Of the arena where they had met the dying man and his torturer there was no sign, just a vast wasteland of rock, sludge and boulders.

They had walked, and walked, and walked.

226

'Hopefully, it should be around this bend,' said the Doctor, his eyes heavy and dark in the light of the captured sunset.

'Didn't you say that before?' queried Anstaar.

'That was then, this is now,' replied the Doctor, defensively. He beckoned Nashaad to follow, and peered cautiously round the edge of the crag in their path.

Anstaar joined him. 'That's it, I remember. That's the opening!' Automatically, she moved forward at a jog towards it.

'Wait, Anstaar!' hissed the Doctor, desperately, but it was too late.

A Kusk, buried up to its waist in the sludgy earth by the cave mouth, had seen her and was redoubling its efforts to get free. She screamed as it lashed out for her leg, stumbling backward as she tried to get out of reach. With a sibilant noise that was half hiss, half roar, the Kusk lunged towards her once again. A pile of mud exploded over her as it managed to pull one huge charred knee free of the ground.

The Doctor turned to Nashaad. 'Stay here!' he ordered, and sprinted over to Anstaar, trying to pull her clear. But the Kusk had seized her leg now, and was twisting it round savagely. She screamed and tried to turn with it, her face and hair grinding into the spongy soil, spitting out clods of earth as she was pulled towards it and out of the Doctor's grasp.

'No!' he cried, and ran at the creature as hard and fast as he could. He bounced off almost comically as he impacted with the hard, cold shoulder, and a swipe of its skinny arm sent him sprawling away. It still held on to Anstaar, who kicked out at it in her panic, aiming for the eye but missing, hitting instead the fierce crack of the mouth.

The Doctor tried attacking again, from behind this time. He reached an arm round the neck but it was almost too thick to get in a hold of any description. He yanked back with all his strength but the hulking creature seemed barely to notice.

'Please,' he yelled, attempting to reason with it. 'Let her go! She's done you no harm!'

The creature turned its head sharply, cracking its skull against the Doctor's. He fell back, stunned, while the creature looked evilly at him and then twisted harder on Anstaar's leg. Where her trouser suit had been ripped away from the leg he could see the muscles and sinews moving round the bone, and a dark stain forming on the skin under the Kusk's fingers.

As the creature opened its mouth in amused enjoyment, a metal foot crashed down on top of its head and punctured its huge eye. It screamed in agony and clawed at its assailant's legs. Nashaad was brought down hard to the wet earth.

'Get away, Nashaad!' yelled the Doctor, running for the Kusk once again. Anstaar was free, and started to drag herself away from the creature. As she did so, she kicked out with her other leg, catching the Kusk a glancing blow that distracted it just long enough for the Doctor to grab its right arm. He tried to keep it from seizing Nashaad's neck, every muscle straining, but the Kusk suddenly swung out its arm and sent him flying backwards into the cave opening.

But Nashaad had used the few moments the Doctor had bought him to get out of reach. The Kusk was furious, its great dark body thrashing about as it struggled to free itself from the earth holding its leg.

The Doctor crawled out to Anstaar, who was moaning and whimpering with pain. Her leg was twisted almost right round, swollen and badly cut, the foot sticking out at an unnatural angle. Anstaar wondered whether she was meant to deliver some brave, humorous line at this point to make light of her injury and pain. Nothing sprang to mind, so she just lay there.

'The platform's more or less intact,' whispered the Doctor to her, excitement on his face. 'That Kusk must've been guarding it when the landscape regressed around it. 'Come on, quick! We can make it.'

'I can't *move*, Doctor,' Anstaar whimpered.

The Kusk was still thrashing and roaring as it struggled to free itself, pounding the earth beneath it, its remaining eye rolling round in its huge socket.

'Come on, Nashaad, quickly! Over here!'

But Nashaad didn't answer the Doctor. He stood watching the Kusk, baffled and upset. He stepped a bit closer, holding an arm out to it. 'Sorry,' he said. 'Didn't mean to hurt you –'

With a triumphant screech the Kusk freed itself and hurled its bulk at Nashaad's slender form. He had time for one short, high-pitched scream before the monstrous body crushed him into the earth, the brown scabrous arms reaching for his throat.

Sam had taken the guns from the dead K'Arme guards. She didn't want to use one, but the size of those giant creatures – and their violence – scared the hell out of her. And she had Tanhith to protect. And that Fettal, whom, against her better judgement, she was helping along even now.

She remembered trying to convince a Thal warrior that fighting and obeying orders you didn't believe in were bad, that they killed your inner spirit. She shuddered at how fatuous her comments must have sounded.

Life was never that simple. Here was a woman who had probably maimed and killed her way through hundreds, maybe thousands of people. And here was Sam Jones helping her, in a determined, sweaty silence. She'd try harder not to preach in future. Maybe she'd let her actions speak for her. Mind you, she couldn't for the life of her work out *what* she was trying to say by doing this.

'Those things are coming this way,' muttered Tanhith, climbing painfully down from the roof of a supply store. Fettal emitted a low groan of terror.

'Quick, in here!' Sam ordered, kicking open the corrugated-iron door of an outhouse full of decaying brukweed, brown and withered in the intense heat of the endless day.

Suddenly they heard a desperate scream. Having helped Tanhith inside the hut where Fettal was already leaning heavily against the pile of vegetation, Sam scrambled out to see what was happening.

In a panic, the weight of the massive creature crushing down hard on his struggling little frame, Nashaad skidded round in the mud until his legs found purchase on a small boulder. He pushed against it with all his strength.

Like a cork popping from a bottle, Nashaad and the Kusk went flying through the air. There was a terrible snapping sound, then silence.

Anstaar raised her voice a little, wincing from the pain in her leg. 'What happened?'

The Doctor's eyes were closed tightly shut. 'His metal legs. They carried him straight into that cliff face. Too fast.'

'Is he…?'

'I think he must be.' The Doctor's voice was a mournful whisper.

'The Kusk –' She started trying to crawl away at the thought of it.

'Nashaad took it with him.' She heard him move over slowly to the bodies. After what seemed like an age, he reported back, his voice hollow. 'They're both dead.'

Anstaar let her head slump against the ground. Her leg was agony. 'What do we do now, then?' She was too tired and hurt too much to take any more responsibility for herself. Leave it to the Doctor. He didn't hesitate in his reply.

'I'm going to bury Nashaad. I'm going to get that platform working. And then I'm going back to the moon.'

'To a base full of those creatures? You're mad! They'll tear you apart!' Anstaar shrieked as the Doctor turned her gently on to her back and inspected her leg.

'It's broken. In lots of places.'

'No more dancing for a season or two, then.' There, it had come. Obligation to cliché fulfilled. 'I can't go up there, Doctor. I just can't.' Anstaar started shivering, despite the warm muggy air. 'I'd rather die here.'

The Doctor looked at her sympathetically, his brilliant blue-green eyes staring deep into hers. 'I'm afraid I've nothing left to wrap round you.'

'You could hold me, couldn't you?' She closed her eyes as she felt his arms slide softly round her. 'Then you can tell me your secret plan for getting us both out of this alive.'

The silence that followed somehow wasn't as frightening as it should've been.

Shielding her eyes with one hand from the glare of the sun, Sam suddenly grasped what it was she was looking at.

A man was running for his life. 'Crichter!' she cried, pleased that he'd got away, but then suddenly scared, unsure what she should do next.

He saw her as he rounded the corner, and pelted with a fast and painful limp towards her. 'You!' he shouted. 'Hey, you!'

Sam shushed him desperately. 'Shut up, don't make them think there's anyone else left!'

'There isn't,' he said, panting. 'They've killed everyone.'

'Not everyone,' she said, taking him firmly by the hand and pulling him towards the shed, anxious in case the Kusks should round the corner and see them standing there.

'What...?' Crichter's voice died in his throat as he saw Fettal slumped against the pile of bruk. 'What is *she* doing here.'

Sam shut the door, quietly and angrily. 'Trying to stay alive like the rest of us.' The heat was so oppressive in the little building that Sam thought she would drown in her own sweat. She fidgeted with her torn T-shirt.

'You stupid freak bitch,' exclaimed Crichter. 'I knew you were trouble right from –'

'That's enough out of you,' said Tanhith, quietly. 'Keep quiet. Those things will be looking for us now you've screamed the place down.' He seemed resigned to the fact.

'You'd have done the same –' Crichter began, but Sam shushed him again.

'I can hear footsteps,' she whispered.

Through a crack in the door, she could see one of the two creatures standing in the hot dusty street, about a hundred metres away. Its huge dark party-balloon head was swinging through the air from side to side, as if scenting them. Sam was reminded of the giant in the story. 'Fe… fi… fo… fum,' she whispered to herself. Then her heart jumped. 'One of them's heading straight for us.'

Felbaac had discovered that Mortayne was familiar with the principles of take-off. 'Once we're in the air, I can take over. The computer will do most of it – it's a programmed flight path back to civilisation,' he'd said. 'Just get us off and out of here.'

He stood brooding as the crotchety little man and his dour companion pored over the aged and cracked controls. He'd checked the computer. It seemed fine. Good – something was going right. When he got away from here he would lie low for a while. He could take the credit for destroying Sangton – surely the old bastard would be dead by now. Yast would help. They could rest up. Regroup. No real rush. His fame would be all the greater for its longevity against the forces of evil and oppression.

There was a sympathetic outpost that would give them supplies just a few days' flight away. It would be tough but he'd endured worse.

'You'd better get thinking about how to explain this mess to the outpost in a way that's favourable to us,' he growled to Yast.

'I don't want to think about it,' said Yast, simply, his expression vacant. 'I don't want to think about anything.'

'Very useful.' Felbaac kicked a wall. To his annoyance, the toe of his boot went straight through a patch of rust and got stuck there for a moment. He hopped back until he managed to extricate it, then looked to see if Yast was laughing at him. He wasn't. He was still just staring into space. 'You're pathetic, Yast.' There was no response.

Felbaac decided to persecute his new crew a little, to show them who was boss. 'Haven't you fixed it yet?'

A low rumble came from the ship's engines, and Furstican looked up at him with the same dour expression. 'I think we have.'

Felbaac clapped his hands. 'Time to leave, then.' He pulled Mortayne away from the controls. Perhaps he would train himself up as a proper pilot in the hiatus to come. Save having to rely on halfwits and incompetents quite so much.

He fed the data into the computer carefully and precisely, and breathed a deep sigh of relief as the ship took off a little shakily from the planet surface. Cool air began to fill his lungs as the ship operated its artificial atmosphere, and it was paradise. No, he decided, there was nothing wrong with his ship. Some random ageing had occurred, just as on the way down. What had happened to the cargo was a freak effect. Things would be fine.

Soon they reached the upper atmosphere. When the buffeting started, Felbaac's confidence was still absolute. It was only a few moments later, when the parched skeleton that had been Mortayne seconds earlier slumped and broke over his back, that he began to panic.

* * *

'Get out of the way,' muttered Tanhith, pushing Sam's frightened face from between him and the door. Wincing at the effort, he grabbed hold of Fettal by the scruff of her neck and pulled her up from the pile of dead weeds. Semiconscious, she barely noticed. Crichter realised what Tanhith was planning, and he, too, pushed Sam aside in silence to help the struggling man.

Sam stood horrified but not daring to speak as the door was flung noisily open by Crichter, and Tanhith used his foot to propel Fettal out into the dusty street, pushing the door to after her.

The direct glare of the sun revived Fettal for a moment as she struggled to gain her balance and failed, falling to the hard dusty floor. Looking up, she saw it.

Fingers quivering and stroking the air ahead of it, its mouth twisted open in a triumphant leer at the sight of its quarry.

'No,' moaned Fettal in helpless terror as the huge creature lunged for her. Her speckled neck was broken before even a cry could escape her parched lips.

Sam saw it all through the crack in the door, then fell heavily back against the soft dead weeds, shocked and outraged.

'It worked,' hissed Tanhith. 'It's going.' He turned to Crichter and Sam. 'Give it a few moments, and we'll follow from a distance.'

Sam stared at him. He met her gaze levelly. 'How could you?' she asked. 'What were you thinking of?'

'You,' he stated simply.

'Oh, yeah, right. Thanks, Sir frigging Lancelot.' Sam turned away.

'You think I've never killed people?' Tanhith snapped. 'I've probably killed more people than you've ever spoken to.' He spun her round violently so she was facing him, but the intensity of the moment was almost defused as he fought off a coughing fit. He took a deep breath. 'Life's cheap, Sam.'

'It isn't,' said Sam, pleadingly. 'How can you say that?'

'It is,' insisted Tanhith. 'Even though I've spent so long convincing myself it isn't. Trying to make mine more valuable by shoring up the numbers of those lives I've taken against it. But it doesn't work. The more you think about it…'

'I thought –' Sam's voice dried up as yet more tears sprang to her eyes. 'I thought it was your – the pain…' Her hand moved to her chest, gently tapping it.

'That?' He tapped his chest too, and smiled faintly. 'Legacy of my incarceration. A reminder. Now it just reminds me of everything I've done to stay alive.'

Crichter interrupted them, angrily. 'When you've quite finished –'

Tanhith turned, raising a fist in warning. Crichter stared murderously at him.

'Stop it, you two, for God's sake.'

Tanhith lowered his fist, and tried to take Sam's hand with it, but she pulled it away. He narrowed his eyes, but whether in pain or in accusation she couldn't tell.

'Come on, Sam. You're going back to the moon to your lovely little friend, aren't you?'

'It's working.' The Doctor had emerged from the cave mouth, and walked over to where Anstaar was lying near the shallow grave that now housed Nashaad, some way from the pile of stones that the Doctor had heaped on the Kusk.

'Is it?' she said, dreamily.

'I'm going up.'

'See you, then.'

'If everything goes well, I'll operate the platform every few minutes. You'll know it's working – it'll glow. I'll keep working it till you come through.'

'See you, then.'

He pressed a hand against her shoulder, leaving it there for a few moments. Then he turned and walked back into the cave.

'The engineer's life trace has been extinguished.' The technician's voice was a hollow rattle.

The Leader spun round to face him. Only five Kusks remained unaccounted for. 'And the troopers in that section?'

'The signals are becoming harder to read as chronal imbalances increase. But one trooper at least is definitely dead.'

'If the signals are unclear, how do you know the engineer is dead?'

The technician paused. 'I felt it important to monitor the progress of the engineer if it located the Prize. I diverted more power to the maenus chip in its sensor to track it more effectively.'

The Leader hissed, but said nothing. How dare the idiot place more value on the scientist than his men, particularly when the Kusk numbers were so small anyway? In total there were now four Kusk casualties, all presumably victims of freak effects of time on the planet's surface. Four dead, to add to the ever-dwindling numbers back home. Would the Kusk race reach extinction before it managed to win its greatest victory?

The Leader considered the death of the engineer. This casualty had clearly affected the technician – now it would be weaker, more isolated. Perhaps some good then would come from the death after all.

'Further power fluctuations observed, Leader,' came the technician's terse report.

'Patch in the extra power you diverted to tracking the engineer,' said the Leader pointedly. 'Our power *must* last,' it stated, with finality.

The matter-transmitter platform suddenly hummed and the opaque glow swirled above it. It took the Leader no more than a couple of seconds to respond to the sight of the Doctor forming before his huge eyes.

'Seize it and kill!' he bawled in his gravelly monotone.

Several Kusks moved eagerly to obey.

CHAPTER TWELVE
GETTING OUT OF HAND

'Wait!' cried the Doctor, brandishing the precious circuitry from the probe as if he were holding a crucifix and warding off vampires.

'Wait!' warned the Leader to his troops in turn. The Kusks froze.

The Doctor's voice rang out through the fetid air in the control chamber. 'I've rigged a destruct mechanism into these circuits. If you kill me I can't deactivate them and your precious prize will be lost for ever.' He smiled. 'I'm the Doctor, by the way. How do you do?'

Felbaac threw off the skeleton and ran to where Furstican was leaning against the monitor screen. Hirath's atmosphere splashed up against the vidscreen, violent reds clashing with purples and yellows in an insane kaleidoscope of colour. The ship was vibrating so much that he thought it would pull itself apart.

'Are you all right?' yelled Felbaac, grabbing the man by his shoulders.

To his horror, he realised that his own hand was blurring, smearing between old age and infancy, first skeletal, then full, fat and fleshy.

He screamed. Furstican was staring at him in horror. 'Your face!' the man exclaimed.

'How can this be?' mumbled Felbaac, feeling his skin loosen around his bones.

The swirl on the screen darkened and the buffeting got worse. Furstican slid heavily to the floor, his eyes shrinking in their sockets as old age seized him too and swung him around and around in the maelstrom of colour.

'So tell me,' said the Doctor. 'Why go to these lengths? Whatever's happened to you in the past, why choose this path?'

'We did not choose that our planet should become caught in war between alien powers,' stormed the Leader. 'The aftermath of war shaped our path.'

'We are few,' interrupted the technician. 'Our race hangs in the balance. We must grow stronger in order to defend ourselves.'

'Be silent,' insisted the Leader. 'You would have this humanoid think us weak?'

The Doctor looked up fearlessly at the sharp teeth of the Leader. 'How could I think anything else? Look at you.' He paused, and moved angrily forward towards the Leader, apparently oblivious to the snapping teeth and keen, hungry stare of those Kusks about him. 'So desperate to learn the secrets your probe has stolen for you. Ready to hinge your invasion plans on a natural disaster, a disarmament treaty, *anything*, ready to gobble up anything at any time that's incapable of offering strong resistance. To take away the choice from other races just as it was taken from you.'

'We cannot afford this diversion, Leader,' announced the technician, rising from its kneeling position on the sticky brown floor. 'We need the datacore.' It walked heavily towards the Doctor.

'Reconsider,' begged the Doctor, backing away. 'Your programming powers must be quite phenomenally ingenious to bring even temporary stability to the forces unleashed by that probe's travel mechanism. You can still use it to take another path. Build defences, protect yourselves. Don't enslave others.'

'Strength *is* protection,' stated the Leader.

The technician kept up its slow advance.

'Wait!' cried the Doctor. 'I travel through time and space, I have knowledge, I'll help you.' The Doctor was speaking so quickly his words were a blur. 'I'll help you if you help me let the people stranded down there escape.'

'Irrelevant,' rumbled the Leader. 'Hirath's surface is on the verge of becoming inimical to all life.'

'No!' cried the Doctor. 'If that's true, then you'll be responsible for the murder of thousands of living beings!'

'Only a start, Doctor,' said the Leader.

Sam allowed herself to be led along by Tanhith. She didn't know what else to do. Following the Kusks had been her plan and now Tanhith was committed to it too. Entirely committed, it seemed.

They'd been walking for what seemed like hours. The gun had dropped from her hand some time ago, and she hadn't bothered to pick it up. Crichter limped in silence beside them. The sun was still fixed resolutely in the sky like a gleaming pin. The landscape was so empty, stark and bright that it looked like a page from a Bible storybook. Sam could hear her grandmother reading to her. The voice blurred and became the Doctor's. Something about revelations. Plagues and curses. The end of the world – of all worlds.

'Sunstroke. I'm delirious. Blondes are crap in the sun,' she announced in a faraway voice.

Tanhith pulled her along. 'Come on, Sam. Don't give up yet.'

'Or you'll kill me?' She giggled, the sound catching in her throat. 'I keep forgetting life is cheap.'

'You brought me back. Well, now you can live out this happy time with me.' He attempted to smile, but his eyes were dark. What had she pushed him to?

She saw movement out of the corner of her eye. Its orange

colouring made it hard to spot against the sand. A cat. A tabby cat. It stared at her for a moment, then sauntered off behind a rock.

Sam stared, and blinked hard. Her eyelids felt full of grit, her mind full of rubbish. Why can't I be a cat? she wondered. Independent. Stylish. Uncaring.

'I saw a cat!' she announced, shaking her head. 'How can that be?'

Tanhith stopped still and grabbed her. He held the back of her head and pulled her face close to his. She squirmed to try to get away, but he held her fast. He kissed her lightly on her caked dry lips. She broke off by dropping her face down, breathing hard. Crichter trudged past them, seemingly oblivious.

Tanhith let go of her. 'That woman was evil, Sam.'

'I know. I just never got close to someone who could kill that way in cold blood before.' She looked at him and shrugged, her voice hollow. 'That's all.'

'Perhaps you don't want a man at all,' said Tanhith quietly, 'just an ideal.'

But Sam had already set off after Crichter and the Kusks.

Felbaac screamed, and the noise reverberated in his ears as the ship spun crazily out of control. Yast's body suddenly slid through from the corridor outside as the craft pitched forward.

'Yast! Yast, help me!' Felbaac's voice was desperate. But as he turned Yast over his heart sank. His aide's black hair had turned snowy white. His skin was so wrinkled it was difficult to discern any features at all.

Decaying consoles detached themselves from rusting walls. Dead terminals sparked and fizzed over the screech of failing engines pushed too far.

I'm not beaten yet I'm not beaten yet –

An explosion snatched his vision and splashed it over the darkness of the bulkhead he smashed against. Trembling, he waited for his eyes to clear, feeling the vibrations of the ship as it began to take itself apart.

The Kusks were heading for the large cave in the mountainside. There was nowhere else for them to go, unless they were planning on walking straight through the rock. But having seen the creatures' power, Sam couldn't rule it out.

Crichter was peering cautiously over the top of a large rock. Tanhith was leaning against it out of sight, looking up at the sky, at the birds that wheeled overhead with their low calls and shrieks. His face was red, badly burnt. His eyes seemed vacant. Sam still felt detached, divorced from events. She watched him, watched the lack of feeling in his oddly handsome face. Felt ashamed of herself, guilty for having wanted him. A murderer. A scared, clinical murderer. The gun looked small in his large hand.

'Your friend,' announced Tanhith. 'Up on the moon.'

'Yes.' Sam looked away from him.

'Do you love him?'

There was no hesitation in her reply. 'Yes.' She looked at the floor, a slightly puzzled expression on her face as if her own answer had surprised her. 'Yes,' she said again, with more conviction, looking at Tanhith. 'I do.'

'Why?' He was staring at her now.

Sam looked down again, then up at the sky, then in all sorts of directions. She found her mouth opening, almost in a smile. 'I don't know. I don't know, but I do. I shouldn't, it's useless –'

She stopped talking and joined Crichter peering over the top of the rock. He ignored her. The Kusks were getting close to the cave mouth, but there was no cover to hide behind between the rock and the Kusks.

Crichter's voice was emotionless. 'We'll be dead if they turn round and catch us.'

Sam was feeling a little stronger. 'We've got to get in there and see how they operate the machinery. If we can't suss it out, we've no chance at all.'

Tanhith looked at her, grasping the general gist of her words. 'Then let's go.'

Crichter looked at them and nodded. They walked out from cover. The Kusks strode on silently some way ahead of them. A feeling that was almost liberating came over Sam. She was walking openly, with nothing to hide. If the Kusks turned round they would no doubt kill her. If they didn't, there was a chance she'd get back to the Doctor. There were only those two possible outcomes, and that made her feel decisive, really purposeful, for the first time in so long.

Sam became almost jaunty in her movement along the dusty surface, and she saw a grim smile break out on Tanhith's face.

Anstaar realised she could see the moon in the sky, frozen along with everything else in the silent tableau above her. She thought of the Doctor up there, somewhere in the future or the past. Busying himself righting all those wrongs, or lying dead beneath the brute club foot of a Kusk? The pile of stones lay to her right, and she spat in its direction.

Then she saw something glowing in the distance. Like the fireflies back home. Two little lights, weaving around. Orange. Getting slowly bigger and brighter out of the dark mists.

Cold panic rose up from her stomach. She'd never find somewhere to hide in time.

Anstaar painfully moved round towards the one place left to go.

* * *

Noise and heat. The blackness – no sight... no, wait – the blackness of space. Pinprick stars. Vision.

'Felbaac,' croaked Yast from the floor. 'Felbaac, rebel of the Outer Worlds... out'a time.' A cackling laugh rattled out of him.

The head of Furstican's corpse nodded in mute agreement as the craft shook and screamed, pitching wildly.

Felbaac ignored him, stretching out a bony emaciated hand to the flight keys. 'Need nearest shelter. The ship will steer us to nearest heat trace. A safe landing.'

He stared at the screen, his eyesight failing him again. Auto lock-on. Let the ship guide them down.

Felbaac patted Yast's lifeless leg. The man's tiny eyes were fixed on his, accusingly. 'We'll be all right!' he said.

The symbols on the navigation screen rolled, then flickered out.

There was a band of golden light stretching beyond the cliff face near the entrance to the cave. Now they were closer it was clearly visible, despite the harsh sunlight.

'What's that?' whispered Crichter.

'The end of this zone and the start of the next, perhaps,' murmured Tanhith.

The band of light crackled and spat, seemed to move backward away from them. A small grove of tall, sinister-looking dark trees with broad leaves and huge clumps of orange berries were left behind, glowing with a strange power.

'Oh, my God,' breathed Sam, recognising the time trees for what they were. 'What the hell are they doing here?'

The soil was darker beneath the weird forest, and a pungent smell filled the air. The two Kusks had entered the cave, and Sam prayed they would not emerge to investigate the change in atmosphere the movement of the time barrier had brought about.

'Wait here,' Sam whispered, and skittered across the hundred or so metres between her and the darkness of the cave mouth. She could sense the coolness within, and closed her eyes, longing to throw herself inside. She could see the dextrous fingers on the slender alien arm operate the touchpad set into the base of the clear plastic platform. Two grey buttons and a large red pad beneath them that was clearly an activation device. The Kusk clambered heavily on to the platform and waited.

Sam turned excitedly back towards the others standing by the strange forest, just as a tremor suddenly rumbled through the landscape. Caught unawares, she fell over backward to the ground. A few rocks fell to the ground near her sprawled body, and she staggered to her feet. She heard a roar of alarm from the cave and a sudden human cry of pain – Tanhith, too, had fallen backwards on to his mashed-up back, into the grove. The howl of pain became a staccato rattling, as the wounded man's cough echoed out like gunfire and the rumble of the tremor died away. She saw Crichter clamp a hand over Tanhith's mouth, and kick him in frustration when it did no good.

She ran back towards them and realised with sick dread that the creatures were following her.

Stuck with a dying man and Hopalong Cassidy and facing two bloodthirsty alien giants, Sam gritted her teeth and forbade herself to cry any more.

The technician had prodded the Doctor back towards the matter transmitter. The Time Lord yanked out his sonic screwdriver from one of his pockets, and held it against the components in the bag.

'Stop there. This device emits sonic wavelengths, enough to scramble the datacore irreparably.' The Kusk stopped its advance, and the Doctor smiled grimly. 'All you'll get from it is gibberish.'

'A useless threat, humanoid,' grated the technician. 'That memory bank is empty. For now.'

The Doctor was taken aback. 'What?'

'After its discovery by the seeker ship, the probe ceased external transmissions. A secondary probe, an inferior, lightweight signalling device, was constructed to track the original probe with the express purpose of draining its acquired knowledge while the computer held it stabilised. It located our probe way below in the planet's crust, and we could at last move in and complete reclamation to secure its knowledge.'

'You mean –'

The Leader strode over and knocked the sonic screwdriver from the Doctor's hand. 'The malfunctioning probe is still deep within Hirath,' he hissed. 'But with these circuits you have brought to us, we can now download the means to conquer untold civilisations throughout history.'

The Doctor's voice was hollow as the technician plucked the bag from his fingers. 'Of course,' he said sadly. 'The *true* prize.'

The Leader leaned down so that his face was opposite the Doctor's, and placed a hand round the humanoid's throat. 'Thank you for delivering it to us.'

Anstaar looked at the platform blankly. Then she noticed a scrap of paper lying next to it. Instructions.

A small tremor shook through the cave. Dead ahead outside, the orange lights were pushing through the warm mist towards her.

'Wait,' gasped the Doctor, choking. 'I may be able to help with your computer. Buy more time, save those people –'

The Leader wasn't even watching him, staring instead at the technician as it connected the datacore to the central computer.

'Can the humanoid help?' inquired the Leader, scratching a talon down the Doctor's cheek, leaving a thin red stripe in its wake.

'The computer is beyond assistance. But the Prize was designed to download the information, bypassing the maenus chips, enabling –'

The Leader's voice broke over the technician's like a rock fall. 'I believe we can dispense with your services, Doctor,' it announced, squeezing harder at the Time Lord's throat.

Felbaac's ship screamed through the silence of space, one unfinished instruction left to carry out.

>> *heat trace autopilot safe landing*

The Leader's gloating face filling his vision, the Doctor felt consciousness slipping away.

>> *safe landing*

Felbaac was trying to remember if his last words had been suitably memorable, and was about to ask Yast's corpse – when their bodies were jellified in the crash.

The ship ploughed helplessly into the moonbase before exploding with tremendous force, a plume of flame reaching up into space as if trying to engulf the stars shining dimly above.

CHAPTER THIRTEEN
NEVER END

An enormous explosion ripped through the corridor and into the control chamber, sending Kusks spinning and scattering like huge, screaming skittles.

The room was plunged into darkness, the siren was still sounding and the Doctor's ears were ringing. He pushed frantically at the body of the Kusk that had landed on him. His hands slipped inside a huge wound in the creature's side – but something was firm within and he pushed against it to shift the glutinous corpse.

He was lying on his back. It hurt to move his neck. A bright light began to flicker haphazardly, and he made out the scene around him as if in a series of still photographs. The technician was struggling at the terminal. The Leader was calling out in pain, his lower body trapped and crushed by a heavy bank of equipment that had toppled over. The matter transmitter still stood, but one of his lashed-up modifications had fallen to the ground, along with a sizeable chunk of the ceiling. Wires spewed out from the wall behind him, and enmeshed within was another Kusk, convulsing, dying, caught in a new hideous pose each time the light flickered back on. At last it stopped moving, eyes dead and black, hanging grotesquely from the mass of cables and wiring.

He heard the technician's voice: 'Systems still operational, but data corrupted.'

The Leader's voice, low and rasping in the darkness, pushing the heavy control unit from his legs. 'Recommence downloading.'

The technician's voice: 'You must evacuate this area. Return to the ship. All remaining power must be diverted to this equipment.'

Hear, hear! echoed the Doctor, cautiously rising to his feet away from the corpse by his side. He crouched closer behind the console as the Leader responded.

'I am your Leader. You may not command me.'

'The knowledge we stand to gain is all. It is the future, the way forward. Lead the others, but leave me. All life-support must be diverted to my operations.'

The Doctor waited to hear if the Leader would respond, but there was only silence. Then the distinctive rumble rolled out into the confusion of the control chamber. 'Evacuate. We must return to the ship.'

The Doctor curled himself up under the back of the console. Science wins, he thought. He reflected sadly that he'd heard only one set of footsteps move to follow the Leader. No one else was left. Hopefully, they'd forget all about him and believe him dead too.

'You shall answer for this insubordination later,' hissed the Leader, before footsteps signalled that he was leaving the chamber and heading into the corridor. 'The damage is severe,' came a slightly higher rumbling voice. 'Come.' The Leader's familiar tones moved off down the corridor. 'Report on the way ahead. We must clear a path if necessary.'

So, some of them had made it. But what could have caused all this devastation?

Suddenly, from his vantage point down behind the console, the Doctor realised some circuitry was perilously close to burning out. If that happened and the computer died completely...

With the noise of the technician's programming echoing under the control desk, the Doctor set about doing something to keep the system operational.

* * *

Sam thought hard. The Doctor would turn the situation to his advantage, use what he had to hand. Why couldn't she have pockets like he did?

Behind her the glowing strip of crackling light seemed to billow as if in a strong wind. The berries of the trees glowed with dark light as if in sympathy.

That was it. Risky as hell, but what did they have to lose?

'Crichter,' she said, 'these time trees can help us. If we can get a Kusk to…' Her voice trailed off. She'd lost him with the first sentence – he was looking at her now as if she was mad.

The Kusks split up, narrowing down any escape route past them.

Crichter turned and limped off through the trees in the direction of the pale light.

'Don't!' began Sam, as another tremor shook the ground around them. Her head spun and the air seemed to blur. Memories of their trek here crowded into her head, filling it till she felt it would burst.

Then the Kusk was towering above her, mouth open and salivating.

The Doctor circled round behind the technician staring so intently at his controls, and peered out into the murky corridor. It was dark, and cold, no doubt due to the explosion, the temperature drop caused either by failing life-support or by the air lost to the atmosphere outside. The Doctor followed the Leader's trail into the darkness.

There was only one thing to do – get back to the TARDIS and try to find Sam that way. But Hirath was huge. Could he really expect to be lucky enough to land next to her? Was it possible that time had already run out for everyone on Hirath?

He closed his eyes and swallowed hard. Yes, it distinctly was.

Ahead the Leader's low rasping voice could be heard, tinged with desperation. 'A spacecraft has impacted into this section. We *must* return to our ship. Clear a path through this debris. Quickly.'

The Doctor tried to think, his mind racing. Auto-sealants must be holding in the atmosphere, but with all remaining power being channelled through to the control chamber, there was no saying how stable they were. Whose ship had crashed here anyway? Had Sam been trying to get back? Sam. Sam Sam Sam Sam Sam. No time, no time...

There was only one thing to do.

He walked purposefully back to the control chamber.

Sam ducked back behind one of the trees as the Kusk lunged for her. She could feel the power in its branches and felt the wet hairs on the back of her neck rise up. Tanhith was still lying on the silty ground, but at least his coughing had stopped. Was he playing dead, or was he...?

The Kusk was circling round to try to get hold of her. She wondered why it wasn't just getting the hell out of here, then realised it was probably having too much fun.

An echoing cry rang out. Crichter. She gaped in disbelief as seemingly millions of him passed by behind her, spewed out by the band of light into flickering patterns dancing off into the distance the way they had come. There he was, his corpse shredded through the last few hours of his life. The other Kusk stared around itself, presumably as terrified as she'd been.

A wind started up, whipping at her hair, at the broad leaves of the time trees. The sky darkened, even though it was filling up with images of the sun. It was as if someone was throwing circles of colour at a russet backcloth.

Seemingly oblivious to anything but its chosen task, the Kusk clutched Sam's shoulder and sneered in triumph as it dug in its claws. Screaming with pain, Sam grabbed hold of a huge bunch of the glowing berries hanging from the tree above her, pulling on them while simultaneously ripping herself free from the creature's grip. Falling backward, she saw the tree glow with light and then vanish, taking the Kusk with it.

She gingerly felt her shoulder and let out a sob of relief, but the movement of the tree back in time seemed to have agitated the swirling light that was attempting to hold their time zone separate from whatever lay beyond. The sky darkened still further, and she crawled towards Tanhith as the remaining Kusk headed remorselessly for them.

The Leader watched his troops clearing a path through the rubble brought down by the crash.

The technician had spoken out of turn. Given an order *he* should've given. He wondered what he would be without the technician on hand to advise, to steer.

Where would the Kusk race be without the technocracy building it upward? What would become of them if they couldn't seize the knowledge they'd invested so much of their hopes in? Of their *science* in?

He looked around him at the devastation. The auto-sealants had pumped in, and hardened white foam now covered the huge hole in the protective hull bulkheads. It had to hold until his troops could clear the path back to the ship. The technician would succeed in taking back the information from the ancient probe. The Kusk race would be different. It would have a glorious history. Many histories.

Science was worthless without solid, hard leadership to channel it into shaping an aggressive, prosperous future.

The Leader knew he had his place.

Abruptly, he lent his bulk to the shifting of the rubble, helping the blue-skirted Kusk struggle with a huge twist of blackened metal wedged between charred floor and ceiling.

'You can't succeed.' The Doctor sat on the scorched bonnet of his Volkswagen Beetle, looking over at the Kusk technician with pallid eyes, barely visible in the gloom of the emergency lighting that had finally kicked in. 'I'll rephrase that.' He got up, and walked slowly over. His voice sounded unnaturally loud in the chamber now so many systems had stopped their quiet, confident humming. 'You don't succeed. You won't succeed. You never did succeed.'

'Your words are meaningless,' grunted the technician, apparently uninterested in the Doctor's continued presence, its fingers delicately flicking over the controls it had wired into the datacore. 'The Kusk race *must* receive this knowledge.'

'Why?'

'To exploit. To grow strong.'

'To conquer.' The Doctor stood directly behind the huge creature kneeling in front of the central touchscreen. The dim light in the chamber made the huge eyes seem to glow green as it watched each new stream of information encode itself into the memory pod. He could see the dents and lumps in the creature's skull and back, half-formed cankers and growths covering the encrusted body.

The technician continued its work. 'The Kusk race will stabilise when a greater powerbase is established, whatever the Leader's own dreams of glory. Peace and prosperity can be achieved. *This* is the real prize,' came the warbling growl.

'No,' said the Doctor, quietly. 'Your race is strong, but it has taken on board a science that is too powerful to control. Your people are too naive, and the temptations you're giving them too great.'

'Through this knowledge gathered for us, they will learn. They will learn much from the other races they will reach out to. Understanding.'

The Doctor moved beside the huge creature. 'You're telling me there will be no invasions, no pillaging of time, no conquest?'

The massive head swung round to face him. The oily growl became more urgent, and the Doctor felt that the Kusk wanted him to understand, or to vindicate itself in some way. 'Eventually, of course. The progression will be natural. But with the knowledge they will glean they will help other races, and continue to learn –'

'Culture exchange at gunpoint? Your newly educated people waiting for the next disaster to befall a planet so they can trample in and subjugate the populace?'

'To share with them our sciences, to create a clean, cultured empire that will –'

'– last a thousand years? A hundred thousand? How many million more when you achieve time transference into the future?' The Doctor was shaking with quiet anger. 'Your culture is barren and so is your philosophy.'

The technician rose to its feet, towering above the Doctor, its voice pitched slightly higher. 'Our race is barren also. We cannot survive indefinitely, our science is not founded on miracles.'

'And successful empires cannot be founded on forbidden foreknowledge.' The Doctor strode over to the matter-transmitter section of the room, reaching for the fallen cables and standing on a collapsed monitor to try to wire it into the fragile ceiling. 'I'm sorry, but, as I say, you won't succeed. Can't.' He twisted in some wiring to a blackened socket. 'Didn't.' A flick of his sonic screwdriver melded two more connections. 'Won't.'

'What are you doing?' came the warning rumble of the technician.

'I'm restoring power to the matter transmitter. I owe it to a friend down there to try to save her.'

'There can be nothing left alive on that planet.'

'I don't believe that, and you can't possibly know for sure.' The Doctor continued his repairs.

'Stand away from that equipment.' The Kusk took a lumbering step towards him, but was clearly reluctant to leave the delicate operations of the memory pod.

The Doctor flashed the creature a steely look, as if he thought his gaze a weapon strong enough to keep it at bay. 'I can't. I'm sorry.'

'Any rerouting of power may cause the information I am downloading to corrupt.'

'Good,' called the Doctor over his shoulder. But the Kusk moved with a frightening speed towards him. The Doctor tried to feint backwards as the creature lashed out at him, but a bony wrist caught him across the temple and he was knocked flying the length of the room.

Rolling over as he landed, he reached out a hand to a patch of wires protruding from a heavy cable pulled away from the wall. 'Just the job.' He smiled grimly, and pushed them into a gaping socket.

A blinding flash of electrical light passed through the matter transmitter and the Kusk technician howled with despair as it staggered back over to the console. The Doctor climbed shakily to his feet.

'The planet is in its death throes,' rumbled the Kusk. 'The link is burning out. There is no more time –'

'Take it from one who knows,' interrupted the Doctor, backing away before the advancing creature. 'There's *never* enough.'

The technician's eyes burnt a deep crimson, its sharp teeth snapping together in anger. 'You have cheated my people of their dreams.'

The Doctor found himself shouting back. 'Your selfish,

infantile dreams of conquest have taken away someone precious to me!'

'What worth is one life against –'

'Don't talk to me about worth.' The Doctor waved an arm angrily. 'You can have no conception –'

The technician's words steamrollered over his own, and chilled him.

'Your friend, coming through. I shall take her from you.'

'No!' The Doctor's head spun round to look at the image forming in the sudden luminescence filling the transmission area. A girl – a woman…

Sam had dragged Tanhith through the thick mud that sucked at her trainers into the cover of the small forest, but she knew it wouldn't take the Kusk long to find them. She'd stopped by a small sapling, its berries bright and tiny.

Tanhith was semi-conscious. 'I remember everything,' he muttered, 'everything that's ever happened to me.' He stifled a cry of pain. 'It's killing me, Sam!'

Sam backed off, all-too-familiar tears welling up in helpless frustration as Tanhith writhed in agony. The growing wind blew through the grove, the sky grew still darker.

'Shan't be sorry to see the back of today,' she muttered. Then an idea hit her. 'Tanhith, listen. This little tree. If it's young, it shouldn't be as strong, should it?' The dying man just stared in painful confusion at her, but she continued. 'Pull on one berry. It should send you back a little way in time. Just one, maybe it'll be a few minutes, or an hour or something.'

He still just stared at her, and the tears came again. 'Look, *I* don't know!' she hissed. 'You can't move, you won't be able to get away in time. It's all I can think of! I'll wait for you, I promise. I'll –'

The Kusk burst through about ten metres away, and roared in triumph. Tanhith reached over to a berry and pulled on it as Sam stood there. He vanished, but as he went Sam saw some trace of determination in his eyes.

He wasn't so keen to die, maybe. Did that make the situation better or worse?

Sam backed away as the Kusk stared in confusion at the patch of ground where Tanhith had been. The creature moved cautiously towards her, perhaps expecting a trap. Could she send it back as she had the other?

Behind the creature, she saw Tanhith blur into view again, and her heart leapt. The plan had worked – she just had to get rid of the Kusk long enough to double back and rescue him.

'You know,' she said, rubbing her streaming nose. 'I really fancy a run. What do you say?'

But the Kusk was already launching itself at her, clawed crusty hands outstretched.

Anstaar screamed as the creature lunged for her, toppling her from the platform. Snarling, it moved to grab hold of her, leaning directly over the transmitter. The Doctor dived back over to the bunch of wires, disconnected them and shoved them back in.

The platform glowed with light once again, and the monster screamed as its head and torso began to peel away out of existence, caught in the milky light. A few seconds later the scream stopped as two brute, club-like legs toppled and fell to the floor. Anstaar lay unable to move amid the debris. The Doctor moved over to her and stroked her hair, tenderly. 'Oh, Anstaar,' he breathed. 'Oh, Anstaar, what have I…' He snatched his hand away from her, looked over at the severed legs of the Kusk and wiped a hand across his forehead. 'It wasn't revenge. It wasn't, it wasn't, but I've lost – and I thought…' The Doctor turned and left Anstaar lying there.

'Doctor!' she called out, hurt and confused.

'There isn't time,' called the Doctor from behind the console. 'Everything depends on whether the link between this controlling computer and the space-time probe deep inside Hirath is still strong enough.' He banged his fist against the touchscreen in frustration. 'Come on, come on... Everything's being channelled into this one room. You can do it.'

Anstaar crawled towards him, shocked at the devastation around her, wondering how this shell could ever have been the place she had lived and worked in for so long.

'What's happening?' she pleaded, gasping for breath.

The Doctor's fingers were a blur of movement. 'Hirath's about to rip itself apart in a temporal explosion.'

'A what?'

'The damaged probe. There's another one down there and it's pushed the planet too far. Hirath's going to take half the galaxy with her when she goes.' Anstaar saw him clasp his head in his hands as he waited for a device to power up. Then he looked at a small piece of smooth, rounded metal. 'They'd never have escaped to put this information to any use even if none of this –' he gestured around the burnt-out room – 'had ever happened. Idiots.' There was pity in his voice. 'Poor, hopeless idiots.'

Anstaar shook her head, struggling to use her good leg to raise herself to a standing position.

'The year,' demanded the Doctor, suddenly, peering at the screen. 'Is it 3177?'

'Of course it is,' Anstaar grunted as she leaned heavily against the console.

'Good, the anchor point still remains.' He looked up, and his eyes cleared for a moment, his gaze less furious and intense. He slapped his forehead. 'I understand now! The moon itself, it's our anchor!' He turned to look at her with new hope in his eyes. 'We must turn back the clock!' He began reconnecting the partially overridden digitpad interface with the computer.

'What?'

'Bypass the real-time anchor. This computer's simulating the passage of time for the probe down there, keeping it stable, yes?'

'All right,' nodded Anstaar blankly. 'It regulates the time disruptions –'

'– by fooling the probe mechanism down there into thinking they all make sense, that all the disruptions are natural, part of the planet, *meant to happen*. It does so by operating a complex set of algorithms that balance out every distortion, every last piece of temporal friction. The unit here, and so geographically the planetoid it's based on, is its anchor – a spatio-temporal reference point. It's really quite clever.'

'Yes.' Anstaar nodded, more because she felt it was expected of her than for any other reason.

'But also stupid!' cried the Doctor with a flourish of his hand, his fingers fluttering deftly over the digitpad he had rewired back into the system. 'Because if I can shift that anchor, convince the probe that we're at a point far in Hirath's past –' one hand slapped down on a pale-green option button on the touchscreen, the other wiped sweat from his brow – 'way, way back to a time when this moon was far, far closer, newly captured by Hirath's gravity, before it drifted further and further out and all the way to here...'

Anstaar looked at him with her wide dark eyes, but his own were staring intently at the information flickering across the screen. She jumped on his train of thought: 'The gravitational shift that would cause –'

'The *simulated* gravitational shift,' corrected the Doctor, 'should be sufficient to convince the probe it should be torn apart.' He sighed. 'A more conventional explosion.' Then he looked at her sullenly. 'The galaxy is saved.'

'But what about us, here?' Anstaar looked beseechingly at him. 'How big will the explosion be? What about the time fields? Will they just dissipate? Will there be shockwaves, will we be affected –'

'We might be far enough out to survive.' He shrugged. 'I don't know.'

Anstaar felt anger surging past her fear. 'And don't you care?'

She looked at his pale face, dimly illuminated by the emergency lighting. His voice, when it finally came, was as faint as the colour in his haunted eyes. 'Always.'

The Leader was unprepared when the section above him collapsed. A shouted warning from one of his troops was far too late, and he fell heavily, trapped under tons of heavy metal.

He could feel bile rising in his throat. It tasted sweet, sugary, and he released a long, frothy groan.

He could feel the debris being lifted from him, but he couldn't feel his legs at all following this latest disaster. 'Ignore me,' he gurgled, angry at his misfortune and perceived weakness. 'Clear the path. Ready the ship for take-off. The technician will soon be finished.'

'Finished' seemed an apt term. He realised that his remaining troops – how many, two or three? – had already moved to complete the clearing of the path, leaving him talking to nobody. Control could be lost so easily. Respect won or lost by a single chance. He knew now the glory he dreamed of would never be. But perhaps these last Kusks could still escape and return home, and remember his fierce love for his troubled planet, whatever happened.

'The Kusk race *will* begin anew!' he called out over the clanking of shifting metal, but no one could hear him.

Sam was running, but the creature was bigger than she was

and just as fast. As it gained on her, Sam found endless memories dizzying her mind.

One suddenly stood out: a cruel trick played on her during kiss and chase in the school playground on the afternoon of 3 June 1989. She was running, chasing after Peter Stokely. He dropped into a ball in front of her, she tripped, went flying, skinned her knees, was crying –

She dropped. The Kusk's huge legs cannoned into her, winded her, but the creature still toppled and fell just as she had done in the playground. A huge tremor shook the landscape once again, and a crack opened up in the parched earth in front of her. The Kusk scrabbled around trying to find something to hold on to to stop it falling. Sam watched in ghoulish fascination for a few moments, then moved off towards the grove of trees.

She stopped.

There *were* no trees, just a patch of evil-smelling earth and a crackling band of power filling the air around the edge of the cliff face. The images of Crichter dotted around into the distance suddenly sparked and vanished as the wind grew stronger, but Sam just stared at the empty space where Tanhith should have been, and screamed.

'The planet's going critical!' yelled the Doctor, his long brown curls almost seeming to stand up on end. 'How far back do I send the real-time anchor? How long since this moon was captured by Hirath's gravity?'

'You really expect me to know?' spluttered Anstaar.

'Too far back and we won't have arrived yet. Lose its reference point entirely and it just won't register. There'll be nothing holding the time-fields in place.'

'"Boom"?' suggested Anstaar, trying to be helpful.

'"Kerboom", to be truly scientific.' The Doctor looked incredibly serious.

'And I suppose if you don't go back far enough –'

'– the gravitational shift may not be sufficient.'

Anstaar stared at him. 'So what do we do?'

The Doctor shook his head, his eyes closed, lips muttering something that could've been mental workings, oaths, or a prayer. Suddenly the eyes snapped open and fixed on her. 'Think of a number,' he ordered. 'Now double it…'

Sam turned and walked robotically towards the cave mouth as the whole planet seemed to pick up her scream of anger and frustration and echo it all around. She glanced back over one shoulder and noticed that the Kusk had managed to extricate itself from the widening split in the planet's crust, and was even now staggering towards her.

She entered the thick blackness of the cave, the memory of the Kusk's operating procedure clear and sharp in her mind. The two grey buttons must be a kind of delay mechanism, giving you time to get on to the platform, she reasoned, detachedly. It had been preset by the Kusk. It would take her back to the moon.

Love, love, love.

She wondered if Tanhith had felt anything when he'd finally been taken by this place. She pressed the buttons, and pulled her clammy body up on to the clear plastic.

A short time later the Kusk entered the cave. Its bulk lent a frightening movement to the darkness. But the dust and the light were already pulling away at her skin and her hair, and her heart.

Leaving the two other survivors to the work of cutting through the debris that blocked their escape from the dying base, the Leader crawled slowly and painfully in the direction of the control chamber. He had to be sure that the knowledge they had travelled so far to attain was safe – that the Kusks' future was assured.

His legs were crushed, unusable. One arm seemed broken and useless too. But he would pull himself forward with his good arm. His spirit and purpose were unbreakable; *this* was what science could not teach. The technician would be forced to witness his spirit. The technician would be reminded once again that science was little without strength.

He heard the voices from outside the door and hissed. The Doctor. And someone else.

'Divide it by four. Now take away the number you first thought of. What's left?'

'Twenty-four.'

'Pity. I was hoping it would be in the region of minus thirty-four million, thirty-four thousand, seven hundred and sixty-eight.'

A furious gurgling roar began somewhere in the pit of the Leader's stomach and rose in volume as it hissed through his jagged teeth.

Anstaar spun round at the sudden noise, and grabbed hold of the Doctor's shoulder. The eyes of the Leader glowered at them balefully from floor level, the arm reaching into the control chamber to haul the huge body along.

'Stop him, Anstaar!' yelled the Doctor. 'He's their leader. I can't leave this now, I can't!' He was wrestling with the controls in front of him, trying to solve problem after problem as his attempts to bypass the alien systems met with alternate failure and success.

Anstaar stared helplessly at the Time Lord. 'My leg's broken!' she reminded him.

The Kusk Leader dragged himself a little closer.

'Get in that purple machine!' He gestured impatiently over his shoulder. 'There should be a key inside. Turn it clockwise and you'll start an engine. Quickly!'

* * *

Sam's eyes were still staring out into the cave, with no lids to shut out the sight of the furious Kusk roaring in frustration in front of her, reaching out into the milky opacity that surrounded and shielded her.

The process hadn't taken this long before. Consciousness showed no sign of leaving her, and nor did the savage creature that was desperate to destroy her, staring at what must be her half-dissolved face. Something was wrong. She was stuck. The howling noise of the maelstrom outside grew still louder.

Oh, God, help me, help me, help me.

Leaning on a shattered tubular cable housing for support, Anstaar took the quickest route towards the Doctor's machine, which involved getting dangerously close to the Leader. He roared again and flailed out his arm, which caught the piping and knocked Anstaar off balance. She screamed as the injured creature rolled over on to its bony back to try to get hold of her, and propelled herself through the dirt and filth on the floor with her good foot towards the Doctor's machine. She realised as she pushed herself along that the Kusk now seemed to be after her, not him. Was that good or bad?

Her vision spun crazily as she twisted round to try to drag herself along on her front. She glimpsed the Doctor, his fingers moving over the digitpad. She saw a dark arch of metal above a large rubber wheel. This purple thing had to be a vehicle. How was she meant to get in?

The Leader reached out a sharp-nailed hand towards her. She saw all six fingers splayed out, ready to grasp her flesh.

The pipe hit the Leader's arm with enough force to knock his hand down. She raised it again, and pushed it into his eye. The Leader's angry roar became one of pain, and he lashed out, sending the pipe flying across the other side of the room into a dark bank of machinery.

Anstaar reached out to a protruding piece of metal and chrome and pulled herself up and away from the thrashing Kusk's reach. There was a handle, a crack in the metal. A door.

She almost screamed as she put her weight on her smashed leg to throw herself inside to the soft seat. Facing her were instruments, a black plastic wheel and a key in a mechanism.

It didn't seem to want to turn. Outside, she could hear the Leader punching at the undercarriage, seemingly trying to force a way in through the bottom of the vehicle.

Sam felt the next tremor even through whatever shielding the matter transmitter was providing. She could see the Kusk before her clutching at its tendril-like ears, screaming out a sound that was surely too high-pitched to come from such a creature.

As she watched helplessly, its skin dried out and cracked, becoming the texture of ancient parchment. The Kusk's ruddy brown colour faded to a cold grey before the beast seemed to shrivel, its eyes narrow and a sickly yellow.

The luminance of the transmission mechanism hid from her the rest of the creature's bizarre death, but its screaming lingered for several seconds before joining the host of demonic sounds from outside. She couldn't feel relieved, not in this horrible, bizarre condition, half in, half out. A spectator in her own body, scared, desperate for a way out – or in – back to safety, back to the Doctor.

Then she realised, as rubble fell crashing in front of her, that the entire cave was falling in.

'Come on…' hissed the Doctor. 'Now!'

He punched in the final codes.

CHAPTER FOURTEEN
THE AFTER-HOURS

Nothing happened.

A collapsed monitor, the hazy picture on its screen rolling over and over, showed the pink mass of Hirath bright against the blackness of space.

And where Anstaar's cable piping, thrown across the room by the Kusk Leader, had hit the exposed innards of the bank of machinery near the matter transmitter, it had pushed together a group of wires that finally conducted enough energy to send a faint radiance of power flickering over the circuitry.

At last the key turned in the mechanism. The engine the Doctor had promised her roared into life. But the smashing against the underside of the car was getting louder, more desperate. The car shook with the chugging of the engine but the Leader's hard, bony fist was hammering closer and closer. Anstaar could hear metal tearing.

Sam could feel the force of the rocks hitting the ground in front of her. The platform was vibrating now. If it toppled over…

Then she felt hundreds of tiny mouths biting at her flesh with renewed vigour. Felt her mind spinning round, tired giggles spill out of her, consciousness fading, rocks falling, her flesh being forced down a plughole with the milky water all around –

'What am I missing? What am I missing?' The Doctor coughed

slightly on the exhaust fumes filling the chamber and stared at the pitching picture of Hirath on the monitor. 'Don't go away,' he muttered.

Anstaar could hear the Leader snarling, choking and roaring beneath her. Finally, with a protesting grinding of metal, the bony, scabrous hand had burst through the floor of the vehicle and was flailing about. Anstaar kicked at it, but it grabbed her good foot and dragged it through the jagged gash in the underside of the machine. She screamed as she tried to pull against it, but with her broken leg she could gain little leverage.

The Doctor's head swung round as Anstaar screamed, and he paused, torn between wanting to help her and having to save the million people he'd never know in this part of the galaxy from destruction.

He rose to his feet. 'Always,' he muttered.

The blue-skirted Kusk approached the control chamber, choking in the gloom as it inhaled the fumes. The last remaining trooper drew up behind it.

'Only one other Kusk life-sign registering,' stated the trooper.

The other Kusk slowly considered the implications of this. 'Technician?' its voice rattled into the darkness. Silence. 'The way is clear. Our ship is powered up for –'

'Stop the Doctor!' came the choking groan of the Leader from somewhere ahead.

The Doctor reacted to his name, then turned back and saw the glowing corner of the matter transmitter, the opaque vortex of light just beginning to form.

'Of course,' he muttered. 'Power drain. No matter how

weak, the synapses are still diverted. My command's not getting through.'

Anstaar screamed again, the noise mingling with the retching growl of the Kusk Leader.

It was impossible to say what figure was forming in the swirl of light above the matter-transmission platform.

The Doctor couldn't bring himself to look anyway.

He looked at the image of Hirath, heard a soundtrack of screaming and roaring.

Two Kusks burst choking into the chamber and moved towards him, arms outstretched.

The Doctor re-entered the final codes. The scanner monitor went dead. Dead. How could he get the power through?

As the blue-skirted Kusk grasped and twisted his shoulder in a vice-like grip, the Doctor reached down deep into the innards of the control desk and grabbed hold of a live conduit.

The Kusk stared up at the twilight sky from beside the rocky grave of its fallen comrade. The sky turned white, blank. An explosion –

The moon filled the ancient probe's decaying sensory horizon for a fraction of a nanosecond before it tore itself apart.

The Doctor's scream rose louder than any other. The computer terminal exploded outward, peppering the Doctor's face with shards of glass and plastic, the force of the blast scattering the two Kusks and knocking him against the far wall with a sickening impact. A surge of electricity crackled outward from the shattered terminal along the metal floor and through the corridors beyond.

The Leader stopped screaming as the current paralysed its wrecked body and the consciousness died in its huge eyes.

* * *

The two Kusks twitched and spasmed as they were shaken and hurled to the ground by the last effects of the lethal feedback.

The Doctor's body shook and convulsed, his eyes clamped tightly shut.

She wasn't dead.

Anstaar didn't know what exactly she *was*, but she wasn't dead. Her foot had come free. The interior of the Doctor's vehicle must have sheltered her from the blast and the power surge. The engine still chugged noisily. It was the only sound she could hear.

She moved painfully to the window set in the door, bumping her head against the metal frame. The glass had been shattered in the blast from what she guessed was power fed back to the machinery along the link between probe and computer. He'd done it. They were still here. *She* was still here.

Anstaar noticed a light swirling like scum on the surface of dark water, in the corner above the matter transmitter. Soon after, almost as if in sympathy with the dead control room, the milky opacity dwindled and died.

Anstaar bumped against a switch with her arm and two beams of light cut through the pitch blackness, dimly illuminating the room. She saw a slight figure in filthy wet clothes collapse forward into the debris and grime hiding the metal floor. A girl – the one who had tried to help her when Vasid had gone mad. It seemed like such a long time ago... Sam. Her skin was red, badly burnt. When the girl raised her head, even from this range, Anstaar could see that the eyes were wild and frightened.

Anstaar opened her mouth to call out, to say something, but no words came. She realised how tired she was, how much she was hurting.

Sam had crawled on her hands and knees over to a shape on the floor. Looking through the glass shield that had stayed intact above the instrumentation panels, Anstaar saw it was the crumpled form of the Doctor. Her dark eyes widened in alarm, but the effort of thinking too hard hurt, and the noisy chugging of the engine was lulling her back down to a sleepy lethargy.

She saw the girl stroking the Doctor's face, gingerly – she must have seen the cuts there. She put a hand either side of his ribcage – then a wail escaped the cracked lips.

Anstaar guessed the Doctor must be dead, then. The Doctor had lost Sam, and now Sam had lost the Doctor. Anstaar watched the girl scream and shout and start crying, seemingly oblivious to anything around her.

Sam pulled at the buttons of the Doctor's shirt, beat his chest, crouching over him protectively.

Tilting his head back, pressing her lips against his, breathing hard, trying to resuscitate, pounding the chest.

Pressing her lips against his – lips hard-pressed –

Kissing him. The jaw moving almost mechanically, hands scrunching up his shirt. Pulling at the fabric.

Light fading.

Anstaar had slumped forward. A blaring noise struck up suddenly from near the steering mechanism, woke her with a jolt, threw her back. Vision swam back into focus.

The girl was at the window, tears streaming down her crumpled face. She looked ridiculously young. 'You're Sam,' she began.

'What are you doing in our car?' Sam sobbed, accusingly, her eyes spiteful.

'I'm Anstaar.' She closed her eyes. 'I was…'

'I don't know – I don't believe –' The words wouldn't leave Sam's mouth. She walked helplessly back to the Doctor's body on the filthy floor.

The control room had become freezing cold, and Anstaar shivered, opening the door and trying to haul herself out. 'I saw you.' Anstaar didn't know what to say. Sam looked at her and collapsed in angry tears.

'You saw me what? What?' The words resounded round the dead room. 'What?' The girl was hitting the Doctor's body, hitting herself.

Anstaar hobbled over. 'But isn't he…?'

'No!' Sam looked at the Doctor's prone body in anguish. She ran from the room, leaving Anstaar alone in the dim light. 'No!'

Anstaar could see a slight layer of frost forming on the Doctor's skin, hiding the cuts and grazes. He looked beautiful, and at peace.

She left him then and hobbled painfully through the littered Kusk bodies in pursuit of the girl. 'Come back! Sam, this place is shutting down. We'll die if we don't get out!'

Sam's voice screamed back at her, hysterical. 'I don't care!'

There was the sound of more debris falling, some way off, ahead of her. 'Sam?'

Silence.

Anstaar wondered if all the Kusks were dead. Nothing stirred in the thick blackness, but that didn't mean –

Then she heard the sobbing, a child's sobs, inconsolable in the darkness.

Why was it dark at night?

Anstaar had always hated the dark.

'Liz and Simon… married…St Oswald's…'

The Doctor stirred, groggily raising himself on to his elbows. 'Anyone there?' Silence. 'We're still here! We did it. "Boom"!' He breathed in deeply. 'Yes, a palpable "Boom"!' Then he sniffed, like a dog catching a scent. His voice came in a hoarse whisper. 'Sam!'

He scrambled to his feet, exuberant, ignoring the pain twisting his body. 'Sam!' This time it was a proclamation. 'Sam, you're here, you're –' he felt the chill in the thin air – 'alive?'

The corridor beyond was shrouded in blackness. 'Sam?' The car was empty, the door ajar. 'Anstaar?'

Silence. Under the car he discerned the stretched-out form of the Kusk Leader. Unsteadily, head spinning slightly from the exertion in the thin air, he dragged the cold, heavy corpse away from the car and looked sadly down at it, swathed in the shadows smeared over the floor. 'All for nothing.'

The Doctor got in the car and drove unsteadily down the corridors. It seemed to take for ever. Every time the car couldn't negotiate round some debris, the Doctor would get out and check that it was either inorganic or dead before driving jerkily over it.

Then he saw the section where the other ship must have come through. The mass of wreckage was unbelievable. And his blood ran cold when he discerned a piece of Sam's top skewered on a jagged piece of metal protruding from the rubble-strewn floor.

'Sam!' The cry echoed dully in the ruined corridors as he rushed out to retrieve the fabric. It was damp with sweat and with traces of blood. But there was no sign of a body. Then he saw a gap in the debris, a narrow gap. She must have gone through. She must be on the other side.

He propelled himself through the gap and rushed through the darkened passageways, stumbling, falling down, always onward.

When he reached the docking lounge he lit a match. The room was empty. Peering through the outer inspection hatch, he saw that the Kusk ship had departed.

Sam had to have come this way – with Anstaar? The gap back there wasn't big enough for a Kusk to get through, but had there been any crew still on board?

The Doctor looked at the dead terminal on the desk, at the logo on the wall in the light of the flickering flame. 'Time is our business…' he muttered bitterly, a sneer forming on his lips. The flame flickered out as the scant oxygen was used up.

He was alone.

EPILOGUE

– don't know if I'm working this right or not. But I hope it's recording. It's a message for you. For you, Sam.

You're going to wake up, I know – well, you will have woken up, I suppose. Sorry, I'm not very good at this – and I bet you're wondering what in the deity's name is going on. But I bet you'll work out how to use this datacube, like I did. Like I think I did.

You're on the Kusk ship. Don't ask me how I got us on board. I had to drag you some of the way – not easy with a broken leg. You were semi-conscious. You'd run right into something, I think. You're in a bit of a state. You were concussed, I guess, and lost consciousness a few – well, I don't know how long ago by the time you watch this. I know I'm not being much help...

The ship's empty. It was left ready for take-off, but I think the crew must've died before they could escape in it. Doesn't smell very nice here but I think the air's breathable, and there's sort of food things and drink things packed away in the next room. I don't know what they're like... There's room to move about, too – those things were so big, you wouldn't believe it.

The ship took off all right, the ascent was pre-programmed, but I can't figure out many of the flight controls. I just know it's taking you away from the moonbase, from what's left of Hirath. I don't know where to.

Not much use, am I? Sam, I'm sorry. I couldn't wake you to ask you, or to tell you, but I was scared this ship would take us far and away from the Thannos system, and from my home. If you travel with the Doctor, and I know you must do, then I'm sure you're used to not knowing where the hell you are. I want to go home, Sam. There's only one escape capsule, and I'm taking it. I don't know if it makes my chances of survival any better or not, but at least if anyone comes looking for Hirath – and they've got to, they must do, mustn't they? – maybe they'll find me too.

So I'm not here, and I'm saying goodbye. I suppose you're wondering why I'm bothering, I mean, we've hardly spoken. But I remember you calling out to Vasid, all that time ago, trying to stop him sending me away. And I saw you with the Doctor. I saw how much he cares about you. Sam, I'm so sorry he's – he's not here, with you now. But he saved us, didn't he? Saved everyone he could. He did it.

Why do I get the feeling that… I don't know, I bet he made a habit of that sort of thing. So full of life – so caught up in everyone's lives. I don't think there was anything he didn't care about in some way or other.

Anyway, I'm going. I've got to go now, I reckon, if I'm to stand any chance of getting back. Good luck. All systems seem to be go. It'll be all right. You'll be all right.

How do you turn this thing –

The Doctor searches for Sam – and for answers –
in the following series of books: